HAMMERED

LEGACY OF MAGIC, BOOK 1

LINDSAY BUROKER

ACKNOWLEDGMENTS

Thank you, regular readers and new readers, for picking up my latest urban fantasy series!

Legacy of Magic is set in the same world as my *Death Before Dragons* novels, so, if you've read those, you can expect to encounter some familiar characters. If you're new, no problem! This is the first appearance of my heroine Matti, and her adventures can stand alone.

Before you start reading, please let me acknowledge the people who helped me put the new series together. Thank you to my editor, Shelley Holloway, and my beta readers, Sarah Engelke and Cindy Wilkinson. Also, thank you to Gene Mollica for the cover design and Vivienne Leheny for bringing these characters to life in the audiobooks.

Now, please enjoy the story...

1

"I DIDN'T THINK THE POLICE USED CHALK OUTLINES ANYMORE." I tried not to feel uneasy about the faded drawing on the floor of the foyer in the house I'd just purchased.

Correction: my small home-renovations business had purchased it. On the advice of my goblin assistant, whom I'd encouraged to take more initiative. Why was I already sure that had been a mistake?

"Maybe a neighbor child with sidewalk chalk was responsible." Tinja waved airily, cog-and-charm bracelets rattling on her green wrist. "I have observed that human offspring will draw on *anything.*"

"Oh sure. And they often wander into locked vacant homes to do their graffiti work."

Tinja nodded, missing the sarcasm. Unlike me, she hadn't been born on Earth, so I couldn't expect her to catch such nuances.

"The owner of the house *was* killed here, right?" I asked. "It's why we got a deal."

A *steal* of a deal. I'd never remodeled a house in Bellevue at all, much less one in the prestigious Bridle Trails neighborhood, with houses on acre lots located a stone's throw from a huge equestrian park. As I eyed the mid-century-modern "diamond in the rough," as the listing had called it, I worried this would be too much to handle.

"It was the *renter* who was killed, not the owner."

"Well, that makes it all right then. Are those bullet holes?" I probed one of several finger-width gaps in the cedar-plank wall of the foyer. Had there been anything magical about the bullets, I might have sensed them lodged in the wood, a talent my half-dwarf heritage gave me. Apparently, this had been a run-of-the-mill mundane homicide.

"Easy to fix with your spickle, right?" Tinja asked.

"It's called Spackle, and you can't apply it to cedar."

"We will get new boards then. If we want boards at all. This cedar is not as tacky as the faux-wood paneling in the last house I drew plans for, but it is *not* suitably modern. Not this much of it anyway. An accent wall would perhaps be acceptable. Come, Matti. I will show you my blueprints. They're *amazing*." Tinja patted the rolled papers under her arm and ambled toward the kitchen, her tool belt clanking.

I wondered if her professors at the university found her supreme confidence warranted. Or if any of them knew she was a goblin. Tinja was enrolled solely in online courses, which did not require she walk her three-and-a-half-foot-tall green-skinned and white-haired body into a classroom.

Before following her, I considered the position of the holes to estimate where the bullets had been fired from. Not from the street and through a window or the front door—not that I'd expected drive-by shootings in Bridle Trails—but from the living room. Had someone been lying in wait for the poor homeowner—renter—when he'd come home?

Maybe I shouldn't have left my war hammer—all that I had

left of my dwarven mother—in the truck. *Usually*, I used it for demoing drywall and cabinets, a purpose the dwarven smith who'd made it surely hadn't intended, but I'd been known to thump bad guys with it.

"Come, Matti," Tinja called regally. "Do you not wish to see the plans?"

"You're my assistant, you know. You're the one who's supposed to be at *my* beck and call." Despite the words, I headed toward the back of the house, peering into rooms along the way. At four thousand square feet, the two-story house wasn't as large as some in the neighborhood, but seeing all the spaces that needed remodeling had the adding machine in my mind tallying thousands of dollars' worth of supplies. Not to mention Tinja's plans involved a master-suite addition over the garage.

"You may beck-and-call me if you wish, but unless you're waving your hammer around, I'm rarely intimidated enough to drop everything and come."

"My body-builder physique doesn't make you quake in your work pants?" I flexed my biceps as I stepped into the kitchen, but the horror of avocado appliances, linoleum floors patterned in green squares, and chartreuse-striped cushions on the banquet table stole my humor. "The cedar planks were beautiful in comparison to this."

"Have you not said you enjoy a challenge?"

"I guess Abbas and I have fixed up worse," I said, mentioning my business partner.

"Certainly. There's not even a mildew, cat-urine, or wet-dog smell in this home, not like in the last one, which featured all of those and more. Not that I'd expect your dwarven nose to take note. Dwarves are used to living in all manner of underground miasmas, after all. On their home world, some of the resorts involve steam chambers where you bathe in sulfuric gases."

"The human half of my nose did note the urine odor." I'd never heard of dwarven resorts and suspected she'd made that up.

"Ah, it is good to know that it is capable. Humans are not known for their sublime senses." Tinja patted a faded laminate countertop. "Overall, this house has been very well cared for. Many things will be simple to renovate in here, and the kitchen is very spacious. Look, we can add a wine cellar in that nook. Or, I suppose you would prefer a cheese cellar for your fancy wheels of cheddar." She grinned at me, aware of my favorite snack.

"*I'm* not the end buyer." As if I could afford this neighborhood for myself. "And for your information, it would be Camembert or Roquefort and a cheese *cave*, not a cellar."

"Don't you keep yours in the carrot crisper?"

"The vegetable crisper, yes. Because there's no room in my tiny house for a cheese cave." I touched a backsplash tile that emanated a hint of magic. My finger tingled slightly. I'd only been inside for five minutes, and this was already the oddest project I'd taken on. "I wouldn't even be able to fit a roommate in my house if she wasn't three feet tall."

"Three and a *half* feet." Tinja jumped, spread her arms wide, and spun a pirouette, almost whacking me with her blueprints. "Matti, I wish you to make more money on this house than the last one. You barely broke even and paid me only a portion of what I'm worth."

"You're a *student*. Most students don't get paid much at all. And Abbas and I don't typically use blueprints."

"You didn't *used* to use them. In the savage and woeful days before you met me. But now I am here. You must do as other house flippers do to maximize profits."

"I really wouldn't need an architect then. Most flippers only paint, replace drawer pulls, and do other minimal—and cheap—fixes." Maybe it was my mother's blood, but I couldn't bring myself to do anything less than the best I could with the money and materials I could scrounge. I was a craftswoman, not simply a *house flipper*.

"There must be a center ground."

"Middle ground."

"Yes. We will discuss it more later. Now, back to business. I am afraid that this free-standing circular fireplace does not belong in the kitchen, and I have removed it from my design. It impedes the flow and is not up to modern building codes." Tinja tapped wrought-iron fireplace tools mounted on the brick below the open hearth and shook her head. "I am learning about human building codes in my classes. They are most quirky. Your hammer is capable of demolishing bricks, yes?"

"Bricks, metal doors, murderers' heads..." I touched one of the window frames, envisioning replacing the old aluminum with wood. "They've all fallen to my mighty—" Something large and furry darted through the backyard, and my senses twanged. Whatever it was, it was magical. "What was that?"

"I believe it is a shifter of some kind," Tinja said as I pressed my nose to the window to peer out. "A werewolf, maybe? I assume they are common here."

"You assume werewolf shifters are *common* in a hoity-toity neighborhood in the most expensive metro area in Washington?"

"There are many trees and ferns, which wolves like very much. They are similar to elves and enjoy nature. Except they hunt in and pee on the nature instead of using it to calm their senses and enhance their magic."

"No wolf better be peeing in my new yard." I squinted into the overrun morass that was far more representative of the *nature* she'd mentioned than a yard. Creeping buttercups had smothered someone's attempt at growing grass, Himalayan blackberry bushes encroached on an ancient moss-covered patio, and towering firs, pines, and cedars ensured that little afternoon sunlight made it to the ground.

"If he has, you can apply your hammer to his head."

Leaves quivered on a rhododendron threatening to consume an old swing set, and I sensed the shifter hiding in the foliage. I couldn't see him, but I *felt* him. As with magical bullets, my senses could detect those with magical blood.

"What do you think he's doing?" I whispered.

"Probably what I said wolves like to do in nature."

"He's *not* doing that." I hoped. "This is private property. *Our* private property. I'm going to get my hammer."

Before I'd taken more than a few steps, glass shattered in the living room. I sensed a *second* magical being, one leaping through the freshly broken window... A fit man in his thirties with a thick beard and mustache, he landed in a crouch, facing me. Despite his human form, he snarled, his dark eyes locking on to me.

Before he moved, my instincts told me he would spring. I darted back into the kitchen and grabbed the fireplace poker from the tool set. As he charged through the doorway, I spun and swung the pointed rod like I would have my hammer.

He saw it coming and tried to duck, but I'd swung many a weapon over the years and was fast. It caught him in the forehead. Had my hammer struck him, he would have flown across the room and into the far wall. The poker lacked its heft, but the blow halted him, and he yowled like a wild animal.

"What are you doing in my house?" I demanded, pulling the poker back for another swing if necessary.

Fur sprouted from his bare arms, and his face contorted, nose and jaw elongating into something lupine.

Knowing he would be more dangerous in his wolf form, I swung again.

This time, he anticipated the blow. Ducking, he charged under the tool and toward me. Not surprised, I whirled and launched a spinning side kick into his gut. His abs were as hard as a brick wall, but my heel connected with enough power to make him stagger back.

Thanking my grandmother for putting me in martial arts as a kid, I hefted the poker to crack him on the head again. I wanted to knock him out or at least convince him to jump back out the window and get off the property.

"The other one is coming," Tinja blurted before I struck. She knelt on the countertop as she peered out the window. "Uh oh. Make that the other *two*. I didn't sense that one before. Maybe he has a charm that camouflages him."

Damn it, why had I left my hammer in the truck? I did *not* want to fight two at once. Three if this one stuck around.

"Never mind." Tinja lowered a wrench that she'd intended to use as a weapon. "Is that an elf? Here, on Earth? How startling."

Before the shifter in the kitchen could attack again, I slammed the poker down on his head. Worried we would face more enemies, I didn't soften the blow, and the strength I'd inherited from my mother dropped him hard. If he'd been fully human, it might have done lasting damage—something my martial-arts instructor would have berated me soundly for—but werewolf heads had the sturdy resilience of concrete blocks.

Tinja swore. Then whistled. What did *that* mean?

After the shifter passed out, I snatched a sidearm out of his belt holster, threw it into the fireplace, and ran to the window, bumping shoulders with Tinja. The second and third werewolves had shifted into their lupine forms and charged out of the bushes—or maybe been *dragged* out of them. With their heads almost as high as a man's, their powerful bodies covered in black fur, and their jaws snapping like steel traps, they battled a foe even more unexpected than werewolves.

A pointy-eared elf in a green cloak, brown trousers, beige tunic—was that *buckskin*?—and low brown boots wielded two longswords ambidextrously. I'd never seen a full-blooded elf in my life. They'd supposedly all left Earth back before I'd been born. What was he doing *here*?

Working together, both wolves leaped for his throat, their teeth flashing. With a stern but unconcerned expression on his face, the elf dedicated one sword to each and parried their snapping jaws without giving ground.

They were powerful and had him outnumbered, but his movements were so fast and fluid that I didn't doubt for a moment that he would win. In fact, he could have finished them at any time.

His eyes narrowed slightly, and one wolf jerked his head back, as if he'd been stung. Or… attacked mentally? I'd heard that full-blooded magical beings could speak telepathically, read minds, and interrogate people with a thought, but I'd never seen it.

"He's *beautiful*," Tinja whispered.

"Which one?" I assumed she meant the elf, as he *was* handsome, with intense blue eyes, a perfectly straight nose, and short blond hair that accentuated his pronounced cheekbones. But with goblin tastes, who knew?

"The *elf*."

The werewolf that had shaken his head backed away from the fight as the other tried to distract the elf. He shifted into his human form, then rolled naked into nearby bushes, reaching for something. Not overly distracted, the elf kept watching him, even as his twin swords blurred, shifting from defense to offense. With a powerful blow, he lopped off the attacking wolf's head so startlingly cleanly that I would have known his blades were magical even if I hadn't sensed them.

"Ack." Tinja scrambled off the counter and flung her hands over her eyes. "Gruesome!"

As the head landed with a sickening thud on the mossy patio, I couldn't disagree. The other werewolf rolled away from the bushes with a gun in hand.

"Look out!" I blurted, not sure if the elf was familiar with firearms. He looked like he'd stepped out of *The Lord of the Rings*.

Not glancing toward us, he strode toward the werewolf. His enemy fired twice, aiming for his chest.

Blades blurring again, the elf deflected both bullets, and I could only gape. Even with *magic*, I wouldn't have thought that was possible.

Cursing, the werewolf fired twice more, but the elf thwarted the attack again, even from scant feet away. The bullets ricocheted into the side of the house, making me duck while thinking of the bullet holes in the foyer.

Though I should have flattened myself to the floor, as Tinja wisely did, I couldn't keep from peering over the windowsill. Before the werewolf could fire again, the elf sprang, slicing a blade through his enemy's wrist. It cut off the hand holding the gun, and the firearm flew free. It struck a drainpipe with a clang. I had no idea where the hand went.

As the werewolf screamed, the elf struck again. For a second time in twenty seconds, someone was decapitated in front of my eyes.

It slowly dawned on me that warning the elf might not have been wise. He might be prettier than the werewolves, but that didn't mean he was a good guy.

What if he disliked half-blooded dwarves as much as werewolves?

2

"Is it safe to look?" Tinja had risen from the floor but still had her hands over her eyes.

Outside, it had grown silent, the birds and squirrels that had been chattering earlier not making a peep.

"Not if you don't want to see two guys' bloody heads." I grimaced, not wanting to see that myself, but until I found out if the elf would be a threat to me, I wouldn't close the shutters on him.

"Gross."

On the patio, the elf drew a square of cloth from a pocket. He fastidiously cleaned his swords before sheathing them, the blood somehow not staining the cloth, then put it away and removed a slender backpack. He plucked free what looked like a large red-velvet bag, shook it out, and picked up the first head by the hair. After tucking it into the bag, he went for the second.

In death, werewolves reverted to human form, which made watching their decapitated heads being stuck in a bag all the more disturbing. With another shake, the bag flattened, and the elf *folded* it.

I'd heard of magical items, such as charms that could allow the wearer some specific and usually trivial power, but this guy had everything out of a *Dungeons & Dragons* compendium.

As the elf returned the neatly folded bag of heads to his backpack, I looked around the interior of the house, gaze lingering on the unconscious werewolf on the floor. "We did *not* negotiate hard enough for this property."

"It was already four hundred thousand under market value," Tinja said. "I did research. As you taught me."

"That was still too much. *Way* too much."

As the elf donned his backpack again, he looked through the window at us, his blue eyes flinty and cold, as if promising we were next.

"Shit." I slunk away from the window. "I'm getting my hammer. You better hide."

After watching his battle, I worried he would kick my ass even if I *did* get to my hammer in time, but I would go down fighting.

This time, as I ran through the house, broken glass crunching under my shoes, I made it to the front door. A second before I pulled it open, something splatted against the wood. Several somethings.

Now what?

I rose on tiptoes to peer through the peephole, wishing I had a few more inches of height. A familiar truck painted with black tiger stripes idled in the street, the driver hanging halfway out as he raised his arm to throw again. More idiots jeered and pointed from the bed in the back.

If I hadn't needed my hammer, and also recognized a woman darting from the walkway into the shrubs, I wouldn't have opened the door. As I did, wrinkling my nose at a rotten-egg smell, the driver dropped back into the seat.

"Freaks!" he hollered, then gunned his truck and drove off,

almost clipping my old beater. It and a sporty EV were parked in the street.

The woman in the shrubs—Zadie, my real estate agent—yelled, "Shit heads!" after them.

Broken shells littered the stoop, and the liquid remains of the eggs dribbled down the door. At least it hadn't been a flaming bag of dog droppings this time.

If I hadn't been worried about the elf, I would have been furious at the ongoing antics of my unasked-for rivals, but I had bigger problems.

"Who were those guys?" Zadie asked. "There can't possibly be gangs in this neighborhood."

"Rival flippers. I beat them out of a property we were both bidding on once, sold it for less than they would have, and they've decided to turn into high-school bullies and torment me now. Are you okay?" Though I should have helped brush leaves off her, we weren't alone on the property. I ran past her and yanked open the truck door to pull out my hammer.

The double-headed weapon radiated magic, and its familiar heft was comforting in my hands. With it, maybe I *could* hold my own against an elf.

"I'm not used to being pelted by eggs when I walk up to a client's house. That usually only happens in *my* neighborhood." Zadie stepped back onto the walkway, brushing off her top, which appeared to be egg-free.

"I thought you lived in a good part of town."

"I do, but I'm kind of an odd duck, you know." Dark-skinned Zadie, with her eyebrow rings, nose piercings, and *Starfleet Academy* logo on her messenger bag, gave me an arch look. "That's why I like hanging out with your group. It's the only time I'm not the weirdest one in the room."

"Is it safe?" came Tinja's plaintive call from the doorway. "My wrenches and screwdrivers are quivering with fear."

"Definitely not the weirdest," Zadie said.

"That's the truth." As far as I knew, Zadie was 100 percent human, versus me, Tinja, and Abbas, my half-troll partner who paused drywalling and painting periodically throughout the day to pray, half the time for his mother's Muslim religion and half the time for his father's shamanic troll religion. He observed an inordinate amount of holidays for his dual beliefs. Fortunately, he was a gifted craftsman and made up for the copious time off. "Though your penchant for swishing wine around in your mouth before spitting it out is a little strange."

As we spoke, I crept to the side of the house and peered through the undergrowth toward the backyard, surprised the elf hadn't made an appearance yet. Had he gone inside? I assumed he wasn't enjoying the whimsy of the rusty swing set.

"Wine tasting is perfectly normal." Zadie trailed me around the side of the house, though she had to be wondering what I was looking for. "You spit it out after you taste it so you don't get drunk before you get to try everything. Rich old guys at wine clubs do the same thing."

"Just who we should let define our normal."

I sprang around the corner of the house and into the backyard with my hammer poised, ready in case the elf was still on the patio. He wasn't. But the two decapitated bodies *were*.

I swore. What was I supposed to do with those?

Zadie saw them and swore even harder. She lunged back around the corner of the house and covered her eyes. Her voice got squeaky as she asked, "Why are there naked *dead* guys on the patio?"

"Because Tinja got the house for four hundred thousand off market value, and it came with some quirks." I peered into the overgrown bushes and trees edging the yard and reached out with my senses, but I couldn't detect the elf's magical blood. Now that I thought about it, I hadn't sensed him when he'd been fighting the werewolves either. That was strange. Usually, full-blooded magical beings glowed like beacons to my senses.

"Headless dead guys are more than *quirks*."

"I'll get them cleaned up." *How*, I didn't yet know. Even though I fancied myself a bit of a secret crimefighter, I didn't make a habit of *killing* people. I only thumped them around to ensure proper behavior. What did one do with shifter bodies? Put them in a barrel and dump them in the lake? Mafia-style? "I wouldn't want you to have to mention them in the listing."

"There's a *lot* about this house I wouldn't mention in a listing in its current state." Zadie backed farther away from the corner, not lowering her hand until she stumbled on a broken paver. She gripped her knees and took a few steadying breaths before continuing. "At least it's in a great neighborhood. And quite the departure from your usual blue-collar flips. Inasmuch as there's blue-collar anything left in the greater Seattle area. You say Tinja picked it out?"

"Yeah. She's encouraging me to go higher end so we can make more of a profit." Never mind that I *preferred* fixing up houses for people who couldn't afford to pay for remodeling on their own. I raised my voice and called into the bushes, "Hey, elf-dude. Would you mind folding up the bodies in your funky bag as well as the heads? This is littering." I waved toward the patio.

Zadie stared at me. "I'm *definitely* not the weird one here."

"Ha ha." When no response came from the bushes, I returned to the front yard.

The elf was waiting on the sidewalk, his weapons sheathed in scabbards on his back and his arms folded over his chest.

Cursing, I jerked my hammer up and dropped into a fighting crouch.

He gazed at me with interest. No, he gazed at *me* with bland indifference, but he eyed the hammer with interest.

That happened often. Even if one knew nothing about

dwarves or the runes etched on the haft and sides of the heads, the large silver weapon looked badass. I wished I knew more about it, besides that it had belonged to my mother.

"Uh." Zadie stepped behind me. She was a half a head taller than I was, so she would have to crouch if she wanted to use me as a shield, but she must have been curious about him, because she didn't. "Who is *that*?" she whispered.

"Who the hell are you?" I called to the elf.

The direct approach had always been my style.

"Where did you get that weapon?" he asked in English, though he had an accent I couldn't place.

Since almost all elves and dwarves had left Earth forty years earlier, returning to their home worlds through portals that some of them could create, there weren't many full-bloods around. I had a feeling this guy wasn't a local.

"My mother." I drew myself up to my full five feet one inches, wishing I wasn't still a foot shorter than he. "What's it to you?" My grip tightened on the haft. Was it possible he'd come because he wanted it? Numerous times over the years, people with half- or quarter-magical blood had sensed its power and tried to take it from me. From a young age, I'd gotten used to defending myself.

"You did not steal it?" His sky-blue eyes gazed into mine, as if he were trying to read my mind. It was unnerving.

"Of course not." For some reason, I almost added that my mother had died when I was four, my father had been carted off to military prison for killing some of the soldiers who'd been responsible, and my oblivious-to-all-things-magical half-sister had once tried to save me from being weird by throwing the hammer in the river. But what business was it of his? "Where did you get *your* weapons?"

They were at least as magical as mine.

"I won them in battle."

Won them in battle? That made it sound like he'd stolen them, as he was accusing me of doing. Killing the owner before taking something didn't make it less of a theft.

"You forgot to answer my introductory question," I said. "Who are you? And why were you killing those guys on my lawn?"

The elf gazed toward the house. I sensed the remaining werewolf inside—he hadn't moved and was hopefully still unconscious. If I could sense him, the elf could too. I hoped he didn't plan to go in and decapitate the guy.

"The two I slew were werewolf shifters from Osgashandril," he said calmly. "Not *guys*." The way he carefully pronounced that made me think the word was unfamiliar to him. "Before joining a local pack on this world, they stole from an orc princess. Her mother hired me to ensure they will steal no more."

"By killing them?"

I surreptitiously released the haft of the hammer to wipe one sweaty palm, then the other. The elf made me nervous. Though I hated to admit it, it wasn't entirely because I'd seen him fight and worried he would attack me. As Tinja had pointed out, he was strikingly handsome, and I always got flustered talking to those types.

My teenage years were long past, but I'd never stopped being awkward around hot guys. It was that tangle of emotions that came over me in their presence, the longing for them to notice me even as I braced myself to cringe when they inevitably said something cruel. Or ignored me altogether.

That awkwardness had been understandable in high school, when I'd been the oddly strong girl who'd beaten all the boys at sports, something that had earned me far more derision than admiration, but I was a thirty-four-year-old successful businesswoman. Or at least one who wasn't mired in bone-crushing debt. You'd think I would have grown some self-confidence by now. And I had. But not in this area...

"Yes." The elf lifted his chin. "I am Varlesh Sarrlevi, traveler, mage, warrior, and accomplished assassin on more than twelve worlds." He glanced at the hammer again before gazing expectantly at me.

"I'm Matti."

His gaze continued unwaveringly, as if my introduction hadn't been sufficient. Maybe he was trying to figure out how a scruffy half-dwarf and half-Samoan woman could have ended up with a magical hammer.

"Mataalii Puletasi," I said, giving him my full name, though I still didn't see what business it was of his. "Neither my kindergarten teacher nor the kids in my class could say Mataalii, so it got turned into Matti."

"I have noticed that many humans in this part of your world struggle with names of more than one syllable. What was the name of your dwarf progenitor?"

"My mother? Dad called her Roxy."

He looked blankly at me. Yeah, that wasn't a dwarf name.

"You know, like *Rocks*. Because she was really strong, even more muscled than me, and when she got mad and yelled, her voice sounded like rocks grinding together." At least she hadn't had a beard, something I'd heard some dwarf women could and did grow.

His stare continued. I couldn't tell if he didn't understand me fully or did and didn't *believe* me.

"It was apparently sexier than it sounded because my dad was super into her," I added.

"Why are you telling him this?" Zadie whispered over my shoulder.

Good question.

"He has more weapons than I do," I whispered back.

"I haven't noticed that's made you garrulous in the past."

I didn't mention the pretty-boy-fluster phenomenon.

"What was your mother's *real* name?" the elf—Sarrlevi—asked.

"It's none of your concern." I should have replied that to *all* of his questions. "This house belongs to me now, and I'll kindly ask you to get off my lawn. Especially if you're not going to take the bodies of the dead werewolves with you." I pointed my hammer toward the street.

Long seconds passed as the elf continued to look obstinately at me, his feet not moving.

Fine, if he wouldn't move, *I* would.

"Come on," I muttered to Zadie and headed for the front door.

She hurried after me. After we stepped inside, I closed it with a resounding thud that left the hinges shivering. The elf couldn't fail to get the point.

Curiosity made me spin and peer through the peephole. More long seconds passed as he gazed at the door. I half expected him to walk up and demand to be permitted to behead the third shifter, but he finally turned and walked away. No, he *glided* away, barely stirring the overgrown grass as he headed not toward the street but to the side of the property. He slipped into the bushes, going in the direction of the equestrian park.

"Why do I have a feeling I haven't seen the last of that guy?"

3

A groan came from the kitchen, the shifter waking up. My first instinct was to run in there and club him into unconsciousness again, so he couldn't cause trouble, but inspiration struck.

"I'm questioning that guy."

"To find out what it's like to be hunted by an elf assassin?" As Tinja, who'd never gone outside, trailed me through the house, she kept glancing back toward the front door. She must have also believed we weren't done with Sarrlevi. "I can't imagine it's a delight. Goblins are often trod upon by the larger and stronger races, including humans, but we're rarely targeted individually by assassins."

"Can humans tell your people apart?" Zadie asked as she followed us.

Since she'd been helping me buy and sell houses for almost five years, she'd become familiar with the magical community in and around Seattle—and in the houses I worked on—but I didn't think she'd met a goblin besides Tinja. Most of their kind lived in the woods outside of cities and did their best to keep to themselves, aside from those who frequented a new coffee shop in

Fremont. Apparently, it drew their kind like a Bug Zapper 9000 drew moths. I stayed away from the place. Rumors said one of the owners was the Ruin Bringer, a half-elf assassin who worked for the Army, and I'd never been able to see the military as anything but evil since they'd incarcerated my father for defending my mother.

"Astute ones can, and I'm very little like my scavenging cousins in the wilds who are happy scratching their unwashed armpits with their wrenches while living in hovels." Tinja sniffed. "I'm a career goblin. I have goals."

When we walked into the kitchen, the werewolf's eyes were open. From flat on his back, he snarled and fumbled at his waist but found his gun missing.

"If you think that's bad, don't look outside." I propped my hammer on my shoulder and planted a foot on his chest to keep him from rising.

He might have fought me, but his gaze snagged on the hammer. He lifted a hand to probe his head where I'd cracked him earlier, hopefully realizing that I could do a lot worse now that I was armed with a real weapon.

"The Dugrogik brothers are dead?" he whispered. He didn't have much of an accent, suggesting he'd been on Earth a while, maybe even born into one of the established packs.

"An assassin got them. What brought you here?"

"They said we'd get rich, that they'd cut me in. I just had to show them how to get here. They didn't know our world, nothing. Not even how to read a map and find an address."

"What *here* would make anyone rich?" I glanced toward the kitchen backsplash, but the tingle-delivering tile hadn't been *that* amazing.

"I—"

A can billowing smoke soared through the broken window in

the other room and cracked against a wall. It clattered to the floor, and the werewolf rolled away from me.

An odor that made the rotten eggs spattered on the door seem delightfully palatable in comparison flooded the room as grayish-blue smoke spewed from the can. My nostrils started watering like Niagara Falls. The shifter coughed, but that didn't keep him from springing to his feet.

I started to lunge after him as he beelined for the broken window, but my throat itched horribly, and coughs racked my body. I couldn't keep from bending over. Tinja ran deeper into the kitchen, but Zadie wasn't fast enough to follow her, and the smoke also doubled her over. The werewolf sprang out the window, dislodging more glass that tinkled to the floor.

Coughing and cursing, I ran for the can, deciding it was more of an enemy than the wolf. Though I tried to hold my breath, my coughs foiled me. I grabbed it anyway and hurled it through the broken window, more clouds of smoke flowing from it. The can hit the patio and rolled into the bushes.

I ran through the kitchen to the back door in a vain hope of catching the werewolf. *What* had he thought was in the house that was valuable? So valuable that thieves from another world had come for it?

But he'd crossed four properties and was heading for the park by the time I stepped into the backyard. Worse, I sensed more werewolves running with him. They must have thrown the can. A pack helping a member escape.

A breeze outside made the smoke less awful but not so much that I wanted to linger. As I stepped back inside and started to close the door, something else caught my eye. The two headless bodies were gone.

"Well, that's a small blessing."

Back in the kitchen, Zadie and Tinja were coughing and wiping their noses with a packet of tissues Zadie had pulled out of her messenger bag. With my nostrils quivering, I walked through the house, opening all the windows that weren't stuck—and manhandling open a few that were—in an attempt to air out the place.

"I'm charging you more than the industry-standard three percent to sell this house, Matti," Zadie called.

"It's going to be a long time before it's ready to list." As I walked back to join them, the front door opened.

I spun, raising my hammer, certain the assassin had returned. But it was Abbas, his toolbox in hand and his head ducked so he didn't bump it on the door frame. His kinky black dreads dangled around his broad face as he peered curiously inside.

"Am I late?" he rumbled, then wrinkled his flat nose as he got a whiff of the lingering odor.

"It depends on whether you're a fan of decapitation and smoke bombs."

"Nope."

"Then you're right on time. Tinja is about to share her vision for the house while I... look around for things the last tenant might have left behind." Like a valuable magical treasure that might prompt my house to be invaded by werewolves on a daily basis until I got rid of it.

This early in the renovation process, things breaking wasn't that big a deal, but I didn't want windows and locks being destroyed after I replaced them. This house was already a huge financial gamble, one I'd started questioning as soon as I'd seen the chalk outline. I should have stuck with the blue-collar fixer-uppers.

"If you find any plaid shirts like last time, I'm expanding my collection. Grunge is making its way back you know." Abbas winked at me.

"Plaid shirts that fit you must be few and far between." I waved at his six-foot-ten-inch frame, barrel torso, and muscled arms. As with most half-bloods, he appeared fully human, those genes being dominant, but some of his size, that kink to his hair, and the stone gray of his eyes came from his troll ancestry.

"Not as much as you'd think. They were originally made for lumberjacks, you know. Lumberjacks are big boys." He lifted his head, eyes growing glazed as he seemed to peer not at the walls but through them. "I assume you know there's magic in this house. Besides your hammer and Tinja's charms."

"I noticed a tingly tile in the kitchen. I haven't done a thorough investigation yet." But I would.

"Want me to rip out the cabinets?" Abbas eyed the broken window. "It looks like you've already started on demo."

"Go ahead, but save some for me." I patted my hammer. "You know I enjoy that."

"Are you supposed to use what's likely an ancient magical weapon for smashing cabinets and drywall?" He'd asked that numerous times before, and it had become an ongoing joke.

"Probably not, but Mom forgot to leave the instruction manual."

"Too bad she's gone."

"Yeah."

It had been thirty years since her death, and I barely remembered her beyond a vague image of pale skin, frizzy red hair, and gentle green eyes, but I did wish she'd survived so that I could have known her. With my dad in prison, Grandpa and Grandma had been the ones to raise my half-sister and me, and, even today, I sometimes grew wistful about the past and wondered what it would have been like to have a *normal* childhood. At least our grandparents had been there for Penina and me. Not everyone was that lucky.

The closets did not hold any flannel shirts, but I did find an array of leftover clothing, dusty boxes full of receipts, and wooden toys that had been whittled with a knife, not manufactured in a factory. Faint magic clung to a few of them, as if the crafter had been an enchanter, though I couldn't tell what the enchantments did. The toys were well-made but nothing worth stealing or invading a home for. An artifact that could have interested werewolves from another world should have banged at my senses with as much magic as my hammer had.

The toys were as dusty as the boxes, and I hoped that whatever children had played with them had grown up and moved on and hadn't been there when the renter had been shot. The police would have figured out what had happened to him and contacted his next-of-kin, I assumed, but maybe there hadn't been anyone to come collect his belongings.

"There you are," Zadie said from the doorway. She'd stopped coughing and sniffling, but her makeup had run, leaving mascara streaks on her cheeks. She frowned around what had been the master bedroom, though it lacked a walk-in closet or attached bath. These houses had been large for the era they'd been built in, but they weren't like modern mansions. "My reason for coming, though I almost forgot it in the chaos, was to let you know there's an offer on the Renton house."

"Will I like it?" I set down the toys and ran my hand over the wood paneling in the back of the closet, wondering if the home had any secret doors or a vault.

"You should. You set it."

"They're not coming in low?" The market had softened since we'd picked up that house, and I'd worried it would take a long time to sell and that we would be lucky to cover our expenses.

"No. Your craftsmanship wows people. It's why I like working with you. Your houses sell right away."

"But you don't like working with me enough to charge less than three percent on your half of the agent's cut."

"Of course not," Zadie said. "Business is business. Besides, you used another agent to buy this house. You're lucky I'm still talking to you."

"Tinja was behind this deal. She has a cousin in the business."

"A goblin real-estate agent?"

"Half-goblin. Hm." I didn't find anything odd about the closet, other than the choice to put wood paneling in it. Outside, the sky was darkening, partially with clouds and partially with the oncoming sunset. My experiences thus far today assured me I didn't want to hang out here after dark. But if nobody was here to keep an eye on things, might more would-be thieves come? Maybe I would ask Tinja to set some goblin alarms. "Let's check downstairs."

Wood creaked under the steps as we descended, emerald-green Berber carpet giving way to black-and-white checkered floor tiles on the bottom floor. Even after turning on the overhead lights, a staggering number of saucer pendants that reminded me of Roswell, it was dark down there. Numerous high windows should have let in the fading daylight, but almost every one was blocked by overgrown foliage in the yard.

A mustard-yellow sectional and a pool table with metal siding that reminded me of old car fenders were the only furnishings left behind. Due to their heft, I suspected they'd been left behind by *many* renters.

"I'll look forward to seeing what you do with this place," Zadie said, a wrinkle to her nose as she looked around. "That pool table might be worth something. That's an old Brunswick, I think."

The fumes of the smoke grenade hadn't invaded the basement, and the air smelled of something... familiar. I couldn't place it, but it reminded me of my parents' apartment before my mother had died. Strange.

I drifted from room to room, trying to detect magic. I felt something, but it was as vague and hard to place as the scent. Almost like the ghost of magic. As if a great deal had been used here once, but whatever—or whoever—had called upon it was gone.

"When do you think this one will be ready to go on the market?" Zadie asked over bangs drifting down from upstairs.

Abbas had gotten to work.

"It depends on how many times it gets broken into over the coming weeks." Using my hammer, I tapped at a few walls, still thinking there might be a hidden vault or secret room. "I wish I'd gotten more out of that werewolf."

"Do you want me to do some research on the house's history for you?"

"I didn't know real-estate agents could search the MLS for information on magical artifacts the previous owners possessed."

"We can't, but I can surf through the county records to see if any interesting permits were filed for over the years." She watched me tap at another wall. "You look like you're trying to find secret rooms. If there were permitted additions done, it'll be in the records."

"I don't think people who install secret rooms get *permits* first."

"It's also possible what's now a secret room is something from the original plan that got walled in at some point."

"True. Sure. If you want to look up the house, I'd appreciate it." I knew how to surf through the county records myself, but since Zadie had admitted I made her job—and her 3 percent—easy, I would happily give her some extra work. "Huh. These tiles look brand new, don't they?"

I'd wandered into the laundry room and lowered my hammer to the floor. The same black-and-white checkerboard pattern continued in there, but the white tiles were a *lot* whiter. The grout was fresh too.

When my hammer clunked against one, the sound was unexpectedly hollow.

I touched a dried brown smudge. "Is that a bloodstain?"

"If so," Zadie said, "I doubt that'll be in the county records."

"Remind me to scour the internet for articles related to the renter's death." I waved toward the ceiling in the direction of the foyer. "It's too bad he wasn't the owner. I'm not sure how easy it'll be to find information on a tenant, but since he died on the premises, maybe a search for the address will bring up something."

I clunked a few more tiles in the center of the room. It sounded like we were on a second floor rather than below ground.

"Let's check." Zadie pulled out her phone.

"We're in the basement," I mused.

"A daylight basement, yes. You're perceptive. That's a good quality in a house flipper."

I shot her a dark look. "I wouldn't expect there to be a crawl-space under a basement floor." I waved toward the ceiling, vents implying the ductwork was between the floors.

Forgetting the bloodstain, I thunked more tiles. Maybe I'd found my secret vault. I tried to pry up a tile, but they were well sealed. As one would expect if the job had been done recently.

I checked the floor tiles in the pool-table room, and they did *not* thunk. Older and darker, the grout flaked away when I scraped at it. The temptation to take my hammer to the laundry-room floor and destroy it to see what was underneath came over me, but did I truly want to tear up something that was in good shape? It wasn't as if I sensed something magical under there.

"The only thing that's coming up under the address are the real-estate listings for the house," Zadie said.

"Really? A guy was murdered here, and it didn't make it into the news?"

"Maybe it was a suicide."

"People shooting themselves in the head don't usually miss a bunch of times and blow holes in the wall."

"I didn't know you were an expert on that." Zadie lowered her phone. "Want to come to the Rose and Lily with me tonight? Tinja's invited too, of course, though I'm not sure they serve her kind."

Since most humans didn't know that goblins existed, that wasn't surprising.

"Is that the bar where they wouldn't serve *Abbas's* kind either?"

"Guys are kind of frowned upon there, yeah."

"Uh huh. I got hit on a lot the last time I went there with you."

"You said it was flattering."

"I said it was less depressing than when I wander into bars full of straight guys who ignore me."

She grinned at me. "If you broadened your horizons a little, you might find true love."

"The elf assassin is a lot more likely to get my motor running."

"Hell, he was gorgeous. Even I could see that. But, uhm, he might not be a good match for you."

"Too hot for someone like me?"

"I didn't say that. But he beheaded people in your backyard. That's not an endearing pastime for a guy."

"If he's an assassin, I think that's his *main* time."

"Yeah. Not endearing."

I eyed the floor again, less sure of that assessment. If Sarrlevi *hadn't* shown up, all three of those werewolves might have sprung through the window and attacked me. Taking that many down with a fireplace poker would have been asking a lot of my combat skills.

A howl drifted to our ears, the sound making the hairs rise on the back of my neck. Upstairs, the banging had stopped, likely for Abbas's sunset prayer, so the eerie sound came through loud and clear.

"Is that a coyote?" Zadie asked.

"Wolf." I thought of the pack I'd sensed earlier. Now that

they'd rescued their buddy, maybe they'd decided to try again to find what they believed was in the house.

"There aren't any wolves in Bellevue."

"You *just* saw werewolves."

"I meant actual wolves."

"Werewolves howl too." I flexed my fingers on the hammer, an idea percolating in my mind. "Maybe I should *let* them break in so I can see what they find."

"What?"

I patted her on the shoulder. "Why don't you go home for the night, Zadie? Do that research on the house if you're inclined. Or visit the bar. I'm going to round up my crew for some nocturnal work."

"After what happened today, you shouldn't stay here tonight."

"Probably not."

"But you will anyway?"

"Yup."

4

"Is it weird to spy on a house your business owns?" Tinja asked from the branch next to mine. She rubbed her nose, and the charms and cogs on her metal bracelets jangled.

"We're spying on those who might *come* to the house," I whispered, "and be as quiet as possible, please."

Trying to take my own advice, I shifted carefully to readjust my weight, not wanting to knock leaves or apples to the ground. Already, my thighs ached from my awkward perch ten feet up an apple tree that an aspiring orchardist had long ago planted opposite a cherry tree in the front yard.

The fruit trees were out of place near the native evergreens that dominated the back half of the lot. They were, however, handy for one wishing to see the front door, the street, the side of the house, and part of the backyard, all from the same perch. If I'd been brave enough to climb higher, I might have been able to see *all* of the backyard, but both my dwarf and human instincts agreed that great heights were to be avoided as assiduously as venomous snakes, workplace bullies, and spiders that sauntered into the shower stall when one was naked.

"For a goblin, I'm being very quiet."

"It's a wonder your people have remained a secret to most humans."

Full darkness had fallen, with no streetlights in the quiet residential neighborhood and only a handful of landscaping lamps on adjacent lots brightening the cloudy night. Now and then, a car drove past, its headlights gleaming on pavement damp from an earlier rain. Hopefully, it wouldn't start up again while we were on our stakeout, but the air smelled of moisture, and the clouds were thick.

"We have means of cloaking ourselves when we travel among humankind," Tinja said. "Haven't you noticed that your neighbors are oblivious to my presence as your roommate?"

"I assumed it was because you weren't raiding *their* vegetable crispers and eating their cheese."

There was enough light for me to see Tinja's teeth flash white against her dark green skin as she smiled over at me. "My people have been known to be discovered or at least suspected of being in an area due to our scavenging tendencies."

"Scavenging is what you do at a junkyard or in a trash bin, not in a friend's refrigerator."

"I have read your dictionary, and I'm not certain the word conveys such specificity."

"I thought we were being quiet," Abbas rumbled from the hydrangea bush beside our tree. Thanks to its lack of a recent pruning, it hid even his tall frame.

Another wolf howl wafted through the damp air. There had been a few in the last hour, each time a little closer. Whether it was the same wolf or one of many, I couldn't tell.

"Tell that to the wolf," Tinja said, bracelets rattling.

I almost told her to take those off, but she faded from my senses, startling me into glancing over to make sure she hadn't fallen. Her small dark shape still perched on the branch.

"What did you do?" I whispered.

"I engaged stealth magic," she whispered back with another grin. "The werewolves won't sense me."

"One of your charms does that?" I wouldn't have guessed she had anything as valuable as a camouflaging trinket.

"The one that looks like a mix of used gum, paperclips, and metal pencil bands."

"Doesn't it look like those things because it *is* those things?"

"Those things and *magic.* I have a cousin who makes them."

Now I regretted ever teasing her about her jewelry. "Can you extend your influence to cover me and Abbas?"

"You, maybe." Tinja shifted closer to the trunk, rattling bracelets promising the camouflaging magic didn't stifle noise, and stuck her hand out to grip my wrist. "Abbas is too far away."

"Can you sense us, Abbas?" I called softly down.

"Not now, no. To my senses, the tree is talking to me."

"How are we going to hide him?" If those were werewolves howling, they would sense our magical auras, something that hadn't dawned on me when I'd been coming up with this plan.

"Ssh," he said. "Someone's coming."

Headlights pierced the night as a black Jeep Wrangler rolled down the street.

"Probably a neighbor," I said before I realized that whoever was driving the vehicle had the aura of a magical being. Not a werewolf but something similar to me. A half-blood. Half-elf?

The Jeep pulled to a stop where my truck had been parked before I'd moved it closer to the park, not wanting to leave evidence that I was still on the property. Because of the large lots, the houses were far enough apart that there was little chance the Jeep belonged to a neighbor in need of a parking space.

"Whoever that is will sense me," Abbas whispered up.

"It's all right. We own the property. It's not like we're doing anything wrong."

"Just hiding out in the dark in apple trees and hydrangeas."

"That we own. That isn't the police, anyway." I was fairly certain the Bellevue P.D. didn't cruise the city in Wranglers.

The passenger door opened. The headlights hadn't yet turned off, so I had a clear view of a fit-looking, dark-skinned woman with short, wiry salt-and-pepper hair. Even though she wore plain clothes, that haircut and her stern face made me believe she was in the military. I stifled a groan. That was even *worse* than the police. What would someone from the military be doing in Bellevue?

The Jeep turned off, the headlights went dark, and the driver got out, tugging something onto her back as she did so. It had a strong magical aura. No moonlight filtered through the clouds, and I hadn't inherited the dwarven ability to see in the dark, but I could tell the second woman was tall and blonde, her hair a bright spot against the darkness.

She looked straight toward Abbas's hydrangea. She was the one with magical blood, not to mention what I guessed was a sword now sheathed on her back—it had an aura similar to my hammer's. *Very* similar. It had to also be of dwarven make. In addition, a bunch of magical charms hung around her neck.

The other woman walked up to the front door, though the house was dark, not a light left on inside or out. She eyed a pile of broken wood by the porch. Abbas had started tearing out a closet full of built-ins that we would replace.

"She's not inside," the blonde woman said.

She? *Me*?

I supposed I should have assumed they hadn't come for Abbas or Tinja. Half-trolls and goblins weren't common in the greater Seattle area, but they weren't as rare as a half-dwarf with a powerful hammer.

"Humor me." The military woman rang the doorbell, found it didn't work, and knocked.

A testament to the years I'd been in the business, I subconsciously added *doorbell* to my mental to-do list of renovations for the house.

"You know that fostering your humor is one of my great passions in life." The blonde woman ignored the house and headed toward the bush Abbas was hidden in, her hand reaching not toward the weapon on her back but a second one strapped to her thigh. Its signature wasn't as strong as the other's, and I hadn't realized it was a weapon at first, but the lumpy shape made me think it was a gun. A *large* gun.

"I thought it was aggravating me."

"While making you throw back your head in raucous laughter, yes."

"I haven't raucously laughed in my life."

"Sadly, I believe you." The blonde woman drew the gun and pointed it at the bushes.

Not wanting Abbas to be hurt, I almost jumped down, but I hesitated, afraid to startle someone with a firearm. She might shoot me on reflex.

Abbas must not have wanted to be hurt either, because he blurted, "I didn't do anything," and stepped out of the bushes.

"Who are you, and what are you doing in there?" the blonde asked.

The military woman left the door and joined her.

"I'm Abbas, one of the guys working on the house."

"From the bushes?" the military woman asked. She had a Southern drawl, a *tart* Southern drawl.

"I had to take a break to pray. I'm Muslim."

"I thought that involved a prayer mat facing Mecca, not hunkering in a shrub."

"I'm also half-troll, and my father was a shaman," Abbas said. "Shamans like nature, so I gotta compromise."

I stifled another groan. I might as well have gone down to talk to them myself. My awkward lies couldn't have been any worse than his.

Throughout the conversation, the blonde woman was gazing toward the trees. Not only the apple tree but those to the sides and back of the property too. Was it possible she knew we were there? Her gun was still pointed at Abbas, but she looked like someone capable of shifting targets in a heartbeat. Or maybe hitting *two* targets in that time.

Since she was half-elven, her senses shouldn't have been any sharper than mine, but elves were known for their keen hearing, more so than dwarves. Maybe she heard us breathing.

"I'm Colonel Willard, and this is Val Thorvald." Why did those names sound familiar? "We're looking for Mataalii Puletasi," she said, pronouncing my name carefully and more or less getting it right, though hearing it with a Southern twang was odd. "She's your partner, right?"

"Uhm," Abbas said.

"Business partner or *partner*?" Thorvald asked the colonel, thankfully holstering her firearm.

"We only know about the business aspect," Willard said dryly.

"Just business partners," Abbas said, apparently deciding he was willing to reveal that. "She went home for the day. Er, *maybe* she went home. Maybe she went out. I don't know. She goes to the bars sometimes."

I realized he was trying to keep them from going to my house, but I rolled my eyes. Whatever they'd thought of me before, now they thought I was a lush who went out with Zadie every night.

With the abruptness of a boot to the head, I realized why these people's names were familiar. Colonel Willard ran the US Army Intelligence office in Seattle, the one few knew about but that investigated crimes perpetrated by magical beings. And Val Thorvald—she was the *Ruin Bringer*, the assassin who worked for the Army and was a part owner of the coffee shop in Fremont.

My blood chilled. I'd spent years avoiding them both, not because I was a criminal, but because the military had never done anything but screw over my family. And the Ruin Bringer? Hell, nobody crossed her path if they could help it. She preyed on her own kind, anyone who went the tiniest bit astray of the law—the *human* laws. It didn't matter if they were trolls, orcs, or shifters. Or half-dwarves. If they committed a crime, and Willard found out about it, she sent Thorvald out to kill the person. She might even have one of those magical folding bags for putting the heads in.

"We have a few questions for Ms. Puletasi," Willard said.

"She's got a phone."

"We want to ask them in person." Willard eyed the house.

Thorvald had never *stopped* eyeing it and its surroundings. She touched one of the charms hanging on a thong around her neck. In the dim light, I couldn't see them, but I could *sense* them. Almost every one was more powerful than anything on Tinja's wrists. Not that I would complain about my roommate's jewelry, not when her sweaty palm and one of her charms were keeping me camouflaged.

Silver mist and an aura of powerful magic arose out of nowhere at Thorvald's side. A huge silver tiger formed, its head almost as high as her shoulder.

Tinja let out an inadvertent squeak of alarm. Fortunately, it was a soft squeak, and I didn't think the pair would hear it, but Thorvald *and* the tiger looked toward our branches. I closed my eyes in defeat. I would have to talk to them. Since I hadn't committed any crimes, they shouldn't have come to arrest—or behead—me. They just had questions, they'd said.

But before I moved, a mallet of realization struck a gong in my mind. The dead werewolves. What if they'd heard about them? And what if they *hadn't* heard about the strange elf assassin? They might only know that magical beings had been killed on my property.

A howl came from the woods. It couldn't have been more than a quarter mile away.

Thorvald's and Willard's heads both turned in that direction, and the tiger rose to all fours, his tail going rigid.

"I've got a few questions for *them* too," Thorvald said, as if she knew the wolves personally.

"Didn't your assassin buddy say he took care of them?"

I gaped. The elf? He'd spoken to Thorvald?

"Sarrlevi is hardly a *buddy*," Thorvald said, "but, according to him, he took care of the ones from Osgashandril, not the locals. The newcomers might have told the pack what they were looking for, why they came to Earth, and if more of their kind will come."

"I do love when fresh werewolves invade Seattle," Willard grumbled. "If that half-dwarf vigilante is wrapped up in it, I want to know."

Vigilante? I wasn't a vigilante. I just helped people who had problems. So what if I knocked bad guys into walls head-first instead of calling the police? There wasn't always time for that.

"It sounds like she's running around with a stolen magical weapon," Willard added. "You *know* what kind of trouble that can create for her and those around her."

"I've a notion."

Stolen? Who had told her that? The elf?

"Sarrlevi got the werewolves he was looking for," Thorvald said, "so I doubt he'll stick around to help if more shifters invade Seattle."

"Would you *want* his help? When you've got a strapping *dragon* to assist you?"

"Zav is on a mission of his own right now, but no. I have no interest in help from Sarrlevi. As if he would give it without being paid." Thorvald shook her head. "He's trouble."

"You only say that because he tried to kill you."

"Which is a legitimate reason to consider someone trouble.

Come on, Sindari. Let's go question a wolf." Thorvald jogged under my tree and into the brush, heading in the direction of the park.

Why did nobody use the street?

Willard lingered, eyeing Abbas. "Tell your partner that we'll be back tomorrow and want to talk to her."

"I will, ma'am."

I hoped the colonel had the keys to the Jeep and would drive it away from the house, but she only walked out to the street and headed toward the park. New howls arose, and I had a feeling the shifters had detected Thorvald's presence and weren't happy about it.

When she was out of range of my senses, I patted Tinja's hand to let her know she could release me, then climbed down from the tree, landing with a grunt beside Abbas.

"Sorry about that," I said. "Thanks for trying to cover for me."

"I meant to do it more smoothly."

"You should have told them that Matti went to Canada," Tinja said. "I have heard that Canada is very pretty and full of trees."

"And probably even more werewolves. Don't worry about it, Abbas. It's hard to be smooth when an Army officer is questioning you."

"You got that right. I don't want any trouble with the law—or the military. My parents would kill me."

"Even your father?" I didn't think trolls cared that much about Earth laws.

"*Especially* my father. His clan stayed here after all the others left, and he doesn't want them on anyone's radar. He would kick my ass if I was the one to bring them to the attention of the Ruin Bringer." Abbas shuddered. "Are we still staking out the house?"

I sighed and looked at the Jeep. Willard and Thorvald would be back. Though I didn't know for certain they suspected me of anything, I didn't want to answer their questions. Or interact with them at all.

"No."

"We coming to work tomorrow?" Abbas pointed at the house.

"Yes. We can't afford to hold this house longer than necessary. We'll just keep an eye out for visitors."

"And hide in the bushes when they show up?"

"Maybe under the basement." If I could find an entrance and learn what had happened to the renter. I had some research to do.

5

"You're not coming for Sunday brunch?" my sister's voice came over the phone's speaker as I wandered around the kitchen of my house in Lynnwood. I was still in my pajamas, swigging coffee and looking for cheese to go with the salami I'd chosen for breakfast.

Tinja favored the sweetest children's cereal she could find for her breakfast, but meats and cheeses were what my mixed blood craved. In my imagination, storage chambers in dwarven tunnels on their home world were filled with strings of salami and sausage and wheels of cheese.

After realizing my roommate had raided the vegetable crisper again, I was forced to dig into the sliced sandwich cheese that I purchased for those days when I didn't have time to cut pieces from something superior.

"It's not a good idea this week, Penina." I didn't admit that I was glad to have the excuse. Spending time with my sister, who refused to believe that I was half-dwarf or that dwarves existed, despite remembering my mother, was worse than dealing with werewolves. "Uhm, if someone comes by your house asking about me, you haven't seen me in a while, all right?"

I wandered back to the laptop open on the counter, a list of the addresses around the Bridle Trails house typed on the screen. As Zadie had pointed out, there was nothing on the web about our new project, nor had I been able to find the renter's name to run a search on him. But if guns had fired the day he'd died, maybe a neighbor would remember it. And maybe the neighbors knew something about the renter too.

"I *haven't* seen you in a while," Penina said. "You canceled the last two Sundays. Matti, I worry about you. Why haven't you found a nice man and settled down? Don't you want children? You're not getting any younger, you know. And *who* would come to our house, asking about you?"

"Nobody, and I'm too busy with work to look for a man." Not to mention the various painful rejections over the years that had left me disinclined to ask anyone out.

"Not the police, right? You haven't done anything *criminal,* have you? With that big hammer? I can't believe you lug that thing around. Ladies carry Chanel, Matti, not a giant sledgehammer."

"They do if they're in the construction business." The phone beeped, Zadie's name popping up. "That's my other line. I need to go. You haven't seen me. Bye."

My sister was in the middle of another scathing comment when I switched over to the new caller.

"What's up, Zadie?"

"I met someone cool at the bar last night."

"Does that mean you didn't have time to research the house for me?"

"I *do* have new information for you. I'm a gifted researcher and can multi-task like no other."

"I'm sure your new love interest will be impressed."

"Obviously. Anyway, I learned that the house was on the

market for two years while the renter was still there. They took it off the market last winter and then put it on again right before you and Tinja put in your offer."

"Mostly Tinja," I murmured.

Though the mystery of the house and what was in it had me curious, I had no doubt it would have been better for my business if we'd skipped this one. This was my punishment for trying to encourage my young assistant to grow as a person—and a future architect and real-estate developer.

"Right, but it didn't sell for two years, even though the price wasn't that bad. It needs work, but, at a glance, it isn't horrific. I asked around my network of agents, and the ones that remember it said the renter scared off some prospective buyers over the years. That's why the owner gave up and took it off the market. Until the renter moved out."

"Moved out or was murdered?"

"The official word is that he moved out. Do you know his name? Maybe we could find out the day he died. If the house went up for sale right away, one might think the death had been arranged." Zadie sounded excited at this prospect. "Do you think that could be it? The owners wanted the money for the house but couldn't sell until he was gone, and, if he wouldn't leave, they had to take matters into their own hands. Maybe they even hired an assassin. Like that elf!"

I rubbed my face. "You've been reading too many mystery novels. You of all people must know that there are eviction processes, assuming the lease was up."

"This is a tenant-friendly state. It's hard to evict people who are making their payments on time and don't want to leave. Just because you tell people they need to go doesn't mean they will. And, hey, I looked at the records of the house, and, up until you bought it, it belonged to the original owners. They bought it when it was built in the fifties, so basically their family was looking at well over a million in equity that they couldn't get as long as their tenant was there."

"There are legal ways they could have taken equity out of the house if they needed it. They wouldn't have needed to *murder* anyone."

"You never met that tenant. Maybe he was horrible and people wanted to murder him left and right. Maybe he was making drugs in the basement."

"I didn't see anything down there to suggest that, but I am going to try to get to the bottom of this." Assuming the werewolves, the government spooks, and that elf assassin would leave me alone long enough to do so. I couldn't believe Sarrlevi had blabbed about me to that Colonel Willard. He'd blabbed *lies* about me and my hammer. I ground my teeth, wishing I'd pounded him in the head.

Loud thumping came from the house next door. The elderly widow who lived there wasn't one for home improvement projects —I'd ended up as her unofficial handywoman—so I frowned and looked out the window. A couple of pale-skinned brutes in black leather stood on the stoop. I hadn't seen them before but was certain they weren't any of Mrs. Ming's seven children or seventeen grandchildren.

When the door didn't open, they pounded on it again.

One kicked over a flowerpot, and it rolled off the stoop, cracking on the walkway. "Open up, Granny. We know your boy is hiding out here, and he owes us money."

A curtain stirred on a side window, one facing in my direction. Ming wasn't looking out at the brutes but over toward me. As if this was a job for a handywoman.

Cursing, I hung up on Zadie, stuffed my feet in my slippers, and grabbed my hammer. The microwave clock said 7:14. It was *way* too early for people to threaten old ladies.

As I hurried over, Willard's words about me being a vigilante came to mind. As if it was wrong to stick up for people who weren't strong enough to defend themselves.

"Go away," Ming called through the door to them. "Nobody is here."

"*You're* here, and we know that scrawny brat lives here too. He missed his payment again this month, so we're going to take it out of his hide."

"You already took it out of the flowerpot," I said. "Go away."

They whirled toward me.

Since I didn't look that intimidating in my pinstriped pajama bottoms, slippers, and oversized T-shirt, I held up my hammer so they couldn't miss it. Alas, it was cloudy, so there was no sun to gleam on its silver surface and highlight the broad heft of the double heads. It wasn't truly silver, being some much stronger alloy that I could only guess at, but any metal hammer hurt when vigorously applied to the side of one's head.

"Who the hell are you?" the flowerpot molester asked.

"The handywoman."

"You better get back in your house, girl. This is no business of yours." The man stuck a hand in his leather jacket and pulled out a switchblade knife.

"Really? You're going to attack me with a weapon with a quarter the reach of mine? Seems smart."

They exchanged scowls, glanced dismissively toward my slippers and the rest of my wardrobe, then strode toward me. Even though my pajamas were far from sexy, I was a little affronted that they didn't check me out—I bet the Ruin Bringer got leered at by bad guys *all* the time—but I would have hit them harder if they had, so maybe it was for the best.

When they got close, the men charged, trying to take me from the sides. They were as much fat as muscle and had the speed of sloths. I whipped my hammer down to knock the knife out of the wielder's hand as I sent a side kick toward the groin of the other.

Since I didn't bother feinting before committing to the kick, he had time to get his arms down and half-turn away, but it didn't matter. My side kicks could break boards, bricks, beams, and other inoffensive construction materials that our instructor brought into the *dojang*. It sent him sprawling across the yard. Unfortunately, my slipper also flew off. One didn't wear such footwear at the *dojang*.

The other man yelped when the hammer connected with his hand, and he dropped his knife. The pain didn't propel him to back away. Instead, fury contorted his face, and he spread his arms and leaped, trying to engulf me in a bear hug.

I dodged the clumsy grasp and jabbed the top of my hammer into his gut. His breath whooshed out, smelling of tuna fish. Yuck. That was an even weirder breakfast food than salami and cheese. In a hurry to push him away, I kicked him in the same spot the hammer had hit. He tumbled onto his ass in the grass.

The other one had recovered enough to creep around to my back, but I knew he was there. Like a home-run hitter winding up for a pitch, I spun and connected, my hammer pounding him in his squishy stomach. He flew toward the sidewalk, struck down, and rolled into the street where he promptly puked.

A car drove up while he was adorning the pavement with his breakfast. I lifted an apologetic hand toward what I assumed was a neighbor heading off to work, but I froze. It was that damn black Jeep again.

6

THE JEEP DROVE AROUND THE PUKING MAN AND PARKED AT THE CURB in front of my house. Willard and Thorvald got out, and I slumped. Why had I assumed they'd been truthful when they'd told Abbas they would come see me at the Bridle Trails property that day?

"He should have told them I was in Canada," I muttered.

Behind me, the door opened.

"Thank you for your help, Matti," Mrs. Ming called as she made shooing motions toward the men, then picked up her mangled flowerpot. "My grandson is not here, but I will check with him and make sure he does not owe anyone money." She scowled at the men.

The one in the yard must have decided there were too many witnesses present to stick around, for he hurried out to the street and helped his puking friend to his feet. They climbed into a truck with tires almost as huge as their hollow heads and drove off.

"You're welcome," I said, though my gaze was locked on the new arrivals.

Thorvald, clad in jeans, combat boots, and a duster, leaned

casually against the front of the Jeep, her arms folded over her chest. A smirk rode her lips as she took in my pajamas and bare feet, both slippers having come off as I'd fought. She was six feet tall, looked like she had the athleticism of a dancer, and was as beautiful as I'd suspected—who'd ever heard of a homely elf?

I promptly hated her.

"Nice bike," she offered, waving toward the 1988 Harley Sportster tucked under the carport.

Unlike the beater work truck that had more dings than a target at a shooting range, it gleamed, a testament to all the time I'd put into fixing it up and maintaining it. I almost asked if she rode but reminded myself that I didn't like or trust her. Either of them.

"Thanks," I said gruffly and headed toward the house.

Willard was already halfway to my front door. When I met her dark eyes, she tapped her wristwatch, as if to say I was late for an appointment. My first impression of her wasn't warm and fuzzy either. If these two had come to accuse me of being a thief, I would see if I could make *them* puke.

Maybe. Thorvald had a lot of weapons. The tiger she'd conjured the night before wasn't around, but I had no doubt she could summon him again quickly.

Scowling, I stuffed my feet in my slippers and walked over to join Willard on my stoop. "Won't you come in, Colonel?"

"I'd love to. Thanks." Willard waited for me to open the door and walk in first, as if my living room might be booby-trapped. I wished it *were* booby-trapped and added that to my to-do list for the house.

Thorvald waited by the Jeep. Because she now suspected this was a bad neighborhood and she needed to keep an eye on it? Given the morning so far, I supposed that wasn't a strange assumption. We were close enough to busy 196th Street that crime wasn't unheard of, but mafia toughs or whatever those two had fancied themselves weren't typical.

More likely, Thorvald was waiting in case I tried to run out the back door and into the next block. With her long legs, she could probably catch me. I excelled at *most* sports, but being on the short and stout side didn't help me a lot in sprints.

Willard sniffed as we walked in, the air smelling of the coffee I'd brewed. From the small living room, I could see into the even smaller kitchen. Tinja, who favored coffee, must not have woken yet or the rest of the pot would have disappeared while I'd been fighting.

"Do you want a cup?" I grudgingly asked while waving the colonel to the chair and love seat. Maybe if I plied her with gifts, she would be less likely to arrest me or whatever she had in mind. She kept eyeing my hammer. I doubted it was because she was an admirer of fine dwarven craftsmanship.

"Yes, thank you."

As I retrieved it, I texted Abbas that I would be late—and not to expect the military women to come to the project house today. I returned with a mug of coffee, deposited it in Willard's hand, and perched on the edge of the chair. She'd taken the love seat. Per Tinja's suggestion, the furniture was arranged "conversation style," instead of as I'd had it before—pointed at the fireplace and the TV. When I'd lived alone, I hadn't needed to converse that often, and I wasn't sure if this was an improvement. Especially not today.

"That was less messy than the aftermath of some of your other vigilante scenes." Willard pointed the mug toward the wall that faced Ming's house.

"Because I'm not a vigilante. I was helping my neighbor."

"As you helped the proprietor of a teriyaki restaurant five blocks away?"

"*Yes*," I said firmly, though it horrified me that she knew about that. That incident had been more than six months earlier. How long had the military been keeping tabs on me?

Dread curdled in my stomach. Maybe, because of my incarcerated father, they'd been observing me my whole life.

"There was five thousand dollars in damage done during that fight," Willard said, "with furniture hurled through the windows and the glass door of a soda refrigerator."

"*I* didn't break those things. The half-orc brutes did." Technically, I may have hit a couple of them and caused them to crash through the windows, but it was a small restaurant packed with tables and chairs. It had been hard to hit anyone without doing damage. "I was keeping the restaurant from being robbed. That's all. If the police and other authorities were better about keeping crime down, the owners wouldn't have *needed* my help."

Willard's eyelids drooped halfway. Maybe that hadn't been the best thing to say. From what I'd heard of her special intelligence office, she was in charge of keeping crimes committed by those with magical blood to a minimum as well as gathering information on the community.

Her phone buzzed, and she pulled it out, reading a text without turning her face from me. Maybe she also thought I would flee out the back.

As if there was a point when they knew where I lived. And had been keeping track of me for years. Creeps.

Willard tapped a short response and lowered the phone. "Where did you get the hammer?"

"My mother." I managed to bite off the *not that it's any business of yours* that wanted to follow the words. "It was hers. It wasn't stolen."

"And she was a dwarf."

"Obviously," I said, waving at myself, though to someone without magical blood, I supposed it wasn't obvious. There were plenty of short, stout humans who had to tweeze between their eyebrows and Nair their bikini line. Not that my pajamas were revealing enough that I had to worry about Willard discovering information on the latter.

"From the dwarven home world of Dun Kroth? Ruled by King Korvik Ironhelm?"

I shrugged. "As far as I know. I was only four when she died. She sang me songs that taught me Dwarven words about smashing spiders and forging ore, not about the governments and rulers of the Cosmic Realms."

"I guess we can't press you into diplomatic work then," Willard said dryly, glancing at her phone again. "There's a goblin in your home?"

"My roommate, yes. She sleeps in."

"I suppose that cuts down on the time she's demolishing your housewares to build things."

"She doesn't do that too often. She's busy helping me on the job and studying for her architecture degree." I hesitated. "She did retool my electric shaver to mixed success when I made the mistake of saying it wasn't strong enough for the needs of my half-dwarven body." So much for keeping the information about my bikini line a secret.

"And now?" Willard didn't bat an eyelid.

"I pruned the arbor vitae with it the other day. The shrubs should recover soon from the small fire that started."

Willard snorted. "Sounds right. I have a goblin informant-slash-assistant who keeps turning my office accoutrements into siege equipment."

I squinted at her, wondering at the subject change. Did she really care about my goblin roommate? Or was she trying to put me at ease before she pounced?

"What was your mother's name?" Willard asked. "Did she tell you that while she was singing dwarven nursery rhymes to you?"

"No."

"You must know. Your grandparents—"

"Are on my father's side and don't know much." The last thing I wanted was for the military to start sniffing around their house. "Not about my mom. Dad had been through a divorce years earlier, and my parents weren't married when they had me. They were just..." My fingers flexed in the air. *In love.* That was what I remembered them saying, but I didn't want to blurt anything that personal to some Army colonel. "Devoted to each other. It was a long time ago. I went to live with my grandparents after my mother died."

"And your father went to military prison."

My throat tightened, though it had all happened so long ago, I didn't know why I was getting emotional. Maybe because I was worried about this new awareness that the military was keeping an eye on me. Were they also watching my sister? And my grand-parents?

"Yes," I got out.

"You don't know then if your mother was the rightful owner of that hammer."

"She didn't steal it. She wasn't a thief."

Willard gave me a pitying look.

"She wasn't, damn it. And why does the Army care about some magical hammer from another world, anyway?"

"These past few years, more visitors from the Cosmic Realms have been creating portals and coming to Earth. Some to hide out. Some to seek things that have been stolen from their home worlds over the years. The elf assassin thought someone might hear about that hammer and come looking for it."

I scowled. That bastard. "Because he's going to *tell* people about it? It's mine, regardless. It's not stolen." I crossed my arms over my chest and glared. "Besides, what about Butch Barbie out there?" I jerked a thumb toward the window. "I'm positive what-ever elf slept with her human parent wasn't the rightful owner of a *dwarven* sword."

Actually, I wasn't sure about that. Dwarves and elves were reputedly allies, so it was possible a dwarf had given or sold a magical sword to an elf at some point.

"She wasn't the rightful owner, and it *has* been a problem." Willard's mouth twisted. "She now has permission from the dwarven king to carry it."

"She's been to the dwarven home world?" Envy swelled within me. "Have you?" From what I knew about portals—which was admittedly little—I didn't think a half-elf or even many full-blooded magical beings could create them.

"I have not been invited off our world, no. But Val has left a number of times. The benefits of marrying a dragon, I suppose."

"Marrying a dragon?" I mouthed. I'd heard rumors that dragons had been seen in Seattle numerous times in the previous year, but not here in Lynnwood. I'd had my head down working, anyway, not searching the skies for winged creatures from other realms.

"The wedding was quite the event." Willard set her coffee mug on a coaster and leaned back on the love seat. "Listen, Puletasi. I've been aware of you for a while, and I've kept an eye on you, given the crimes that your father committed—"

My jaw tightened, a muscle ticking in my cheek, and I wanted to cry that she didn't know the whole story. I didn't know the whole story, either, but I knew he'd been defending my mother. He'd been trying to keep soldiers from killing her. I'd been there. I knew.

"—and I haven't judged that you were malicious in your vigilante practices, but with your greater-than-human strength and that weapon, you *are* a threat to those around you, whether you want to be or not."

"I am not. I've had martial-arts training. My grandparents encouraged it so I could learn to control my temper—and my punches."

"When we drove up, a man was puking in the street."

"Because he was harassing my elderly neighbor."

"I saw him go flying. If he doesn't have broken ribs and organ damage, I'll be as shocked as a rabbit caught in an electric fence."

I glowered mulishly at her. "If his organs were still healthy and perky, he'd be right back here tomorrow, harassing Mrs. Ming."

"Nonetheless, we live in a civilized society, governed by laws that must be obeyed. There's enough surveillance footage out there of you throwing people through windows that a judge would have you arrested."

"And are *you* going to attempt to have me arrested, Colonel?"

She could try...

Her phone buzzed again. She lifted her eyes heavenward, then held up a finger and walked to the door. After opening it, she called out, "If you want to have so much input on this meeting, come inside."

"I was just letting you know about the potentially dangerous goblin approaching the kitchen," Thorvald called back.

"You know as well as I do that a goblin heading toward a coffee maker isn't a threat." Willard shut the door and returned to the love seat. "I appreciate my independent contractors, but they're much more of a handful than my regular soldiers."

Guzzling noises came from the kitchen where I did indeed sense Tinja. When she peeked curiously out, her white hair sticking up like a bird's nest and a mustache of creamed coffee on her upper lip, I tried to shoo her back to her room. This meeting was looking to end with me in trouble, and I didn't want to get her involved.

"Some of them are effective though," Willard continued, glancing at Tinja but not commenting on her, unless the *I-thought-so* expression that crossed her face counted as a comment. "*Very* effective, I'll admit. Thorvald gets the job done."

Her eyes narrowed as she regarded me again.

What was that look supposed to mean? That she valued her half-elf and hadn't appreciated me calling her Butch Barbie?

"I may regret this," Willard said, "but I'd like to give you an alternative to the life in prison you're doubtless heading toward."

How many surveillance cameras had I been caught on, damn it? And would a court really convict me? When I'd been *helping* people?

"You know your way around that weapon," Willard said. "I'd like to give you an opportunity to prove yourself worthy of working for my office as an independent contractor."

My mouth dropped. Whatever I'd expected her to say, that hadn't been it.

"Work for the government?" I blurted, not bothering to hide my distaste. "The *military*?" The same people who'd killed my mother and arrested my father and kept him in jail without hope for parole for the last thirty years? Was she out of her mind?

"It's better to work for it than against it," Willard said.

"The hell it is," I muttered, glancing toward the kitchen.

Tinja, her mug held in both hands, was watching with wide eyes.

Willard's eyes only narrowed again. Maybe it wasn't a good idea to suggest to a career officer that the people she worked for were awful. But I was not only appalled by her suggestion; I didn't trust it. Or her. I didn't know these people. They might be setting me up. What if she gave me a mission, ordering me to shoot a magical bad guy—that was what Thorvald, the *Ruin Bringer*, was known for, after all—and recorded it all and gave it to the authorities, claiming she'd had nothing to do with it? They would believe an Army colonel over a house flipper. I had no doubt.

"Can I think about it?" I asked, afraid she would arrest me that minute if I flat out said no. "I already have a job."

"Using your magical power to replace toilets and ceiling fixtures, yes."

I scowled at this suggestion that my work was trivial. I was a craftsman. A crafts*woman*. The people who bought the houses I worked on loved them.

"I wouldn't insist that you give up your work," Willard said. "Thorvald takes other jobs on the side. I would only expect that when a mission came up that would be up your alley, you would make yourself available for it. You would be compensated for your time, of course. The military pays its independent contractors for their work. If you're curious, you can ask Thorvald about it."

Oh, sure. The Ruin Bringer. Just the kind of person I wanted to invite out for coffee and a scone.

"I'll think about it," I said.

"Of course." Willard rose and handed me an ordinary business card with Colonel Willard and a local number listed on it. Whatever her first name was, she didn't hand it out to strangers.

Before leaving, she gave my hammer a long look, probably imagining all the trouble that might come looking for it.

I hoped that wouldn't be the case. It had rested in my grandparents' umbrella rack by the door for fourteen years, until I'd moved out and they'd agreed it ought to go with me. A few people had tried to steal it from me over the years, but it wasn't a magnet for trouble.

Or it hadn't been before now.

7

AFTER HEAVING A CABINET ONTO THE GROWING PILE IN THE BACK OF Abbas's truck, I looked toward the bushes at the side of the property. I didn't sense anyone, I hadn't heard any howls all day, and nobody had leaped through the windows to get into the house. The handful of cars that had driven by had seemed local. One person with a poodle hanging out the window had given me a thumbs-up, maybe glad the place was getting a facelift.

The quiet should have put me at ease, but it felt like the calm before a storm. I wished it had occurred to me to ask Willard if she and Thorvald had learned anything from the werewolves in the park the night before. But I would swallow my tongue before calling the colonel's office. I wasn't convinced they weren't setting me up for something.

"My truck do something to you?" Abbas asked as he came up with the kitchen sink in his arms.

"What?"

"You're scowling at it like it bit you." He heaved the sink atop the pile. "That's about all we can get in there. Time for a dump run."

"I'm scowling at the world in general. Your truck hasn't offended me terribly today."

"Good to know. Your dour attitude have to do with those Army people?"

"Among other things. Would you trust the military?"

"Oh, hell no. Military, government, pharmaceutical companies —they're all out to screw us." He grinned at me.

"Which is why your family immigrated to the US."

"Well, what's the saying? When you're out of clean clothes, you gotta pick the least dirty shirt in the laundry pile. There was a no-troll tolerance policy back in Syria."

"I've heard that's true in a number of countries."

Tinja, who was off picking paint colors at whatever home-improvement store didn't mind short green customers, had told me goblins had also been eradicated or driven out of some nations. Others, like the US, pretended the magical beings who'd come to Earth didn't exist. There were plenty of videos online of everything from orcs and ogres to dragons and wyverns, but the government and mainstream media painted them with the same brush as UFOs and chemtrails. Hoaxes.

"I have wondered why that is." Abbas dragged a plaid sleeve across his forehead to wipe away sweat. "Ninety percent of trolls and other species don't cause any problems and just want to live in a world that isn't under the thumb of the tyrannical Dragon Council and their horrible Justice Court, but some *do* make trouble. Why do other countries tolerate that?"

"I guess I always assumed the full-bloods, thanks to their magic, were pretty good at hiding out."

"Huh." Abbas pulled out his keys. "You want me to come back after the dump run?"

"No. People should be returning home from work, so I'm going to call it a day and talk to the neighbors. I'm still trying to figure out who killed the renter—and what his name was, for that matter." Earlier, I'd called the previous owner of the property, using the number Zadie had dug up, thinking to ask a few casual questions, but nobody had picked up. It hadn't even gone to voicemail. The family lived out of state, so I couldn't easily pop by in person. The neighbors would have to do.

"Maybe it's better not to know." That morning, Abbas had scrubbed away the chalk outline.

"If more werewolves are going to break in, I'd like to know why."

"Didn't you say once that it was better to be ignorant of a house's history? So you aren't morally obligated to list possible turn-offs when you sell it?"

"I was referring to meth labs and lead-based paint, not murders."

He rolled his broad shoulders, slapped me on the back, then got in the truck. "See you Thursday," he called out the window.

"Tomorrow is Wednesday."

"Holiday." His grin flashed in the driver-side mirror as he rolled away.

"Why don't you pick up a few more religions while you're away?" I called. "It's taxing to work more than three days a week."

He waved out the window but didn't otherwise reply. Since he'd hauled out more debris and done more dump runs than three normal humans would have managed during the day, I couldn't complain *that* much. And, as I caught a dog walker peering oddly at me as she hurried past in the street, I decided yelling at co-workers might not be professional.

Hm, if the woman lived in the neighborhood, maybe I should ask her a few questions.

"Ma'am?" I called, approaching slowly since the dog was eyeing me warily. My fault, of course, for presuming to stand in the neighborhood he considered *his* territory. "Do you live in the area? Do you have a second?"

She gave me an equally wary look. Maybe it would have been wiser to start with a neighbor who didn't already think I was weird.

"I need to get back to make Rufus's dinner," she said.

Rufus rucked up his hackles and flattened his ears.

I stopped several feet away. "I was wondering if you'd known the man who rented this house previously. He left a lot of stuff behind, and I'm trying to find his next-of-kin so they can come get it." Not exactly true, but if I did learn that information, I would happily hand over the contents of the closets.

"Next-of-kin?" she mouthed. "He *died*?"

"Uhm, yes."

If she hadn't heard about that, she might not be a close neighbor. Going by the number of bullet holes in the wall, a gun had been fired numerous times. It was hard to believe the neighbors wouldn't have heard the shots, and someone had to have seen the ambulance and police cars that had presumably come. Unless the murderer had used a silencer and dumped the body in the nearest lake. For that matter, I was surprised nobody had shown up after the werewolves' gunshots the day before. Nobody except Willard and Thorvald.

"He wasn't that old, was he?"

I spread my arms. "I don't know anything about him. That's why I'm asking around."

"I live half a mile away, and I only come this way to get to the park, but he was a gruff, surly man with bushy red hair, a big beard, and eyebrows like caterpillars. He yelled if Rufus peed on his mailbox, and I heard he threatened anyone who came up to his door. Threatened with *violence*. It didn't tempt me to visit or learn his name. Maybe try the people across the street." She waved toward a house at the back of a large lot; it was barely visible through the trees.

"I will. Thanks."

Before leaving, I locked the front door, though I was thinking of returning to tear up the floor in the basement. Earlier, Abbas and I had poked around down there, trying to find a hidden door, but if there was access from inside or outside the house, we hadn't located it. We'd skimmed through the inspection report to confirm that there'd been nothing about a *sub*basement in it.

Dogs barked in the house across the street as soon as I knocked on the front door. When it opened, I braced to defend myself against Dobermans shooting out, but overly exuberant Irish Setters leaped on me, greeting me like a long-lost cousin.

"Well, you're friendlier than Rufus," I said, trying to see the owner beyond the red-furred dog head and a tongue attempting to wash my eyeballs.

"Cain, Abel, sit," the woman in the foyer said, pointing to the tiles at her side. "Sorry, ma'am. They love people."

"As long as they don't love to *eat* people." I'd left my hammer behind, not wanting to intimidate the neighbors—or make them think I was odd for toting such a thing about.

"They just lick them."

I gave her the same story I'd shared with the other lady.

"Mr. Gruff has—*had* been in that house for the entire twenty years we've lived in the neighborhood," she said.

"That's not really his name, is it?"

"No, but he never introduced himself. His mail ended up in our box a few times, but it was always junk addressed to *resident*. He yelled if anyone came to his door, and he had a big gun that I saw him wave a few times, threatening everyone from teenagers on skateboards to the landlord trying to talk him into leaving the property."

As she spoke, I sensed someone with magical blood in the

back of the house, someone heading in our direction. The signature was faint, suggesting perhaps one-quarter magical heritage, but I tensed, not certain if this would be an ally.

The man stepped into view—the woman's husband, I assumed—a tall, lanky fellow who might have had an elf ancestor. He looked me up and down, and I assumed he could also sense that *I* had a magical ancestor, but I didn't know how aware of the magical community he was. A lot of people who'd grown up and had otherwise normal lives didn't believe anything but what the government told them about our ancestors.

"You're asking about the neighbor?" he asked.

"Apparently, he passed," his wife told him.

Again, I found it odd that the neighbors hadn't known about the shooting, especially a neighbor directly across the street.

"Straight to Hell, I'd guess." The husband looked me up and down again and must have guessed at my heritage, because he said, "He was part dwarf, I think."

"Oh?"

"Maybe *all* dwarf. He wasn't that short, but I could tell he was magical. A lot more than me."

His wife patted him on the chest and looked like she wanted to shush him. Maybe she didn't encourage him to speak about such outlandish things to strangers. Or anyone.

"His gun was magical too," he added, not quelled. He patted her back, as if to say he knew what he was doing.

I hadn't sensed magic from the bullets lodged in the walls, but a firearm could have power without the bullets being anything special. With a start, I realized they might have been silver bullets. What if the werewolf problem had been going on for some time and that was who'd gotten the renter in the end?

"I don't suppose you know where he got the gun?" I asked.

"He never talked to us. Never talked to anyone except to tell them to stay off his property. You might check with the food-truck lady downtown. The one who makes and sells magical guns."

"Food-truck lady?" I'd never heard of such a person, but I also had never had a need or interest in owning a firearm. The hammer was sufficient for my needs.

The dogs, who'd been sitting obediently on the floor, swished their tails. Maybe they knew the word *food.*

"Yeah. I forget her name, but the truck is the Crying Tiger. I think you have to go after dark to get items from the *special* menu."

"Why do you *know* about these things, honey?" his wife whispered.

That only earned her another pat.

"Is the owner of the truck magical too?" I asked.

"Part gnome, I think," he said.

The wife rubbed her face, her cheeks pink with embarrassment. Maybe such topics weren't socially acceptable in the neighborhood.

"If he bought the weapon from her, she might remember him," the husband said, then lifted a hand and stepped back.

"We're glad you're fixing up the house," the wife said. "Have a nice night."

"If no werewolves invade the property, I'll attempt to do so." Right away, I regretted the words, realizing she would think them odd, but she and her husband only exchanged long looks before closing the door.

Maybe the werewolves were a known problem in the neighborhood.

"The pitfalls of living next to a huge park," I muttered, walking back toward the street. Maybe I would visit that park one of these days to see if I sensed anything, but the tree-filled expanse took up almost five hundred acres and had something like twenty-five miles of trails. I would happily work all day at tearing out walls and installing cabinets, but my lip curled at the thought of tramping through the woods. "An elf, my mother was not."

I tried a couple more neighbors, but they either weren't home or claimed not to know anything. On a whim, I asked if they'd spotted any wolves in the area. They'd all shaken their heads and shut their doors on me, hastily ending the conversation when that came up.

After returning to the house, with twilight creeping over the neighborhood, I stood in front of my truck and debated what to do next. Solving mysteries wasn't my expertise and, beyond worrying about shifters breaking into the house to steal who knew what, the werewolves weren't really my problem. All I was there to do was fix up the house and sell it as quickly as possible.

And yet... if the renter *had* been part dwarf, I felt a kinship to him. It bothered me that this guy, grumpy and surly or not, had been murdered in his own home and nobody had cared or investigated it. It crossed my mind that he might have been defending something more than his own house. Why else so assiduously threaten everyone who came close?

Beyond all that, I worried that Abbas and Tinja, and even Zadie if she came by at the wrong time, could be hurt because we'd taken on this project.

"Park, food truck, or stakeout of the house tonight?" I muttered, thinking of going home to trade the truck for my motorcycle. After dark, there shouldn't be any normal people in the park to complain about someone riding a motorized vehicle on the non-motorized trails.

Since Willard ought to be giving me time to *think about* her offer of employment, I probably didn't need to worry about her and Thorvald showing up to interrupt a stakeout tonight. And if there were magical beings in the park, I might be able to sense them and find them quickly, without having to trek for miles. As for the food truck... I dug out my phone.

"I have stored the paint cans in the paint-storage room in your house," Tinja answered cheerfully.

"You mean the shed beside the carport?"

"No, the shed is full of some projects I've started, as well as materials I've acquired."

"If you mean the aluminum cans, mattress springs, and broken air conditioner in there, I'm aware of those *materials.*"

"Yes. I've acquired more. They're all excellent materials for goblin projects."

"Where *is* the paint? And why didn't you bring it here?"

"The home-improvement store would not deliver it to that address," Tinja said, not answering the first question.

Why did I have a feeling paint cans were piled in my living room or bedroom? "Why not?"

"They said it was blacklisted and would not say more."

"All right. Can you do me a favor? Have you heard of a food truck called the Crying Tiger?"

"Of course. A quarter-gnome woman owns it and is always happy to feed goblins, providing we can pay, of course."

"I think most restaurant owners are happy to feed people who pay."

"Not everyone is happy to feed *goblins*. We are a unique clientele."

That probably was true. "Do you know anything about another line of business the owner is in? Such as making magical weapons?"

"I have heard that, yes, though I believe she may have closed that side of her business recently. She is a partial owner of the Coffee Dragon in Fremont. That may keep her busy."

"Is that the same coffee shop that the Ruin Bringer is a partial owner in?"

"It is. Many goblins and other members of the magical community gather there."

Given that Tinja said she was something of an outcast among her people, because she'd moved to the city and wanted to learn to build in the *human* way, she always knew a lot about the goings on of goblins and other magical beings.

"I need to know if she remembers selling a magical gun to someone who might have been half-dwarf. Or *all* dwarf. And lived here. Our mysterious renter. Can you find her and ask?"

Tinja didn't have a car or even a bicycle, but she had a knack for finding ways around town when she wished. As far as I knew, she didn't take the bus.

"I can check," she said. "Do you know when he would have made the purchase?"

"No. I know very little."

"That is distressing since you are my mentor."

"I know very little about *the renter*. My wisdom knows no bounds in other areas. Such as the proper storage of paint cans."

"I will check."

A howl came from the direction of the park. The part of the park nearest this neighborhood.

"Thanks, Tinja. Let me know what you find. I'm going to cruise through the park and then stake out the house tonight. Or at least stay late to work on projects inside and see if anyone interesting comes by."

"Like a pack of werewolves? They are furry and mean, not interesting."

"I'm not sure that's true of all of them, but I'm inclined to agree when it comes to this pack."

"You will not be able to camouflage yourself if I'm not there with my charm," Tinja said. "Will your presence not deter them from intruding?"

"They're probably arrogant enough to think they can handle me even if they sense me."

"What if they *can* handle you?"

"A couple of werewolves won't be a problem."

"There could be a couple *dozen* in that pack."

"If they kill me, then you and Abbas get to keep all the profits from the house flip."

"That is not very reassuring, Matti."

"I agree. I'll try to live."

8

Old Harleys weren't known for being quiet, but I made as little noise as possible as I eased past the no-motorized-vehicle signs and onto the trails of the park. Maybe Willard was right and I *was* a vigilante. But I was a logical vigilante. If this park was overrun by werewolves at night, I would be a fool to be caught on foot in here. As I'd told Tinja, I was confident I could handle a couple of shifters. The entire pack... could be problematic.

I touched my hammer to make sure it still jutted from the saddlebag. Maybe one day, I could find a special weapons sling so I could carry it on my back, the way Thorvald did her sword. She had arms long enough, however, to draw a weapon that way. I'd probably get mine stuck.

As I rumbled down a trail paralleling the east boundary of the park, the branches trimmed back to accommodate horses and riders, I tried to sense magic among the towering trees. The werewolf howls had originated in the park; I was sure of it. But halfway through, I'd detected nothing but the occasional bat flapping off, disturbed by my noise.

At an intersection of trails, I thought I felt something, but it disappeared before I could identify it. I stopped my motorcycle and cut off the engine, listening with my ears as well as stretching out with my senses. It had seemed close, but now... nothing.

The faint rumble of freeway traffic came from the west, a reminder that the park was in the middle of the city, with only the old neighborhoods right around it feeling suburban, almost rural, instead of urban. Maybe the werewolves had gone out for dinner at the nearby Vietnamese restaurant or hit up the bowling lanes for a night of betting on their prowess.

"I do not believe that conveyance is permitted in this park," a male voice spoke from not ten feet to the side of the trail.

I grabbed my hammer as I sprang from the Harley, landing in a crouch and facing the threat. The threat I couldn't sense.

It took me a few long seconds to realize I recognized that voice. "Sarrlevi?"

"It is good that you remember my name," he said, the darkness hiding him.

"Well, you know, it's wise to know the names of assassins." The better to avoid them...

"Yes. I did not expect you to come visit me."

"Visit *you*? I came looking for the werewolves that keep howling at night like lovestruck coyotes seeking mates."

"I am not as familiar with this world as you, but I believe coyotes howl as part of a territorial display."

"Thanks for the tip. What are you doing here? And why did you think I would want to visit you? And what did you tell that Army colonel about my hammer?"

A howl sounded on the far side of the park. Ah, the werewolves weren't bowling after all.

"I am relaxing in the only quasi natural area in this metropolis that offers a modicum of peace to keen elven ears and noses, though the scent of burning fossil fuels and sounds of thundering car engines reach me even here. As I said, I did *not* expect you to visit me. And I informed Thorvald that a possibly stolen dwarven weapon of great power was across the waterway from her, in the hands of a mongrel plumber."

"I'm not a plumber," I snapped. "Not that there would be anything wrong with it if I were. My grandfather is a plumber."

"I observed you removing a cylinder from under a sink today. Is this not the purview of those in the plumbing profession?"

"The garbage disposal, and we were removing *everything* that was broken or old. It's not—" I gaped at him, my grip tightening on the haft of my hammer. "You were watching us work today? *Why?* I thought you got the werewolves you were looking for."

Why was this guy still on Earth? If he was an assassin renowned for killing people on twelve worlds, he surely didn't consider this his home turf.

"I have been observing you."

"You admit to being a stalker?"

Another howl drifted through the trees, the origin closer this time. A second howl came from another corner of the park.

Uneasily, I realized the werewolves sensed me—or they'd heard my motorcycle—and since Sarrlevi's aura was camouflaged, they might not know he was there. They were coming for me. How many of them? Two I might be able to handle, but more?

"A stalker?" Sarrlevi didn't sound like he'd heard the term, at least not in the sense I meant. "I am an assassin, and I frequently stalk my prey."

"Am I your prey?"

"No. You are insignificant."

"Thanks so much. Because I'm a plumber?"

The darkness made it difficult to tell, but he seemed to cock his head. In confusion? "Because you have not, as far as I know, traveled from this world and made powerful enemies in other realms. Enemies of the type who can afford to hire me."

"You're an elite assassin who charges a hooker's hourly rate, huh?"

He hesitated. "I *am* an elite assassin."

"Camping out in the park and keeping an eye on me *because*...?"

"If you *are* the legitimate heir to that hammer, then that is of interest to me."

"Why? Why would an elf care about dwarf matters? And what did you mean when you said this was a *weapon of great power*?"

Sarrlevi sighed. "Are you another Earth inhabitant with a weapon created by a powerful smith and enchanter who hasn't the faintest idea about its capabilities?"

I growled, grip tightening so much that my knuckles ached. "It hits things real good without leaving a scratch. That's all I need to know."

"*Any* dwarf-made weapon has that attribute." He sounded exasperated. "This world is such an overrun den of ignorance and willful stupidity that I can't fathom that Lord Zavryd'nokquetal spends time here. Thorvald must be extremely skilled at coitus."

"Oh, yuck. I don't want to hear about that. I—" I halted, sensing two werewolves approaching from a side trail.

I moved to stand in front of my motorcycle, putting it at my back and being careful not to let *Sarrlevi* be at my back. While I doubted he was aligned with the werewolves, not after killing two of their buddies, he wasn't aligned with me either. Not if he'd been peering through my window all day and thought I was lying about my claim to the hammer. He wouldn't likely help me, and he might impede me.

Relieved that I only sensed two werewolves, I waited in a crouch until they glided out of the trees, huge furry gray creatures with yellow eyes that gleamed in the night. They padded shoulder to shoulder toward me.

I expected them to shift into human form and braced myself

for nudity, but they merely sat on their haunches. One gazed past me and the motorcycle to where Sarrlevi was—or had been. I couldn't sense or see him anymore.

This territory belongs to the pack of the Night Warriors, one of the wolves spoke into my mind. *Those who intrude upon it have no respect for us and must expect to be slain.*

"Really? Like all the dog walkers and horseback-riders who use this park during the day?"

His yellow eyes closed to slits. *Those who intrude upon it* after dark *and bring noisy road vehicles into it have no respect for us and must expect to be slain.*

"Let me offer a counterproposal. You tell me why your people are fishing for artifacts at the house I just bought, and I won't thump you both on the head with my hammer."

The wolves' ears didn't flicker, so it was probably only my imagination that Sarrlevi sighed again at this suggestion that I only knew how to hit things with the precious magical weapon.

We are not cowed by half-blood mongrels. If you want to deal with soft *werewolves who kowtow to human whims, go to Wolf Winery.*

The weakling bootlicking pack that owns the establishment and serves humans will surely accommodate you.

"What do you want at the house?" Deciding threats might not work on these guys, I tried another tack. "Like I said, I'm the new owner. Maybe I can help you find it. I doubt I want whatever it is, and having people break in while I'm trying to renovate is a problem."

You seek to trick us. You know what lies beneath, and you want to keep us from it, just as the previous guardian did. We smell your dwarfness on you and know you are the newest guard dog to snarl from the stoop.

"No kidding? And what were these dwarven guard dogs seeking to protect again?"

The wolves growled, lowering as they prepared to spring.

Once you're gone, there will be nobody to keep us from finding it.

"Did you kill the last guy?"

Instead of answering, they sprang at me.

Something buzzed past my ear as I leaped to the side, tucking myself between two stout trees so that only one wolf at a time would be able to attack.

But a knife lodged in the eye of the one who'd been speaking, and he dropped to the ground, clawing at his face. The other wolf must not have noticed for he landed and lunged toward me without pausing. He was fast, and I jabbed with the hammer instead of raising it for a swing. I didn't want to risk leaving my torso open.

The weapon would have struck between his eyes, but he dropped low to avoid it. He snapped toward my shins. Not wanting to back up and trip on the undergrowth, I held my ground, jerking the hammer down at the same time as I kicked at his jaw. Fortunately, I wore my leather riding boots instead of shoes that would have been more vulnerable to fangs. My foot collided with his snout. He bit at it, but the hammer came down next. It thudded onto the back of his spine.

Yelping, he backed onto the trail again. It had been a hard blow, but he shook it off and crouched to spring again. A shadow moved to his side, a sword blurring out of the darkness. Sarrlevi.

Before the werewolf could dodge, the assassin brought his blade down with amazing swiftness. With a crunch and moist thud, it cleaved the wolf's skull down the middle.

Stomach roiling, I looked away. Never had I considered myself squeamish, but Sarrlevi had a thing for annihilating heads.

"I didn't need any help," I said as he pulled his blade out and cleaned it. He'd already plucked his knife out of the other werewolf's eye.

He'd only taken one of his twin long swords from its scabbard.

Maybe such meager foes didn't require the effort of pulling out two.

Once he sheathed his weapon, Sarrlevi faced me, not caring that a body lay two inches from his boots, brain matter and blood oozing from the destroyed skull. Maybe elves didn't worry about bloodstains since they could magic things clean.

"Is it not customary on this world to thank someone for assisting against a foe?" he asked. "Or did you seek the honor of defeating that one in single-handed combat? If that is the case, I apologize. I did not hear you challenge him and assumed these shifters were merely pests."

They were, but... "I like to fight my own battles against enemies. I'm not even sure yet that *you're* not one. Besides, I wanted to question them. I'm trying to solve a mystery here."

"Did you think the post-battle questioning would be more effective than the pre-battle questioning?" Sarrlevi must have been able to hear the telepathic half of the conversation.

"Yeah, because my boot would have been on his head in the *post-battle* version."

"I see. As I said, you are too ill-traveled and insignificant to have garnered the attention of those capable of hiring me, and I have no need for a dwarven hammer, so I am not an enemy nor a threat to you."

"Despite peeping in my window all day."

"Correct."

"You're just fascinated with me because of my half-dwarven beauty and allure."

He gazed blandly at me. It wasn't an outright scoff but somehow conveyed that. It ruffled my feathers.

"Will you give me a sample of your blood?" Sarrlevi asked.

I rocked back. "What?"

"Only a small amount. I have a magical device capable of analyzing blood and determining one's heritage." He held up a hand. "No, that is a simplification. I do not know how to explain this exactly in your language. It would not be able to spit out your entire lineage unless there is a match with a known bloodline that is held in its memory."

"Are you still trying to figure out if I'm the rightful owner of this hammer?" I assumed it wasn't my Samoan heritage that fascinated him. "You just said you aren't interested in stealing it from me, so why do you care?"

"The hammer means little to me. That is correct. It is what you possessing it, assuming you spoke the truth and it wasn't stolen, could signify. Will you give me a sample?"

"What could it signify?"

Sarrlevi opened his mouth, but an angry howl came from the other side of the park. Several angry howls.

"I think they got back from bowling and realized we killed their buddies," I whispered.

"You did not kill them. I did. If I must, I will slay the rest of the pack, but they are little challenge, and it is not honorable to slay mediocre opponents."

"Has anyone told you how arrogant you are?"

"Many people, yes." His eyes narrowed. "Not all of them live."

"Because you can't take honest feedback or because you were in the middle of challenging them to honorable battle when they spat the words?"

"The latter is closer to accurate."

The howls sounded again, closer. The wolves must have already crossed half the park.

"I'm getting out of here." I stepped toward the Harley, hoping I could outrun—out*ride*—an angry werewolf pack. I was already deciding on my route, a direction that would lead them away from the house, when Sarrlevi gripped my arm.

"I must have a sample of your blood," he said.

"No, you must not."

"Come to my camp, and I will ensure the pack doesn't find you."

I hesitated. The Harley was fast on the highway, but I wouldn't be able to zoom down the dark park trails. It was possible the wolves would catch up to me before I reached a street. Some might already be waiting at the park entrances, poised to cut me off, to trap me.

"All right," I whispered, hearing branches breaking and leaves rustling as the wolves drew close, too incensed to bother with hiding the sound of their passing, "but I'm not giving you my blood."

Gripping my arm, Sarrlevi guided me past the motorcycle and into the trees. We'd only gone ten feet, the Harley and trail still in sight, when a weird zing of magic buzzed my nerves. We stepped onto a mossy patch of ground framed by trees, with a soft glowing orb resting next to a cot with a pillow and a blanket. The backpack I'd seen Sarrlevi wearing the day before leaned against the cot—I hoped the heads weren't still in it, rotting nastily.

Within his camp, I could abruptly sense his aura. His *powerful* aura. Even though he'd claimed to be a mage as well as an assassin, I hadn't guessed he might be a strong one. Right away, I was glad I hadn't picked a fight with him. He could probably kick my ass with his magic without ever lifting a blade.

Do not move off the moss rug. Sarrlevi told me telepathically as he pointed down at it.

Only then did I realize it *was* a rug and not natural growth on the forest floor. Had he brought that with him? Along with his camping stuff? Who traveled with their own *rug*?

Also, do not make noise. My camp is magically camouflaged, and they should not detect our scents, but they will hear us if we're not careful.

I turned in time to see the wolves run out of the woods and onto the trail, pausing to sniff the fallen shifters. My poor Harley stood scant feet away, vulnerable to their whims, and I had to stifle a groan, certain they would slash the tires. If I'd realized that Sarrlevi was only taking me ten feet off the trail, I would have rolled it over the roots and ferns to hide it with us.

Angry snarls came from the wolves as they investigated their dead kin. The light in Sarrlevi's camp, apparently as camouflaged from the outside world as the rest of it, wasn't bright, but its glow next to me made it harder to pick out the details on the dark trail. My senses more than my eyes told me that there were eight or nine werewolves out there. There was also something else, something still coming.

What is that? I asked, not sure if Sarrlevi would hear me. As far as I knew, I had no ability to telepathically share my thoughts.

Something more powerful than the others. It may lead the pack.

That didn't answer my question.

He gave me a long look. Though he'd released my arm, he stood close enough that he could grab it again if he were so inclined. *You are not respectful to your superiors.*

What makes you think you're superior to me? I asked, not willing to believe that superior *power* meant one was a superior person.

It should be obvious.

What, on your world, assassins are better than plumbers? Which I'm not, by the way. I'm an entrepreneur.

Instead of answering, Sarrlevi turned his attention back to the trail. The more powerful being hadn't come into view yet, but it was approaching.

It is a brysarrusi. *They are very powerful. It may see through my camouflage.*

Uh.

Several of the angry wolves stalked toward my motorcycle. I tensed and hefted my hammer. Only Sarrlevi's warning that something more powerful was coming kept me from charging out to defend my baby.

One of the wolves lifted his leg to pee on the Harley. I clenched my jaw. Another wolf came over and did the same. Two more shoved their shoulders against it, and the motorcycle tipped, falling against a tree with a thud.

Sarrlevi gripped my shoulder, pressing firmly down and pointing at the moss rug.

Yeah, yeah, I'm not going anywhere. Though I *did* hope the werewolves came one by one to the house so I could punish them for their actions. *I* wasn't the one who'd killed their buddies. I glanced at Sarrlevi, wondering if it was horrible to fantasize about werewolves pissing on his cot.

The wolves left the motorcycle to sit and face the approaching being. Heavy footfalls sounded before it came into view. It didn't sound like a wolf. To my senses, it radiated the same kind of power as Sarrlevi, maybe more.

Whatever it was, it was definitely a full-blooded magical being. Something from another realm that had come and set itself up as the pack leader?

Finally, the shaggy creature came into view, the *huge* shaggy creature. It moved like a gorilla, walking on two muscled rear legs but touching the ground occasionally with its forelimbs. It had the fanged snout of a wolf, the barrel chest of a sasquatch, and the glowing yellow eyes of something out of my nightmares. Even with a hunch to its upper back, the thing had to be eight feet tall. Something told me that if I kicked it in the chest, I would bounce off. I wasn't positive even my hammer would hurt it.

The wolves dropped to their bellies, facing it.

You have not brought me the artifact, it rumbled, projecting its thoughts to everyone, *nor a sacrifice to ease my hunger and increase my power in this world.* The creature looked toward the motorcycle, and its nostrils twitched.

It had better not be thinking about eating it.

An elf was here. And a mongrel dwarf. Why did you not bring them to me? I hunger for fresh blood.

All right, this thing was creepy. I looked at Sarrlevi, trying to tell if he was disturbed, or if this was all part of a day's—a night's—work for a well-traveled elven assassin.

The brysarrusi *are from Osgashandril,* he said without looking back at me. *They rule over the shifters there. That is why many of them have fled to your world, where predators greater than they are few.*

I thought dragons were the reason other races fled and came here.

They are not the only powerful predators in the Realms. Though the brysarrusi *are not the fastest or most agile foes, they have tremendous regenerative power that makes them difficult to kill. Further, feeding on the life blood of others, the sacrifices they call for, makes them even stronger and faster to heal for a time. I once battled one, cut its head half off with a sword, and watched as it lifted a paw, pushed its head fully back onto its neck, and in scant seconds all was healed.*

Before, Sarrlevi had oozed nothing but arrogance, sounding like he believed he could best any enemy, but he was grim as he spoke of this creature. That worried me, and I didn't make a move and barely breathed as it spoke to the wolves.

Until my phone beeped with an incoming text.

Sarrlevi gave me an incredulous look as the wolves *and* the *brysarrusi* looked in our direction.

9

Return to your domicile, Sarrlevi said. *I will lead it away.*

I lifted my hammer. *I can help.*

But he'd already sprung away, drawing both of his swords.

The wolves started to charge at him, but he was so fast that he reached the trail first, vaulting over the half-tipped Harley and toward the *brysarrusi's* head. Two wolf snouts snapped at him. He slashed them even as he soared toward the more dangerous foe.

Abandoning his camp, I rushed out with my hammer raised. He might not want my help, but I refused to cower and hide while someone risked his life for me.

His blades coming in from multiple angles, Sarrlevi sliced at the head of the hulking creature, his momentum still carrying him through the air. He twisted impossibly to avoid its jaws and the powerful forearms it raised to slash at him with long claws. When gravity finally caught up with him, he somersaulted and came down behind the *brysarrusi.*

Roaring, it spun and lunged for him, as did most of the wolves. Sarrlevi ran backward down the trail, taunting them in the Elven language.

Two wolves remained by the Harley and turned as I crashed out of the ferns, my footfalls not as light as those of an elf. Afraid but angry at them and the whole situation, I smashed my hammer into the chest of the closest shifter, hardly caring if it turned out to be a fatal blow. The werewolf snapped at the weapon, but its teeth could do nothing against dwarven metal. It flew off the trail and into the trees.

Before I could attack with the hammer again, the second wolf lunged in from my left. I pounded a side kick into its chest to halt it. That wasn't as tremendous a blow as the hammer could deliver, and it held its ground and whipped its head downward. Jaws snapping, its fangs pierced my jeans and my flesh before I fully retracted the kick. The sharp pain made me yell, and I swung the hammer again, smashing the wolf in the side of the head. It crumpled beside the trail.

Howls and snarls drifted back from the side trail, the rest of the werewolves and *brysarrusi* chasing Sarrlevi. Though I hated leaving him to deal with that by himself, I didn't know if I could catch up.

"Not on foot."

I eyed the Harley and moved to the tree it leaned against. Had it fallen to the ground, its five-hundred-pound frame would have been too much for even a half-dwarf to lift, but, with a great snarl of effort, I shoved it upright and straddled it.

Firing the Harley to life, I turned and took off in the same direction Sarrlevi had gone. The wheels rolled over the arm of the first werewolf he'd killed, and I grimaced. The early-morning park goers would be in for a grisly walk.

Though it was foolish to ride full speed on a forest trail in the dark, I pressed the Harley faster than I should have, afraid Sarrlevi would lose against so many enemies. He could doubtless handle a few werewolves and maybe even the *brysarrusi* alone, but all of them together? Nobody was that good.

Even though I hadn't decided if he was an enemy or not, he *had* helped me. I owed it to him to return the favor.

Ahead, a wolf with a limp came into view. Sarrlevi must have struck it, for it had fallen behind. When it glanced back, I urged the motorcycle faster and rose up on the floorboards like a horseback rider in stirrups. It turned to face me, fangs leering as it crouched, prepared to spring.

I flashed the headlight before raising my hammer, and the wolf blinked, startled. That gave me the second of distraction I needed to get close and knock him off the trail. As he tumbled into the trees, a new injury to add to the limp, I rode past.

The trail curved, then intersected with another, and I had to slow down. The roar of the Harley made it hard to hear which way the battle had gone, so I turned it off to listen.

But the park had fallen silent, as if elf, wolves, and monstrous creature had disappeared into another dimension. Maybe they had.

All I could hear was the rumble of cars on the freeway, the noise louder on this side of the park.

"Damn," I whispered, wishing I'd been more help.

The wolves I'd dropped hadn't even been a threat to Sarrlevi. But maybe I could question one of them. More than ever, I wanted to know what the hell was going on.

Turning the Harley on the narrow trail was awkward, but I managed while branches scraped at my back and head, then rode back the way I'd come. At the bend where I'd attacked the wolf, I slowed, expecting to find him recovering from the blow. Not that much time had passed, but I didn't see him or sense him.

When I returned to the spot where Sarrlevi had been camped, the two wolves I'd hit there were also gone. So were the bodies from the original fight. That made me uneasy, especially since I didn't sense anyone magical nearby.

Reluctantly, I drove toward the park exit, intending to go back to the house. After all, Sarrlevi, the peeping Tom, knew how to find me there.

As I neared the start of the trail at the edge of the park, my instincts twanged a warning, and I slowed down. I still didn't sense anyone magical, but something told me to make another awkward turn and find a different exit. As I rode deeper into the park again, I glanced back and glimpsed a man peering after me, shining a flashlight into the woods.

Whoever he was, if he had a flashlight, he probably wasn't a werewolf. The police more likely, ready to give a ticket to the miscreant driving a motorcycle through the park at night.

Worried the other exits would be guarded as well, I rode down a trail that passed close to the road and veered off into the ferns. A log almost ended my detour, but I found a way around it, silently apologizing to the old Harley for trying to make it an off-road vehicle. No wonder Thorvald had a Jeep.

Finally, I reached the road, glancing left and right for patrol cars—or werewolves—before riding into the open. It had gotten late, and the street was empty.

I was tempted to go home instead of to the project house, but Sarrlevi would show up there when he came looking for me. And he might be injured. Hell, *I* was injured, my shin and calf throbbing where those wolf fangs had gotten me. If not for Sarrlevi, my house, with the first-aid kit under the bathroom sink, would have been the better choice.

"I'll just swing by to check."

As I drove, I remembered my phone and wondered who'd texted me to start that mess. A note from my sister popped up, asking if I would change my mind about Sunday brunch. She promised to make mimosas and had an accountant *friend* she wanted me to meet.

I groaned and stuffed my phone back into my pocket. Even if I'd had dating on my mind that week, an *accountant* wouldn't have been a natural match for me. Not unless he refinished floors or worked out at the *dojang* on the weekends. I was open to the idea of opposites attracting, but that was too opposite. Someone that normal would think I was weird.

A light was on inside the house when I rolled to a stop across the street. A light that I hadn't left on.

Abbas's truck wasn't there. It was possible that Tinja could have gotten a ride over to bring the paint, but I didn't sense her goblin aura. I didn't sense Sarrlevi's powerful elven aura either. That might not mean anything though; he could have wrapped his magical camouflage around himself again.

Even though I had a hard time imagining werewolf thieves turning on the lights in the houses they burglarized, I drove farther down the street and parked in the shadow of an overgrown bush before getting off. I also opted to go around the side of the house and enter through a back door, but not before checking numerous times for creatures with magical auras.

The werewolves, and probably that *brysarrusi* too, knew exactly where I was working. If I hadn't been bound to the house by a huge mortgage, I would have bailed on the job.

No, maybe not. More than ever, I wanted to know what was going on here.

The back door was still locked, and, as I fished out the key, a faint moan emanated from inside. It sounded more like the moan of the wind than someone in pain, but if that creature had clobbered Sarrlevi, he could be in there, making pitiful wounded sounds.

When I pushed the door open, smoke wafted out, and I jerked back in alarm. Had someone started a fire?

But the gray haze didn't smell like smoke or anything burning. If anything, the wispy air was cool against my cheeks. Like mist or fog.

Neither was something I expected to find in a house. Scowling,

I eased inside and pressed my back against the wall, listening intently for noise. The strange fog curled around my legs, the left throbbing from the werewolf bite. I wondered if I ought to get a tetanus shot.

Again, I tried to sense magical beings—or artifacts—in the area. All I detected was the backsplash tile that I'd noticed before. The mist wasn't coming from it. It seemed to be emanating from the walls.

The light coming from the front room was visible through the kitchen door, and I eased in that direction. I'd swept up the wood shards and insulation before we'd called it a day, so there wasn't much debris on the floor, but the haze made it hard to see, and I accidentally kicked a piece of drywall across the room. It clattered against a baseboard, and I tensed. If someone was in the house, they would have heard that.

When nobody charged out to confront me, I continued toward the front room, the mist thick about my legs. Another moan sounded. From inside, it seemed to come from the basement. Or maybe the hollow space *under* the basement that I still hadn't found a way to access?

The phone rang, startling me. Expecting another brunch entreaty, I frowned down at it, but it was Tinja this time.

Before answering, I peered into the living room. The ceiling lamp was on, but nobody lurked inside. The entryway closet door that had been closed earlier stood ajar.

"Hey, Tinja. What's up?"

"Are you all right? You usually answer my messages promptly and eagerly."

"Promptly, at least. I'm walking through a misty house and about to brain whoever is crouching in the closet." I didn't bother to keep my voice down, since I'd already announced myself by playing drywall soccer.

"Does that mean I should wait to tell you about my visit to the Coffee Dragon?"

"Yeah, give me a sec. And I thought you were going to the Crying Tiger."

I stuck the phone in a pocket and strode toward the closet with my hammer raised. I yanked it open, ready to smash a werewolf invader. But the closet was empty, save for more of the mist that swirled out on the draft. Another moan wafted up from somewhere below.

"I prefer it when my enemies just attack me." I refused to believe the house had suddenly become haunted. Someone was messing with me. But why? The thieves wanted an artifact, right? Not me.

Unless they blamed me for the deaths of the werewolves in the park…

But if they did, they would have charged over to kill me, not to mess with my mind.

Tinja's muffled voice came from my pocket, and I pulled the phone out again.

"What did you say?" I headed for the stairs leading to the lower level. Maybe when I found the source of the moans, I would have my answers.

"Nin Chattrakulrak was not at the food truck, but her assistant directed me to the Coffee Dragon, where many foolish goblins were swilling coffee and playing dangerous dice games."

"You swill coffee too," I pointed out.

"Not at night. I must sleep well so that I am bright for my studies in the mornings."

"What makes a dice game dangerous?"

"Dice being launched from a catapult and bouncing off the walls and into people's ears and eyes."

"That would do it." My shin throbbed as I maneuvered down

the stairs, the mist thickening around me. I had a feeling I was leaving blood all over the floor. Sarrlevi might only have needed to trail me to get his sample. "Kook," I whispered.

"Yes, they were kooks. I find my goblin brethren juvenile."

"Not everybody can be as mature as you." At the bottom of the stairs, I flipped the light switch to turn on the overhead lamps. Nothing happened.

Light still filtered down from above, so the power wasn't out. But here...

Sighing, I tapped my phone's flashlight app. It barely pierced the gloomy mist, and I couldn't tell if anyone had been down there. The pool table appeared unmolested. I headed to the laundry room, wondering if someone else knew about the hollow floor.

"What did this Nin say?" I asked quietly, not attempting to pronounce her last name. "Did she know of or remember selling a gun to our renter?"

"She said she's sold many magical guns over the years and didn't keep the addresses or even ask for identification from her clients. She also informed me that she is no longer in that line—"

I glanced at the phone, afraid I'd hung up on her as I'd been using the flashlight. The call had ended, and when I tried to redial, it didn't connect. There was no signal, the phone informed me.

"You had a signal twenty seconds ago." I'd moved into the laundry room—the floor was still intact—and stepped back out into the pool-table room to see if that made a difference. Nothing.

A moan drifted through the basement. It seemed to come from the walls all around me, not the floor.

"I don't believe in ghosts," I announced to the mist and moans, though I'd seen enough odd things in my life—usually magically inspired odd things—that my disbelief was tenuous. Maybe, if the renter had died horribly here, his eternal spirit *did* remain.

He'd guarded the house in life. Why not in death?

A soft thud came from upstairs. The door shutting?

Something clattered to the floor in the kitchen. That was no ghost. I wasn't alone.

10

IGNORING THE THROBBING IN MY CALF AND THE UNPLEASANT sensation of my jeans drying against my gouges, I hurried up the stairs to confront whoever was making noise in the kitchen. The mist followed me, but I barely noticed it as I sprang through the doorway with my hammer up.

Only to find Sarrlevi slumped against the sink, drinking from his cupped hand as water flowed. He'd heard me coming and watched my approach but regarded my fighting stance with unconcerned eyes. Or maybe those were *glassy* eyes. He was in rough shape.

Sweat gleamed on his forehead and dampened his short blond hair, short blond hair stained red with blood on one side. Holes punctured his tunic, and, when I flipped on the light switch—thankfully, it came on—I spotted more blood dripping onto the floor at his feet.

"FYI, we haven't installed the filtration system yet," I said, because blurting something like *you're hurt* or *oh my God* seemed inane.

"Why does all the water on your world taste dreadful?" Sarrlevi rasped, the corners of his eyes tight with pain.

"There are chemicals in it to make sure it's safe to drink."

His upper lip curled. "I will hope your plumbing skills improve what comes out of this water source."

"My skills improve everything." I might have reminded him that I wasn't a plumber, but scowling and yelling at a bleeding man—elf—seemed inappropriate. Instead, I lowered my hammer and stepped toward him. "Do you need..." He looked like he needed sutures, drugs, and heavy-duty bandages. At the least, a comprehensive first-aid kit. "A hug?" I finished lamely.

It was something my sister would have said. As a mother of two, she had more honed maternal instincts.

He blinked. "A what?"

"Never mind. I'm sorry you were hurt. Did the creature get the best of you?"

Sarrlevi lifted his chin. "I got the best of *it*. Unfortunately, not a fatal blow, but it should be curled up, forced to hibernate and regenerate itself for a time. What I was not prepared for was one of the werewolves having a semi-automatic—I believe that is your term—firearm loaded with magical bullets that could pierce my armor. Thorvald has a similar weapon, but I failed to anticipate scruffy werewolves being so well armed. Had I *only* been facing the gunman, I could have deflected the bullets, but he climbed a tree and fired from the branches behind the *brysarrusi* while I battled it." He shook his head. "It was impulsive of me to leap into that battle without preparation beforehand. Usually, I am not so unwise."

He squinted at me, as if it were my fault. Technically, it *was* because of me that the creature had appeared within spitting distance of his camp, but he could have stayed out of the trouble.

Why hadn't he? What interest did he have in me? In my *blood*?

"Do you want me to take you to the hospital?" I couldn't

imagine explaining a pointy-eared elf without any form of Earth ID to the ER, but he needed help.

"No." Sarrlevi took another drink from the sink, then lifted his tunic to reveal a fine chain-mesh vest with three bloody holes through it. "Most of the bullets bounced off."

"We need to get out the ones that didn't. The hospital—"

"Is not necessary. I recovered my camp and will attend to my wounds shortly. I merely came to see if you escaped the park."

He looked toward my leg. I wasn't nearly as much of a mess as he, but blood darkened the ripped jeans, so I couldn't hide the injury.

"You've been wounded," he said.

"Yeah, werewolf fangs are sharp. Who knew?"

Sarrlevi lowered his tunic. "I will assist you with your injuries so that you may resume your plumbing work tomorrow and improve the water."

I lost the battle not to scowl. From the glint in his eyes, I was fairly certain he was mocking me. I shouldn't have let him know it had irked me to be called a plumber. "I'll be sure to install a top-of-the-line reverse-osmosis system so your palate isn't offended when you slurp up my tap water."

"Yes. Do so." His imperious nod made me think he believed it was my duty to ensure only the finest of Earth's offerings reached his lips. "Come." He pointed to the floor next to him.

My jaw clenched. I was amazed he hadn't snapped his fingers. But if he could use his magic to take the pain in my leg away, it was worth doing as he asked. Though he should have been worrying about his own wounds.

Sarrlevi frowned at the mist that wreathed my legs as I walked.

"You did not install a new magical device, did you?" he asked.

"No." I glanced toward the backsplash tile.

"That is merely a dwarven luck charm." Waving dismissively toward the tile, he limped to the circular fireplace in the center of the kitchen. He walked around it, eyeing the brick structure from all angles.

I didn't sense— No, wait. I *did* sense something. My gaze drifted upward, toward the chimney. Something even fainter than the tile was up there. Inside? Nothing was visibly stuck to the outside.

Sarrlevi leaned his head into the open fire area, grimacing as he twisted to look up. He reached up, couldn't get to whatever it was, and used some magic to knock it free. It fell into his waiting hand.

He straightened and held it on his palm, an underwhelming oval river rock. If I hadn't sensed magic emanating from it, I would have assumed someone had stuck their favorite stone up there for safekeeping.

"This is orc magic," Sarrlevi said.

"Orc? Not werewolf?"

"Orc." He stepped into the kitchen doorway, drew his arm back, and hurled the stone into the woods. Considering his injuries, it flew impressively far.

"One of the neighbor's houses is over there," I said, glad his throw wasn't followed by the shattering of glass.

"Their yard may now be plagued by mist."

"*That's* what was creating that?" I waved at the haze. Had it been in the *yard*, I wouldn't have thought anything of it since fog and mist were natural in the Pacific Northwest. "Could it cause the lights not to turn on? And, uhm, moaning to come from the walls?"

Sarrlevi gazed at me.

"You didn't hear the moaning when you arrived, huh?"

"No. I could not tell what its full capabilities were, but I would guess someone was trying to scare you away from the house."

"To more easily break in and investigate it?"

"Perhaps. I am unaware of what is drawing the werewolves—

and others." Sarrlevi slumped against the doorframe.

"That makes two of us." I waved at his injuries, again feeling that he should prioritize his bullet wounds over my gashes. "Do you want to sit down somewhere?"

Where I would have him sit, I didn't know. Other than the couch and pool table in the basement, the house had a dearth of furnishings.

"I have my cot with me if necessary."

"You brought your camp *with* you?" I looked toward his backpack, wondering if everything I'd seen, including the moss rug, fit in there. "Because you're planning to move into my backyard?"

Only after the words came out did I realize he might construe them as an invitation. It wasn't.

I was more inclined to like him, arrogance or not, since he'd risked himself to lead the *brysarrusi* away from me, but it creeped me out that he wanted a sample of my blood and had been spying on me. He could be cozying up because he wanted to find whatever it was the werewolves wanted. Or for another reason altogether.

"You work here only during the day, correct? So this domicile is available at night."

It took me a moment to realize what he was implying. "You want to move into *the house*? You don't even like the water."

"Not move into, no." Sarrlevi shuddered. "This world is loathsome. But if you'll permit it, I could stay for the night, recover from my wounds, and then place magical wards around the house that would make it difficult for all but powerful magical beings to walk through."

"You can set booby traps to keep the werewolves out?"

"Likely so. A dragon could eradicate my traps, but none of them have shown an interest in your home yet, correct?"

"*Yet?* Are they likely to?"

A faint sneer curled his lip as he looked around the kitchen. "I wouldn't think so. They prefer caves, and whatever treasure the werewolves believe is here, it's likely dragons could make with their own magic."

"That's a relief. I guess. Don't take this the wrong way, but why would you be willing to help me protect the house? Especially when you're injured and probably want to be anywhere but here."

He gave me that unwavering and hard-to-read gaze again. "I offer this in exchange for the blood sample we discussed."

He glanced toward my injured calf, and I couldn't help but wonder if he was thinking of simply *taking* the blood sample.

"What do you want it for? And why are you keeping an eye on me?"

"Research."

"That's vague."

"Until I can confirm or refute my hypothesis regarding your identity, I will not discuss it with you. You may simply be a mongrel thief."

What identity was it he thought I might have? My mother, as far as she and my father had told me, had been a refugee hiding out on Earth. She might even have been a criminal back on her home world.

A chill went through me as I considered for the first time that she might *not* have been the rightful owner of the hammer. As I'd promised, I hadn't stolen it, but what if she had? Before I'd been born? What if that was why she'd come to Earth?

The thoughts stirred panic in me, but I tried to hide it and give a casual response. "Aren't I mongrel regardless? That's what you full-bloods call those of us with mixed blood, isn't it?"

"It is, and you are," he agreed.

"So, what identity could I have that would interest you?"

His eyelids drooped halfway. "Among other things, I can confirm if you are the rightful owner of that hammer or not."

"I am," I said with less confidence than I'd had the day before.

"But if I weren't, what would it mean to you?"

That sneer returned. "That every hour I linger in this hovel of a world is a further waste of my time. Do you agree to this arrangement? This domicile *needs* protection."

"Of that I have no doubt." I sighed. "Fine." I bent, shoved up my pant leg, an ill-considered action that brought tears to my eyes when the denim tore away from the wounds that were attempting to heal, then propped my foot on a counter. "Have at it."

"A pinprick with a needle would have been sufficient." Sarrlevi removed his backpack, not quite managing to hide a wince of his own.

"The werewolves thought fangs were more appropriate perforation tools." I wondered what a DNA sequencer would spit out if I took a sample of *his* blood to someone at the university. Were elves like frogs and 90 percent similar to humans? More similar than that, I supposed, since they, like dwarves, could breed with humans. That made me wonder if all the races, even trolls and orcs, had come from the same world long ago and been split apart by the gods or some other powerful entity. Dragons, perhaps? Dragging us off to different places for one large science experiment.

Sarrlevi pulled out a thin gold-trimmed container that I would have guessed was a sewing case, but it contained vials, swabs, and green gauze as well as needles.

"Do you take blood samples from randos on other worlds often?"

"Randos?"

"Random people."

"Not random people, no. Specific ones." Thankfully, he didn't stab me with a needle—though I supposed it wouldn't have been a horrific wound in comparison to the gouges weeping blood down my leg. He simply swabbed one of my wounds with the green gauze.

"That's not made from moss, is it?"

"It's a versatile substance. If I didn't have magical aids, I would use it as a dressing for my wounds." After Sarrlevi finished, he tucked the sample into an empty container, which disappeared into the backpack.

Too bad. I'd been curious if he had a microscope in there that he would pull out.

When I started to pull my leg back, he held up a finger.

"Hold."

I thought about saying something snarky, but the moaning in the basement had stopped, and mist no longer permeated the house. I didn't know if that magical stone would have harmed me, but nobody liked remodeling in a fog, and I wasn't sure I would have found the source on my own. To reward him for his removal of the object, I held my snark.

He pulled out a small spray bottle, a cloth, and a pad made from wide strands of woven grass. After moistening the cloth in the sink, he dabbed it against my gouges to clean them. I grimaced, even the light cool touch eliciting pain, but the task didn't take him long.

"Shouldn't you be cleaning your own wounds first? I appreciate your help, but yours are a lot more grievous. That said, is there any chance you have tetanus shots in there?"

He gave me a flat look that suggested mongrels were very foolish. Or maybe that was his stand-in look when he didn't know what I was talking about. "I do not. And I will meditate to heal my wounds more quickly."

"That will get the bullets out?"

"I have already incinerated them with magic."

"Handy."

"Yes."

Sarrlevi murmured something under his breath, and the grass pad expanded to something he could wrap around my leg. He squirted whatever was in the bottle on it and pressed it to my mangled flesh. It was cool and blessedly refreshing, creating the effect of a gel with a numbing agent, and I relaxed, filled with such relief that I had to grab the counter for support, lest I melt to the floor.

"The swelling will go down," he said, "and you should be able to walk on this tomorrow."

"Thank you. Do you want me to spray you down and wrap you in grass?"

His blond eyebrows rose. "That is not necessary. As I said, I can tend to my own wounds. I will set up my camp in your domicile. When I've rested enough for the task, I will set the wards."

"Do you want help with that?" I wouldn't mind learning how to set wards that could keep intruders away.

"I do not."

"You don't like me very much, do you, Sarrlevi?"

He gave me the bland gaze again. "I am indifferent to you."

"Because I'm a mongrel? Or are you indifferent to and stiff with everyone?"

He finished wrapping my leg and waved for me to set it down, then tucked the items back into his backpack. It took me a moment to realize he wouldn't answer my question. Maybe he *did* have a thing against mongrels and was attempting to be diplomatic about it. Stiffly diplomatic.

"How much stuff can you carry in that little backpack?" I pulled my pant leg down and gingerly leaned weight on my foot. The grass wrap continued to seep numbing coolness into me. "It seems to defy the laws of physics."

"It is a magical backpack."

"So physics doesn't apply?"

"Magic works within the bounds of physics, but clever crafters find workarounds."

"*You* didn't make the bag, did you?" I wondered if he thought himself terribly clever.

"No." Sarrlevi withdrew what looked like the elven equivalent of jerky and set it on the counter. It might have been made from meat or smashed mushrooms—the dried state made it hard to tell—but either way, if that was his dinner, it didn't look that satiating. He had to be hungry after fighting and running all over the park. "I have few hobbies besides my sword work and fitness and striving to be the best assassin in the Cosmic Realms. When you are good at what you do, people pay a premium for your services, and you can afford expensive—and handy—magical items."

"I've heard that."

He scrutinized me. "Perhaps you should train with such an end goal in mind. For a mongrel, you are strong and not completely lacking in fighting ability."

"Your warm praise is making my lady bits tingle."

His mouth parted, puzzlement in his eyes, and he glanced at my chest, though only briefly. Probably dismissively. "I fail to see how a professional assessment of your aptitude should result in tingling."

"It was sarcasm. Don't they have that in the Cosmic Realms?"

"Few are sarcastic with assassins."

"Because it's not suitably respectful?"

"Among other reasons. I will rest and then apply the wards." Sarrlevi picked up the jerky, slung his backpack over his shoulder, and walked slowly across the kitchen. His hand strayed toward a bullet hole in his pants—in his *thigh*—but he didn't allow himself to limp again. Maybe assassins weren't supposed to do that in front of mongrels.

He stepped into what had been called the *butler's kitchen* in the listing but what I thought of as the pantry. It was lined with cabinets and shelves, with a crumb-filled toaster from a past decade—possibly a past century—sitting on a counter.

I thought about mentioning the existence of bedrooms in the

house, but it wasn't as if they were furnished. Besides, maybe he wanted toast when he woke up.

"You may leave," Sarrlevi called out as a green glow emanated from the pantry. The little light globe he'd had in his forest camp? "I will have healed and applied the wards by morning."

"I'll be able to walk back onto the property, right? And Tinja and Abbas need access too." I gripped my chin, debating if I wanted to leave him here alone.

If he were inclined, he would have all night to hunt for the valuable whatsit the werewolves, and apparently some orcs, were after. But did I care if he found it? Whatever it was, I would prefer it out of the house so everyone would leave the place alone. Maybe I ought to *encourage* him to look for it.

"Yes." A faint groan followed the word. As he lay down?

Maybe I ought to encourage him to rest and forget about the wards. I felt bad that he didn't have real food, first-aid supplies beyond what he carried, or anything to drink besides tap water, which was offensive to his refined elven tastebuds.

A whisper of magic teased my senses, and the pantry door shut.

"I guess the social part of our evening is over," I muttered.

Outside, I circled the house, checking for werewolves, orcs, and shaggy, clawed, gorilla-like creatures. But maybe the fight in the park had worn everyone out, for the property was devoid of intruders. I returned to my motorcycle without encountering or sensing anyone and yawned as I sat on it.

The temptation to head straight home and crash in my bed came over me, but I caught myself looking back toward the house. Sarrlevi had healed my wounds and risked his life for me. While I doubted his motivations were altruistic, and suspected his interest in me would vanish as soon as he found out how mundane my blood was, he *had* likely saved my ass.

Sighing, I headed to the grocery store instead of home.

11

As I returned to the project house, a grocery bag balanced between my legs, I didn't sense any magic emanating from the property. My trip had been quick, since the store had been about to close, so Sarrlevi was likely still meditating. Hopefully, when the wards were installed, I, and those they were meant to repel, would be able to sense them.

Admittedly, I had little experience with wards and had only vague notions about what full-blooded magical beings could do. The few I had encountered had been trolls and shifters, not elves.

I went in the front door, not trying to be quiet. Startling an assassin sounded like a bad idea. He might leap out of the pantry and lop off my head.

"Sarrlevi? I brought you some food and drinks."

He didn't reply, and I didn't sense him. That was the norm, though, so I assumed he was camouflaging himself from enemies.

"And friendly bringers of food," I muttered, heading for the kitchen.

It had crossed my mind to go home and simply have a pizza delivered to him, but it had been easy to envision him springing onto the stoop with his swords raised to assault the driver. Also, I had a hunch elves were snooty and might turn their noses up at something as pedestrian as pizza. At the least, *he* was snooty.

For that reason, I'd gone to the organic-foods store and spent far more on his dinner than I would have on my own. But who knew what elves ate?

The pantry door was closed, but green light emanated from the crack underneath. It amused me to imagine that the glowing sphere was the equivalent of a night light or even a teddy bear that he carried everywhere for comfort, but I assumed it had something to do with camouflaging his camp.

"I brought some food, Sarrlevi." I took items out of the bag, certain his keen ears would hear me through the door. "Turkey meatloaf, blackened tempeh, a deli sandwich, and, in case elves are vegan, a huge container of Emerald City Salad. It's got kale and wild rice and other things that sounded elfy. We've also got three kinds of cheese—I'll help you with those if you're not interested, but you should try them. Do elves have cows? And milk? Cheese is *fabulous*. My favorite food. You'll like the Gouda, but if you want something semi-local, check out the Tillamook sharp cheddar. It's from Oregon. There are three different kinds of drinks. Do you like sparkling water? Kombucha? If not, you can knock yourself out with the beer. Finally, there's a box of chocolates. And carrot cake too. Do elves have a sweet tooth?" I held up the large single-serving square, the moist frosting-drenched cake looking scintillating inside its clear container, and vowed to eat it myself the next day if he didn't. After a harrowing fight in the park, a girl needed desserts. I'd already sampled one of the chocolates. "There are some bandages and antiseptic in here too in case you run out of grass pads."

My chatter didn't result in a response or even a sound from the pantry. Since I couldn't sense his aura, it occurred to me that he might not be in there.

Or—my gut knotted as a new thought occurred to me—he might have lapsed into unconsciousness or worse from his wounds. Even though he'd seemed indifferent to the injuries, acting as if being shot numerous times wasn't a big deal, such severe wounds could have killed a normal person. Just because he'd incinerated the bullets, or so he'd said, didn't mean they hadn't done damage.

"Sarrlevi?" I crept toward the door and reached for the knob but paused, that image of him being startled and springing for me with his weapons returning. Or him just being pissed that I was intruding on his healing time. But if he needed medical attention, I needed to know. I didn't want to return in the morning to find him dead in my pantry. "Are you all right?"

When no response came, I eased the door open. And gaped.

Sarrlevi had set up his cot and spread his moss rug, the ends furled up against the cabinets and shelves along the walls, and rested his swords and a number of daggers on the counter within reach. He lay on his back on the cot, naked except for a pair of brown underwear—the word *loincloth* came to mind—and several of the woven-grass bandages. One was wrapped around his thigh, one his arm, and three stretched across his torso, hiding the bullet wounds.

They *didn't* hide that he had an amazing physique full of powerful muscles with scant body fat softening his form. I couldn't pull my gaze from him. Numerous old scars marked his body, but they did little to detract from the fact that he was a sculptor's dream muse. No, they only stirred my curiosity. How many times had he almost been killed over the years? And how many years had he been alive and worked as an assassin? Fifty? A hundred? More? He appeared no more than thirty, but elves were reputedly long-lived.

Something between a groan and a growl of irritation came

from him, and he lifted his head from the small green pillow on his cot to frown at me.

"Sorry," I blurted, lifting my hands and turning my face to look at the toaster instead of him. Heat scorched my cheeks, as if I'd stuck my head between the coils and turned it on. "I didn't mean to look. Er, come in. I mean, I *did* mean to come in, but only to check on you. To make sure you weren't dead. And to bring you food." I pointed at the groceries spread out on the kitchen counter, as if he wouldn't believe me. "I thought healing would make you hungry. And fighting. And all the things you did tonight."

I was burbling, damn it. When he'd been a warrior bleeding in my kitchen, I hadn't been thinking of him as a cute guy, or any kind of male of the species at all, just a wounded elf. But I was flustered now, and when I glanced to check his reaction, I couldn't help but see *all* of him. I jerked my face away again, afraid he would think I was checking him out.

And maybe I had been. Not *intentionally*. It was hard not to look when someone was almost completely naked on a cot in one's pantry. I hoped he'd been too busy healing to notice.

"Elves do not mate with mongrel dwarves," Sarrlevi stated.

Shit. He *had* noticed my interest.

More heat, as well as indignation, scorched my cheeks. "I didn't come to *mate* with you. Just to make sure you hadn't died and to tell you food is here if you want it."

Sarrlevi rose from the cot, his movements not as stiff as before, and stepped toward me.

I started to skitter back, the pantry feeling far too claustrophobic now, but he startled me by grasping the top of my head. His grip wasn't painful, but it was *firm*, reminding me that elves also had greater strength than humans. He hadn't reached for his weapons, or I would have kicked him and jumped back, but his reaction alarmed me. What if there was some rule about mongrels looking at naked elves, and I'd deeply affronted him?

His face was stony, and seconds passed as he stared at me with his hand on top of my head. I grew aware of how much taller he was than me—and that the grass bandages hadn't fallen off when he'd stood. One stretched across the hard bulge of the pectoral muscles in front of my eyes. Some stupid part of my mind had the passing thought that it was too bad elves *didn't* mate with mongrel dwarves, but I soundly chastised it. He was an arrogant prick, and he was acting like I had threatened him. No way was I interested in anything intimate with him.

"Want to let go of me?" I asked, irritated when my voice squeaked. I wasn't *afraid*. I was just... Hell, I didn't know. Discombobulated. "You're supposed to tip delivery drivers, not palm their heads like a basketball."

Something tickled at my mind, almost like a touch inside my brain. Was he reading my *mind*? It felt more ominous than the telepathic words he'd shared with me earlier.

Finally, he released me. "I accept your offering of food."

"I'm so glad." I backed into the kitchen. "I hope you didn't think I meant to attack you."

"Had I thought that, I would have grabbed my weapons, not your head. Your look was one of sexual interest, not impending violence."

"I'm *not* sexually interested."

"I have been targeted by females before who wish to manipulate me." Sarrlevi sneered. His favorite expression. He must not have had a mother who'd told him his lips would get stuck like that if he made that face too often. He also looked toward the food I'd spread out on the counter, his gaze lingering on the chocolates. They had caramel inside and sea-salt crystals on the top. A sane person would have drooled over them. If anything, his sneer grew more pronounced.

"That's your fault for being pretty. You should have been a

dwarf. Apparently, nobody has sexual interest in them." Or their half-blood offspring...

I shook my head, shoving away the self-pity. It wasn't as if nobody had ever thought I was hot. I'd had a few boyfriends over the years. There were men who liked strong women who beat up criminals. Thus far, they'd all tended to be guys who looked like they'd spent time in prison yards—more than one *had* spent time in a prison yard. Unfortunately for my libido, I was more drawn to pretty guys. And, apparently, pretty elves.

But *not* this one.

"Dwarves are interested in other dwarves," Sarrlevi said.

"You know that from reading their minds? Is that what you were doing?" I pointed to my temple. "Because on Earth, we consider that rude."

"As if anyone on this benighted world has manners."

"Manners enough not to read people's minds. Did you find what you wanted in there?" I wasn't positive he'd been able to read my thoughts, so I watched his face, wanting confirmation. If he had that ability, I would have to be careful what I thought around him.

"Somewhat." His expression turned sour. "Dwarves are naturally resilient to mind probes, and you appear to have inherited some of that predilection."

"I'm not sad about that." I hadn't been aware that I'd inherited anything more from my mother than her strength and stamina, but if she'd given me a hard head that kept nosy elves out of my brain, good. Even better if it irked those nosy elves.

"I do believe you do not intend to manipulate me or lure me into your bed," Sarrlevi said.

"No, I do not." I couldn't keep from rolling my eyes. You get caught giving a guy one short ogle of his bare chest... "You're a tool, you know that?"

"I have the honed body of a *weapon*, not a simple tool."

"Oh no, you're *definitely* a tool," I said, not caring that he probably didn't know what the insult meant.

Sarrlevi gazed coolly at me, some of his powerful aura seeping out of the camouflaging magic cloaking him. I swallowed, reminded that he was dangerous because of more than his sword-fighting abilities.

"I have recovered sufficiently," he stated. "I will set your wards and return to the forest. The coarsely barked trees are not as abrasive as the mongrels on this world."

"Probably because you're not accusing the *trees* of trying to seduce you." I grabbed my hammer and headed for the door.

Earlier, I'd been longing for my bed, but, after that irritating encounter, I was too riled up for sleep. Hitting something sounded more appealing. Or *someone*. But clubbing an elf in the head with a hammer after bringing him dinner might send mixed messages. Besides, as much as I hated to admit it, I was positive Sarrlevi could kick my ass in a fight. Knowledge that also made me want to hit things.

Instead of heading for the front door, I veered down the stairs. While he was setting wards, I would find out what was under the laundry-room floor.

12

NORMALLY, I DIDN'T DEMO HOMES IN THE MIDDLE OF THE NIGHT, BUT the houses here were far enough apart, with trees and dense foliage between them, that I doubted thumps from the basement would disturb anyone. *Gunshots* apparently didn't disturb or even attract notice in this neighborhood.

"Weird place, much?" I mumbled.

At least the mist had disappeared. After checking once more for a possible entrance to the hollow area underneath the floor, I hefted my hammer and smashed the tiles. Porcelain flew, pieces ricocheting off the washer and dryer. It didn't take long to reveal a plywood subfloor underneath, something I'd yet to encounter in a basement in the Seattle area.

"Should be the foundation down there." After my earlier thumping, I wasn't surprised that it wasn't, but I *was* surprised that there wasn't a trapdoor of any kind.

More tiles fell to my hammer, and I pushed the broken pieces into a pile, trying not to think of the work I was adding for myself. The plywood was also new and in good shape. Once more, I hesitated before tearing into it. But I wanted to know what was down there, damn it. If I ended up finding nothing more than a root cellar or someone's Cold War nuclear bunker—I'd encountered both on old properties before—then oh well. One mystery would be solved.

But as I pounded the hammer into the plywood, a strange zing went up my spine. It reminded me of when I'd walked into Sarrlevi's camp in the forest, but this didn't feel like elven magic. It didn't feel like dwarven magic either.

"Hm."

Another zing plucked at my senses, but it didn't come from the floor that time. I sensed Sarrlevi moving around in the yard and realized he was setting his wards. Maybe I'd been wrong, and both zings had been a result of his tinkering.

My hammer had opened a hole in the plywood, revealing the edge of a joist and a dark space below. I took a couple more careful swings, preferring not to damage the joists, then tore away the broken plywood.

The faintest tingle of something magical touched my senses as dank earthen air wafted up, teasing my nostrils.

"My bet is on root cellar, not bunker," I muttered, pulling away more wood until I found another joist. "That is definitely spaced farther apart than the standard sixteen inches. Hell, that's more than twenty-four. Tinja's building-codes instructor would sputter in horror."

Interestingly, the joists were old, the wood dark with moisture damage.

"So, who replaced the subfloor and finish floor and not the joists?"

Whatever was giving off the slight magical aura ought to be what the werewolves sought. It wasn't coming from the yard. I was sure of it and envisioned a sword-in-a-stone or golden chalice or whatever enticed the minds of thieves from another realm. I imagined chucking it over the trees in the same direction that Sarrlevi had thrown the stone.

I set my hammer down and used my phone's flashlight to shine light below. The beam cast light deeper into the darkness than I expected. But it weakened before it touched the earthen ground more than ten feet below. Twenty feet below?

"Why is this so deep? Nobody needs to store carrots twenty feet below ground." No, it was more than that. The basement was already partially underground. "And I'll note the lack of a moisture barrier down there. Such shoddy workmanship."

I dropped to my belly so I could lower my arm and the phone into the dark space, wishing I had a bright camp lantern instead of an app. The light barely reached a wall, one more than ten feet from the hole. Thick wooden support posts lined it, reminding me of a mine shaft. Halfway to the wall, the floor joists switched to beams the same thickness as the posts. That was past the washer and dryer and the wall so not under the house anymore.

A series of fast scrapes sounded, almost startling me into dropping the phone. I grabbed my hammer as I swung the light toward the noise, visions of skeletons and zombies coming to mind.

The light flashed on something's furry backside as it skittered into a hole in the earthen wall and disappeared. Was it a den? Or a tunnel up to the yard? If so, that creature had dug a long way under the house to get down there.

"Weird. Just like everything else here."

Leaf litter, fur, and feces dotted the packed earth underneath the hole, suggesting the creature had been using the spot for a while. Wondering what had drawn it to tunnel so deep, I swung the light in the other directions. Three walls were earth with wooden supports. And one... was made from bright red bricks, the mortar so new it gleamed against the dark backdrop.

"I bet you were done at the same time as the new floor. And what is it exactly that you're walling off?"

As I moved my light around, something metal glinted on the packed-earth floor. A coin? No, it wasn't the right shape.

Another zing plucked at my nerves, and, as if a light switch had been turned on, I sensed a magical perimeter around the house. Sarrlevi was hard at work.

I wondered if he had a rope. I'd practiced falling and rolling a few zillion times in my life and was confident I could jump down without hurting myself, though my healing leg might object to such activity, but getting back out would be difficult. The hole I'd torn open was at least ten feet from the walls down there—more like fifteen to the brick wall—and even with dwarven strength, I doubted I could climb up and swing myself from joist to joist and pull myself out.

"That's a job for an elf," I muttered.

I rose, intending to jog out to ask Sarrlevi if he had a rope in his backpack of impossible physics and let out a startled squawk when I almost ran into him. Distracted by the new magic around the house, I hadn't sensed or heard him approaching. At least he was clothed now, so I didn't have to worry about accidentally ogling his chest.

"I was coming to find you," I said as he looked blandly from me to the hole and back. "Do you have a rope?"

His gaze went back to the hole.

"I've got one back at my house, but if I go home, I'm not coming back tonight. The investigation will have to wait until tomorrow." Not that he cared. But *I* did. I was dying to know what the brick wall had been built—*recently* built—to hide. And what was glinting on the floor? A piece of trash that had fallen out of someone's pocket or something significant?

"I do have a rope." Though his face was as bland and stoic as ever, Sarrlevi sounded tired.

He probably hadn't had enough time to fully regenerate his body before I'd interrupted his meditation.

"If you let me borrow it, you can take a nap while I explore," I offered.

"Assassins do not *nap*."

"Dude, you travel with your own cot, pillow, and rug."

"Assassins do not nap while others go into danger," he amended. "Or sleep in primitive circumstances if it's not necessary." He eyed the ceiling, the hole, and the washer and dryer. His expression haughtily conveyed that the entire house counted as primitive.

I decided not to argue, but the place would be amazing once my team finished remodeling.

"You think there's danger down there?" I pointed at the hole. "So far, I've only encountered a mole or a gopher."

"You sense the magic?"

"Yes."

"A *gopher* did not create it."

"I assumed it's the artifact the werewolves are looking for and that the now-dead renter was protecting."

Sarrlevi didn't argue, but he didn't look like he agreed. "I'll get the rope."

While he was gone, I pondered the logic of the situation. Someone had killed the renter, presumably to get at what was in —under—this house. But if they had gotten the item, why would the werewolves and maybe some orcs still be looking for it? Had they not received the memo that it was gone?

And if someone *had* gotten it, why had they covered everything up afterward? It wasn't light work to build a brick wall and put in a new floor.

When Sarrlevi returned, he carried a coil of slender rope made from long strands of braided grass. If it hadn't emanated faint magic, I would have doubted it could hold up a ten-pound dumbbell, much less a half-dwarf. He dropped the end by the edge, then tossed the rest into the hole.

Startled, I lunged to grab the end before it fell in, but it had affixed itself to the floor.

"Handy," I said.

"I am, yes." Sarrlevi hopped into the hole before I could offer the snarky reply that his comment deserved. He didn't use the rope.

I leaned over and shined my light down in time to see him rising from a crouch. It crossed my mind to jump down after him —maybe he would be impressed by, or at least not disappointed in, my mongrel moves. But I might hurt myself trying to perform such a feat in the dark, and then I would feel like an idiot. Instead, I pocketed my phone, grabbed my hammer in one hand, and used the other to shimmy down the rope.

It held snug, but it was so thin that my descent felt awkward. Or maybe it was having the agile elf observing me that made it awkward.

When I landed and pulled out my phone again, I realized he hadn't been observing me at all. He'd already moved over to the brick wall and rested his hand on it. His head tilted as he considered it.

"Want to see how effectively a dwarven hammer can demolish a brick wall?" I walked over, thumping the haft in my hand, though I wanted to investigate more thoroughly before knocking anything down. Especially since it was possible this house didn't have a proper foundation. I couldn't believe the home inspector had missed all evidence of this.

"Don't you think you should figure out why the wall exists before knocking it down?" Sarrlevi asked.

"To hide something, I assume." Though, as I'd just been considering, the order of events didn't make a lot of sense to me. "The magic is coming from behind it, right? Not the bricks themselves?" I rested a hand on them and was startled to find the wall warm.

Maybe that was what had drawn the gopher. Winter had passed, but I could imagine cold animals having been drawn to a heat source.

"I believe the wall itself is enchanted, actually," Sarrlevi said. "It feels like gnomish magic. It's possible the wall was built to keep something *in* rather than people out."

That was a chilling thought. But did it make sense?

"From what I learned from the neighbors, the likely part-dwarven renter was guarding this house for a long time. Years. And he got surly and barked at anyone who came near the property."

"That is typical behavior for a dwarf."

I snorted. "I'm just saying it sounds like he was guarding a treasure."

"What if he was protecting the neighborhood?"

"From what? Nothing could live locked up in a dungeon for years. It's not like there's a door." At least not that I'd been able to discover. "Or air holes."

"Threats exist that do not breathe."

My earlier thoughts of skeletons and zombies returned. But that stuff wasn't real, was it? I'd heard of legitimately haunted houses, but I'd yet to see one. This place was the closest I'd gotten.

I lowered my hammer. "Are you saying I should leave the wall as it is because some vile magical thing might be back there?"

"I'm merely offering possibilities to consider before wantonly destroying something."

"Right, because you only think it's appropriate to wantonly destroy things that have bounties on their heads."

"I am an assassin, not a bounty hunter," Sarrlevi said coolly.

"What's the difference?"

"I am hired by those who can afford me to perform a specific task. I don't compete against other riffraff for the chance at winning a prize."

"So bounty hunting is a lesser occupation and beneath you."

"Yes." One of his eyebrows twitched. "Is not *plumbing* beneath you?"

"No, it's not. But it's not all I do. I'm good at a lot of things."

"I see."

I clenched my jaw. His tone wasn't exactly sarcastic—apparently, elves didn't have sarcasm—but it pissed me off anyway. Probably because of the superior tilt to his chin with everything he said.

Reminded of the shiny object I'd seen, I swung the light around to search for it. There. It was a bullet—no, the casing from a spent round. I held it in my palm and stared at it. If the renter had been killed in the foyer, why had someone been shooting down here?

I put it in my pocket, thinking someone more familiar with guns might be able to tell what kind had fired it. "If the wall is enchanted, does that mean my hammer wouldn't be able to break it down, even if I decided to?"

"The hammer's magic may be more powerful than the enchantment. I don't know. It's possible it could zap you with lightning and hurl you across the chamber."

"Is that a joke?"

"Your experience with magic is limited, I see."

"We don't have a lot of it here on Earth."

"Your people will fall quickly if dragons ever decide to tame this wild world and bring it under the talons of the Dragon Council."

"Don't be too sure. Humans are a feisty bunch."

His only response was the familiar haughty, I-know-more-than-you look.

"I'm beginning to see why you became a weapons master." I walked around the perimeter of the chamber, shining my light on the ground in case there was something else of interest on this side of the wall.

"I crave physical challenges, exhilaration, and testing myself against others."

"I assumed your attitude got you beaten up a lot as a kid, and you got tired of it."

A pattern of stones embedded in a corner opposite the brick wall drew my eye. I crouched to study it and almost missed that Sarrlevi didn't reply.

I looked back at him. "I'm not right, am I?"

The image of him being stuffed into the elven equivalent of a middle-school locker came to mind. It shouldn't have tickled me, but he was so damn pompous that it did.

"Elves, even elven young, rarely bully each other." Sarrlevi hesitated, then added in a lower voice, "They simply ostracize you if you don't act appropriately."

"Did that happen to you? Did they kick you out of elf land?"

His chin came up again. "A powerful elven assassin goes where he wishes, whether he's invited or not."

"Definitely kicked out," I muttered, a little curious about his upbringing and how he'd gotten himself ostracized but far more curious about the stones. I dusted them off, wondering if the pattern they'd been arranged in had a meaning and if they *marked* something.

Originally, I hadn't been that interested in what was hidden down here that the werewolves wanted, but that had been before I'd learned this was all tied in with dwarves somehow. If the renter had been a half-dwarf, then I identified with him, whether he'd been surly and grumpy or not. I hadn't met that many half-dwarves, and other than my mother, I'd never met a full-blooded dwarf.

I remembered her saying that most of her people had gone back to their home world before I'd been born. That it had grown too dangerous for them here, too difficult a place for them to live. If she'd ever said why she stayed, I didn't remember it. I'd assumed it had been because of her love for my father.

When I brushed the stones, one was loose. The earth under them wasn't packed as compactly as elsewhere. I hesitated before pulling out the loose stone, Sarrlevi's warning of lightning strikes coming to mind. I didn't sense any magic in the area, but maybe I should get his opinion first, however haughty it would be.

"Sarrlevi?" I turned to find him leaning against the brick wall, his cheek pressed against it and one hand splayed in front of his face, fingertips touching the stone. "Are you performing a Vulcan mind meld?" Even if he was blond, his pointed ears couldn't help but bring to mind memories of Mr. Spock. "That's not a Horta."

His eyes opened, and he looked at me.

"Never mind. Can you let me know if these stones might mean anything important before I try digging here?" I waved for him to come over.

"I was attempting to determine how far the brick wall extends and what's on the other side, but elven magic is far more attuned to the above-ground world. If you'd received instruction from a dwarf master, you might be able to use your magic to understand the earth and rocks and ore and such, but I trust you haven't."

"I can do a few card tricks, but that's it." I pointed at the stones, hoping to divert him before he insulted me for being a mongrel. Though it was interesting that he'd suggested I might be able to learn magic. If I could find a dwarf master...

"They are arranged in a symbol favored by the dwarves. It indicates the heart or love."

I blinked. Someone's proclamation of love wasn't what I'd expected to find down here. Not that any of this was within expectations thus far.

"It doesn't necessarily mean romantic love. It can also speak of a bond of friendship or the relationship that comrades who go into battle have." Several zings pricked at my senses, and Sarrlevi looked toward the ceiling. "Someone has triggered the wards. *Multiple* someones. I will check."

He strode to the rope, leaped ten feet to catch it halfway up, and climbed out of the hole in under two seconds.

Though I knew I should go with him—it was *my* house, after all—a weird feeling came over me that this might be my only chance to poke around down here. I scraped at the stones and earth, but the ground wasn't as loose as I'd thought, and I didn't make much progress with my nails.

Another zing plucked at my senses. I hoped that meant the wards were keeping intruders out, not that someone was assaulting the house, but it stirred urgency within me.

Using the metal butt of my hammer, I poked and dug. In my truck back home, I had crowbars and all manner of tools, but I'd had to ride my motorcycle over to stalk werewolves in the park.

Grumbling, I finally made progress, digging several inches down. I was about to give up, not wanting to leave Sarrlevi dealing with the problem by himself for too long. Then the weapon clunked against something that wasn't dirt.

I dropped it and clawed with my nails, feeling the outline of a small metal chest. No magic emanated from it, so I doubted it was what the werewolves sought, but *I* sure wanted to know what some dwarf had buried and put a heart symbol atop.

Hoping it wasn't booby-trapped, I unfastened the lid and eased it open. A gold signet ring rested atop a stack of faded Polaroid photos, crossed hammers on a flag engraved in blue on top of it.

I shuffled carefully through the pictures, looking at stout bearded men and a couple of women—one also bearded—in clothing that varied from denim and flannel to something more like buckskins. One man had a hammer slung over his shoulder and wore a suit of armor. Another matched the description the neighbor had given of the renter. Eyebrows like caterpillars indeed.

Had he been a half-dwarf renter or a *dwarf* renter? The short, stout people in the Polaroids looked exactly how I imagined dwarves would look.

It was hard to tell how tall they were without a normal human standing by for reference, but they certainly seemed like they might be closer to four and a half feet than six.

The second to the last Polaroid made me freeze and stare, the woman so familiar I struggled to process what I was seeing. "Mother?"

If she hadn't been almost exactly as I remembered her, with frizzy red hair, a broad face, and green eyes, I might not have recognized her after thirty years.

Whatever photos my father had possessed had disappeared the night their apartment burned, the night Mother had died and he'd been arrested. After thirty years, my memory had grown fuzzy, but that night remained etched in my mind. My four-year-old self hadn't understood what was happening, but their faces as they'd fought against intruders in camo uniforms shooting rifles at them weren't anything anyone would forget.

The last Polaroid also had my mother in it, standing with her arms around her comrades in a group picture. They were the dwarves from the other images, and they were underground somewhere, with an orange light on a pedestal glowing behind them. Or maybe that was a glowing magical artifact?

I poked into the chest, hoping for more clues, but the ring was the only other item. The inside of the chest was lined, and no moisture or outside air had seeped in, so everything was well-preserved. It was hard to tell how old the photos were, but I hadn't seen anyone wandering around with a Polaroid since my youth. I didn't think they even made film for those instant cameras anymore.

Your authorities are coming, Sarrlevi spoke into my mind.

What? Why? I'll be right up.

I tossed my hammer through the hole, stuffed the chest in my hoodie and zipped it up, then climbed the rope. As I raced up the stairs to the main floor, the sound of sirens permeated the walls. Orange light flickered, coming through a front window. Fire?

Sarrlevi? I attempted to project my thoughts, but I had no idea how telepathy worked.

When I opened the front door, I almost tripped over a body sprawled on the stoop. A human body in a police uniform.

13

I GAPED AT THE BODY ON THE STOOP, BLOOD POOLED ON THE CEMENT underneath it, and struggled to process how it had gotten there—and the ramifications. Unless that police uniform had been stolen, this wasn't—hadn't been—a werewolf.

My first thought was that Sarrlevi, not understanding the significance of such a uniform, had killed the man for trying to get to the house, or that something with the wards had gone horribly wrong, but the side of the officer's head was smashed in. A blunt object had struck him, not a sword. Burn marks on his exposed skin might have been caused by the magic of the wards, but they weren't what had killed him.

The clash of steel in the street, the noise audible over the approaching police sirens, made me lift my gaze and look for Sarrlevi. A fire burning in a tree by the mailbox threw orange light over the pavement, but if that was Sarrlevi fighting, he and his opponent weren't in view.

Unfortunately, two police cars parked in front of the house *were* in view, as were the bodies of more dead officers. One was stretched across the walkway, and two more had fallen by the open doors of their cars, as if they'd been yanked out and killed. The firelight burned brightly enough to illuminate another man's smashed head—another death from a blunt weapon.

I couldn't help but glance at the hammer gripped in my hand. Was it a coincidence that someone else had a blunt weapon? Or... what if someone had deliberately chosen a hammer similar to mine? To cast suspicion on me?

The sounds of the sword fight halted. Someone snarled—it didn't sound like a human voice—and then only the noise of the sirens remained.

Sarrlevi? I tried calling telepathically again.

I might have called his name aloud, but the flashing lights of police vehicles came from down the street, preceding the arrival of more cars. Again, I glanced at the body on the stoop, and terror washed through my veins, along with the certainty that if the police caught me, I would end up in jail.

As I stepped back, intending to close the door and run out the back, I glimpsed a dark cloaked figure in front of the bushes on the side of the yard opposite the fire. A hood pulled over his head made it hard to make out his face, but I sensed his aura and caught the glint of a tusk as he turned to look at me. An orc. Standing over there like a coach masterminding the plays in a big game.

Running out the back of the house *would* have been wise, especially since the police cars were driving into view, but my legs propelled me into the yard. I had to catch that orc and force him to confess to what he'd done.

I sprinted toward him with my hammer raised to strike, but he threw something onto the grass and stepped back into the bushes. Smoke billowed upward.

Holding my breath, I ran through it. He wouldn't get away that easily.

The smoke quickly formed a gray cloud that my eyes couldn't penetrate, but I sprang, swinging at the bushes where he should have been. The hammer struck only branches, and I sensed him running into the yard next door.

"Stop right there!" a police officer cried from the street.

Though I doubted he could see me through the smoke, I dove in case he fired. Branches clawed at me, and I hit the ground hard, a root jabbing me in the ribs. The chest I'd tucked in my hoodie almost flew free, but I caught it, not wanting to lose my only clue to what was going on—or photos of my mother.

Scrambling on hands and knees, I crawled through the bushes toward the neighbor's property.

Gunshots fired, bullets whizzing past above me at head level. Gulping, I stayed low. The police had seen their fallen comrades and were deathly serious.

I squeezed through a fence hidden by the brush, came out of the leaves, and almost crashed into a fountain rising from a manicured garden layered with bark. The smoke hadn't drifted over to this yard, and I could see a house with lights on, someone peering out a window. In the street, two uniformed men appeared, running over from my house.

I rose to my feet so I could run, but I stayed low, racing around the house and into the backyard. I leaped a fence like a thoroughbred and passed through the yard of another house. A dog barked uproariously at my passage, making me wonder if this was a vain effort, if there was any way I would escape.

Then an explosion came from the direction of my property. The house? One of the police cars? My poor motorcycle that I'd been forced to abandon?

I didn't know, but when I ran out into the next street, there weren't any policemen waiting for me. I cut across another yard, then found a trail that led toward the park. Into the den of werewolves and monsters from another realm was the last place I wanted to go again, but it was the only place I could imagine avoiding the police for long enough to think and figure out what had happened. Besides that at least one orc had been in the area, likely standing inches outside where Sarrlevi had put down the wards.

If he had put down the wards. What if he'd been doing something other than what he'd promised and was in league with the orcs?

No, I'd sensed him applying that magic, and I was certain he had been the one sword-fighting with someone in the street. The orcs responsible for killing the police, I hoped. I also hoped that he'd left behind some orc bodies, that they'd had hammers or maces in their hands, and that the police would figure out *I* hadn't had anything to do with the deaths. The *murders*.

The source of the sirens started moving. Police cars searching the neighborhood?

I made it to the street that paralleled the park and looked both ways before running across. As I shoved my way into the ferns on the opposite side, a police car turned onto the street. Had the driver glimpsed me? I hoped not, but there was little doubt that they would search the park regardless.

With nothing but my hammer, the chest of photos, and the clothes on my back, I made my way onto a trail and ran down it, wanting to come out of the park on the far side. And hoping I wouldn't run into any shifters or monsters along the way.

My phone buzzed, and I jumped. I pulled it out but didn't recognize the number. Maybe the police were calling.

Say, Matti, we'd like to arrest you. Can you give us your location, please?

I paused under a tree to text Abbas and tell him not to come to the project house in the morning, that there'd been... an incident. I also warned Tinja that I wouldn't be home that night and that she would likely have visitors. She might want to disappear.

Not waiting for a reply, I put the phone on airplane mode, then turned it off completely, having some vague notion that the police might be able to track me through it if I didn't. They might be able to anyway, but I couldn't bring myself to abandon it alongside the trail.

I slumped against a tree, the sirens penetrating the woods. A dog barked. A nearby resident complaining about the noise? Or had the police called in a K-9 unit to track me down?

I started running down the trail again, though I didn't know where I was going or how far I would get. I was tempted to head back to where Sarrlevi had been camped, but he'd moved his belongings to the house. Still, maybe he would think I would return to that spot, and he could find me there.

But did he *want* to find me? Whatever interest he had in my blood couldn't be worth all the hassle he'd endured tonight.

"I hope if those orcs tear down that brick wall that whatever horrible thing is trapped back there eats them," I snarled, then paused.

Sirens were now coming from ahead of me. And from the far side of the park as well. More dog barks sounded. They were surrounding me.

"Why the hell aren't they looking for the orcs instead of me?"

"They may be searching for both," a calm voice said from behind me.

I spun. Sarrlevi.

I'd never been so pleased to see his haughty face. It was too dark to read his expression, but I was sure the adjective applied.

"What happened?" I blurted.

"Chaos."

"I *know* that."

"When I stepped out of the house, I found several orcs testing the wards from various sides of the property. I warned them that I was protecting the place and that they would suffer great pain if they attempted to advance. They threatened to rip off my penis and shove it down my throat. Orcs are crude."

"Yeah."

"They said that the prize would be theirs once they got rid of the new dwarf—you, I presume—and that they were tired of waiting. They also said I had no right to claim it. I asked them what *it* was but didn't get a response. One of the orcs was a shaman and attempted to use magic to scare me out of the way. It was ineffective. I used *my* magic to attempt to read his mind and got a few glimpses of urgency, of them wanting to hurry to beat the werewolves and whoever else had learned about the artifact, but two cars arrived and interrupted. Your authorities, I believe."

"Yes." I thought of the two cars parked out front and assumed they'd arrived before the others had been called. Had one of the orcs called and reported a crime to bring the police to my address?

"I camouflaged myself, believing your authorities had detected the orcs and arrived to deal with them."

"Probably not. The police usually hand over problems with magical beings to that Army unit in Seattle." I snorted, realizing I'd now met the person in charge of *that Army unit.* Colonel Willard. Then I groaned, certain she would be called in on this. She already thought I was a vigilante. What would happen when she found out a bunch of policemen had been killed on my property? Would she send Thorvald to hunt me down?

Would the police even need her help to find me? I couldn't camouflage myself, and if I tried to check into a hotel or even buy a meal using my debit card, the authorities would be able to track me down. Criminals must have had a much easier time in the old days when everyone had used cash and hadn't had chips in everything they carried.

"The shaman threw a smoke bomb," Sarrlevi said, "which revealed my camouflage, and I ended up fighting two orcs in the street as more noisy vehicles arrived."

"I heard that."

"I dispatched them, but some of the authorities ran at *me*, waving their firearms and insisting that I lower my weapons."

That must have been when I'd been scurrying through the bushes while being shot at. "I assume you didn't."

The hilts of his longswords were visible behind his shoulders.

"No, I sprang into the tree branches and leaped away." Sarrlevi looked past my shoulder, then turned his head left and right, his pointed ears cocked. "Your authorities are blocking the exits from the woods, and several groups are entering with dogs."

"Looking for us," I said grimly. "Or at least me."

I suspected Sarrlevi could disappear easily enough if someone tried to arrest him. "Will you help me get out of here? I can't attack those people. Not the authorities. Not human beings. That some already died on my property..." I shook my head. "I think those orcs might have been trying to get me thrown in jail as a suspect. And I'm afraid it could work because..." I didn't want to explain my father to him, how he'd been sentenced to life in a military prison with no hope of parole, but a long-ago overheard comment by one of my grade-school teachers popped into my mind. *The apple doesn't fall far from the tree.* "Just because."

Sarrlevi gazed thoughtfully at me, and I had the sense that he didn't want to get involved, that, as I'd been thinking earlier, he'd needlessly been attacked and injured several times because of me. He'd already gotten my blood sample. Was there anything else I could offer him?

The barks of dogs were coming from numerous directions, and flashlights probed the woods in the distance. I'd always thought of this park as huge, but, with police charging down the trails from all the entrances, it might only take them minutes to locate me.

"If you can get me out of this, I'll help you with your quest," I offered.

"My quest?"

"Whatever you're curious about when it comes to my mother. I assume that *my* blood doesn't interest you all that much and that you're looking to learn more than whether I'm the rightful owner of my hammer. Why would an elf assassin even *care* about a dwarven hammer?" I raised my eyebrows.

"You will help me," Sarrlevi agreed, then lifted a hand toward a gap in the trees beside the trail.

Magic hummed all around us as a large silver disc formed in the air, its glow pushing back the shadows and highlighting his angular face.

I almost blurted a protest, certain the glowing disc would act as a beacon. If I could see the flashlights of the police, there was no way the officers wouldn't see *that*.

But Sarrlevi gripped my arm, startling me to silence. "Step through with me."

"Through? We're going somewhere?"

"Mongrel woman, do you not know a portal when you see it?"

"Over there," came a cry from farther up the trail.

As I'd feared, someone had seen the light.

I took a step toward it—the portal—but I must have moved too slowly for Sarrlevi. As footfalls thundered toward us, he swept me over his shoulder. I barely kept from crying out, remembering that the police had shot first earlier and not asked questions at all. All I did was smash my hand to my chest to keep the iron box from tumbling out of my hoodie. I almost clunked Sarrlevi on the head with my hammer.

He took three running steps, not disturbed by my weight over his shoulder, and sprang into the middle of the silver disc.

14

My stomach dropped as reality blurred and strange magic flowed all around me. While we traveled through the portal, I lost all feeling, all sense of my body and Sarrlevi carrying me, instead existing in a dream-like state. Seconds or hours might have passed, and I wouldn't have known the difference.

With a flash of silver, the physical world returned, and Sarrlevi landed on a wood floor. I was still draped over his shoulder, legs dangling down his chest, my nose pressed into his back, and his arm keeping me in place. The iron chest fell from my hoodie and clanked to the floor. Cursing, I squirmed free of his grip, afraid to have it out of my grasp for even a second.

"You will not be in danger here," Sarrlevi stated, facing me.

The silver light from a disc—a portal—identical to the one he'd created in the park disappeared, but moonlight streamed in through a large window overlooking a lush green ravine. We'd appeared in a room—no, a *bed*room. The large bed hung from thick green vines that appeared to grow *into* the high beamed ceiling. The walls and floor were made from polished wood or maybe bamboo boards, and furniture carved from a spongy gray substance—some kind of giant mushroom?—rested around the room. The dressers, bookcases, and chairs were nothing like what you would find in a furniture store in Bellevue.

Magic radiated from numerous objects, the walls, and even the ceiling. A floating fuzzy ball drifted past, landed on a dresser, and rubbed itself over the top. Dusting? One of the chairs had a magical aura. Even the bed radiated power. Maybe Sarrlevi had the elven equivalent of a Magic Fingers mattress.

"Where are we?" I eyed the bed, though the window was what drew me, and stepped forward, a feeling of serenity coming over me as I gazed upon the ravine. Far below, trees grew along a river, the silver light from not one but two moons reflecting on the water. Lush greenery rose up the steep slopes, and if there were any other homes in the area, I couldn't see them. The whines and buzzes of insects I'd never heard before, along with the soft hooting of a nocturnal creature, drifted up from the trees.

"One of my homes."

One of? How many homes did elven assassins typically have?

"Uhm—" I turned to face him, "—you being offended because you thought I wanted to jump your bones and then bringing me to your bedroom sends kind of a mixed signal."

His eyes narrowed. "You will not sleep here. Come." He waved toward a rounded doorway.

"I wasn't planning to sleep at all," I said, though my eyes were gritty with fatigue—crawling through that smoke hadn't helped them—and I *did* need rest. It had to be one or two in the morning. Or it had been back home. Here? I had no idea what time it was or even where here *was*.

Nor did I know how to get back. For good or ill, I'd put my fate in Sarrlevi's hands, and I still had no idea what he wanted from me.

But I'd asked for his help, and he'd given it. I would be a polite guest until I figured out what to do back home, assuming he would let me return.

As I followed him past glassless windows that let in a gentle breeze and down a wide walkway overlooking the lower level of his home, a part of me wished I could stay there for a while. It looked like the kind of place one found in brochures for tropical vacation destinations. I couldn't, however, abandon my problems —or my life. At the least, my sister would be aggrieved if she couldn't continue to attempt to set me up with nice *normal* men with whom I could live a white-picket *normal* life.

At the far end of the walkway from his bedroom, Sarrlevi opened a door to a guest room. The walls were covered in spongy gray instead of made from wood, but the same fuzzy balls floated through the air, landing on furniture and swishing away dust. I touched one of the vines supporting a hanging bed, the mattress well above my hip level, and was relieved it wasn't any higher, or I would have needed a ladder.

"I require rest." Sarrlevi remained in the doorway as I looked around, taking in gilded mirrors, a furry brown rug as soft as rabbit or mink, and a marble fountain burbling softly from a corner of the room. "Creating portals is taxing, as is healing one's wounds. Figure out what you want to do, and I'll return you to your world in the morning."

"Thank you."

"If, for some reason, you wish to leave the house during the night, alert me first. There are numerous security measures in place to ensure enemies can't get in. The wards and defenses here are far greater than what I had time to lay around your property." Irritation entered his tone as he added, "No orcs will hurl dead humans through them."

"Are there things outside that would attack me if I wandered?" The ravine appeared peaceful and serene, and, even if I didn't have elven blood, I could feel the draw of such an enchanted place. "Beyond your defenses?"

"Many. This is one of the wild worlds. There is little in the way of civilization, besides what amenities you bring yourself. The dragons and some of the lesser species come here to hunt."

"If you don't personally know how to make a portal, is there a way to leave?"

"No. But that's true of all worlds."

So I was trapped. Or at least at Sarrlevi's mercy. Well, it was better than being in jail. I wouldn't get a hanging elf bed in jail. Still, it bothered me that I didn't yet know the reason for Sarrlevi's interest in me.

I looked toward him, catching him leaning against the door frame for support, but only briefly before he straightened, his usual haughty mask replacing the fatigue I'd glimpsed.

"Don't take this the wrong way," I said, "because I appreciate you getting me out of there, but I'm not sure if..."

His blond eyebrows rose.

"I'm not sure if I should trust you," I admitted, hoping he wouldn't be offended or call me an ungrateful mongrel.

Sarrlevi snorted. "Of course you shouldn't. I'm an assassin. Assassins aren't altruistic."

He stepped back and closed the door, leaving me in the fanciest guest room I'd ever stayed in. Hell, it was the fanciest *room* I'd stayed in. My little house was cute and cozy since I'd remodeled it, but it wasn't posh. And the shrubberies had a tendency to catch fire, due to Tinja's tinkering projects.

A twinge of homesickness came over me, and I wished I were in my own bedroom, with my life back to normal. My version of normal, not my sister's. One where nobody attacked me while I was renovating houses and where dead police officers weren't thrown on my stoop.

I imagined Willard and Thorvald prowling through the yard,

blaming me for the deaths, finding my trail, and figuring out I'd gone through a portal, then hunting me down. I might be able to hold my own against Willard—she'd looked tough, but she wasn't magical—but Thorvald? She had a sword at least the equal of my hammer, and she came with that tiger. Not to mention she was apparently married to a dragon.

"Not fair," I muttered, taking off my shoes and socks and letting my feet sink into the plush rug. "I can't even get an elf to look at me without sneering."

Not that I wanted Sarrlevi's interest. Even if he hadn't been arrogant and prone to calling me *mongrel woman*, he was too dangerous to lust after. I didn't know if he'd had time to check my blood in his magical microscope yet, but I doubted it. What would happen when he did and he learned that it wasn't what he'd hoped for? He might toss me back into the middle of the werewolves.

"He can try." I pulled out the iron chest to look again at the photos.

Figure out what you want to do, Sarrlevi had said. A good idea. I needed to have a plan of action when he dropped me back on Earth.

In addition to my mother and the dwarf that might have been the renter, there were six others in the photos. I supposed most had long since returned to their world, but was it possible some of them remained on Earth? Hiding out in the Seattle area somewhere?

Probably not or the death of the renter would have brought them forth, but then again, maybe not. If as much time had passed as I suspected since the Polaroids had been taken, the dwarves might have lost touch. News of the renter's death had been quashed too, so it was possible the others hadn't heard about their lost comrade yet.

I brushed my fingers over a photo of my mother smiling as the armored dwarf made a gesture over her head. Maybe it was the dwarven equivalent of rabbit ears. The house mystery aside, I wished I could find one of these dwarves to talk to, if only so they could tell me more about my mother. I remembered so little. And I couldn't ever remember her smiling and laughing, not with real humor. She'd occasionally smiled at me and my father, but it had always been reserved. Haunted.

Unfortunately, there wasn't any writing on the backs of the Polaroids. No names or dates. Nothing helpful.

"I wonder if any of you guys are on Google," I mused, aware of apps that could do image searches based on photos. The dwarves probably weren't internet stars, but the urge to check washed over me. I even reached for my phone before I caught myself. "I kinda doubt there are satellites and servers on a wild world."

That would be my plan though. As soon as I got back, I would run a search and hope to get lucky and find evidence of one of the dwarves living on Earth.

"Let's hope the orcs and werewolves aren't demolishing the house in the meantime."

Hopefully, the presence of the police and Sarrlevi's wards would keep them from gaining access that night.

I yawned and rubbed the back of my neck, fatigue setting in. Wishing for my pajamas and a toothbrush and toothpaste, I wandered to the corner of the room with the fountain.

The area looked vaguely like it might be a bathroom. A dressing screen offered privacy for a mushroom-shaped seat with a hollowed-out bowl. A toilet? I stared at it for a long minute, not certain in the least. There was no water inside, no sign of a tank. What if it was a piece of art? And I peed in it?

For all I knew, elves went outside under the trees. Or maybe in the fountain. It was large enough for someone to sit in, though it was more likely to be a tub than a toilet. Sarrlevi would think I was an idiot—*more* of an idiot—if I couldn't figure out where to do my business.

Maybe balancing on the window ledge and going into the ravine would be safer. But what a thing to have to explain if I fell out and had to be rescued as I dangled bare-assed from a root below the house.

I decided to risk the mushroom bowl. It undulated under me as I finished, the gel-like edges flexing against my cheeks, and I sprang free, afraid I'd broken it. Or irritated it. Despite my fear, my waste disappeared, and it stopped undulating.

I washed my face and swished out my mouth in the fountain, since it was the closest thing to a sink and the water appeared to drain. I checked a dresser, wondering if Sarrlevi had any pajamas or nightgowns for his houseguests. What I thought was a drawer startled me by not opening as I would expect, instead flipping a door up and extending garments on a shelf.

Very revealing garments. I blinked as I held up a long sheer gown. Either Sarrlevi *really* relaxed when he wasn't wearing his armor and work clothes, or he invited female guests over and they stayed in the room. Hints of floral perfume wafted from garments in another cubby. Not being big on perfume, I was tempted to shove everything back in, but my own clothes were filthy after my workday and dual trips through trees and bushes.

Hoping Sarrlevi wouldn't be offended, I grabbed the shortest of the revealing gowns—they all looked like they'd been made for tall lanky elves rather than short stout dwarves. After shrugging out of my clothes, I tossed them on a seat. There were towels by the fountain, so I did my best to wash myself before putting on the clean garment.

As I dried an armpit, a green ceramic cylinder levitated in the air and sprayed moisture at me. I almost shrieked in surprise. A basket floated in from behind and blew dried flower petals at me.

"What the hell?"

I lunged for my hammer, hefting it and backing away from the fountain, but the floating cylinder gave chase. It kept spritzing me liberally. Some of the spray got in my eyes and stung.

"Damn it." I swung, connected with the cylinder, and sent it flying across the room so hard that it lodged in one of the spongy walls. "You need to educate your guests on your house's amenities, Sarrlevi," I snarled, though I assumed he'd gone to bed and wouldn't hear me.

The smashed cylinder bleeped softly from the wall. I took a swing at the flower-petal-hurling basket next, but it flew up near the ceiling and out of my reach.

As I wiped the spray and petals off me, the door opened. That time, I did shriek, spinning to face what might be a new threat or —worse—Sarrlevi standing there. I was naked and dripping water and whatever that cylinder had sprayed on me. A metal platter floated out of the room with my clothes dangling from tongs.

"No!" Cursing again, I raced after it.

Those were the only clothes I had, and my phone was in the pocket of the jeans. I sprang through the doorway, catching my clothes as the platter was about to fly over the railing toward the lower floor. But the tongs held them tight and wouldn't release them. Even my dwarven strength wasn't sufficient to pull my clothes free, but I did keep the platter from leaving with them. It whirred and ground in the air, emanating magic as it tried to continue on its way with my stolen garments.

"Let go," I growled, keeping ahold of them with one hand and lifting my hammer with the other. "Or I'll do to you what I did to the cylinder."

"Really, mongrel woman," came Sarrlevi's voice from a few paces away. "Is it necessary for you to destroy *all* of my housewares?"

"This thing is stealing my clothes," I blurted, scowling over my shoulder at him. Barefoot and bare-chested, he wore nothing but satiny pajama bottoms and lingering grass bandages on his chest.

"It's the laundry device. It will return them in the morning cleaned. It assumes that when people undress, they want their clothes laundered." His brows rose and, for the first time since I'd met him, amusement lurked in his eyes as he regarded me. Regarded my nudity.

Mortified, I released my clothing, only belatedly realizing that I had nothing but my hammer to cover my modesty with. Well, if those sheer dressing gowns were what he gave his guests, he was used to seeing female flesh. Maybe not *half-dwarf* female flesh, but my bits were presumably the same as elf bits, if differently proportioned.

"I sensed the destruction of a soap dispenser," he said, "and came to see if you needed instruction on the amenities of the house."

Soap dispenser? I touched some of the stuff the cylinder had sprayed on my damp body and decided it *did* have the slickness of glycerin or whatever *wild worlds* used in soap.

Sarrlevi's superior amused smile as he regarded me—a gentleman would have looked away, damn him—didn't make me want to admit I'd overreacted.

"I do not need instructions, no, thank you. I punished your *soap dispenser* because it was overly familiar." I pointed after the platter whisking my clothing away. "And my phone is in the pocket of those jeans. Electronics can't be *washed*."

"Ah." Sarrlevi lifted a hand. Even as the platter carrying my clothes disappeared through another door, my phone floated up to the walkway and landed firmly in his grip. Eyes glinting, he asked, "Are you *sure* you don't want any instruction?"

"No, I do not." I held out my hand.

Though he'd demonstrated he could levitate objects, Sarrlevi walked the phone over himself. As he placed it in my hand, he reached for my shoulder, fingers brushing my bare skin.

I was tempted to draw back, alarmed by his proximity. And his *familiarity*. But I stood rooted, a little zing of pleasure running down my arm at his touch. With his lips quirked, he plucked dried petals off my shoulder and out of my hair. His bare chest was close enough that I could have leaned forward and licked it.

Which I had no interest in doing. Scowling and shaking my head, I backed up, but I ended up bumping into the door frame and almost dropped my phone. Why was I such a discombobulated mess?

His smirk only made everything worse, and I imagined him comparing me to the beautiful elven women who usually visited him in his home. I was sure *they* knew how to use the soap dispenser and go to the bathroom.

"Please refrain from destroying any more of my housewares before morning, my mongrel guest." His eyes were still glinting.

Damn it. I'd liked it better when he'd been sneering.

"My name is *Matti*. I know you know it. We introduced ourselves while you were accusing me of being a thief." Stung far more than I should have been, I scrambled back into the room and slammed the door shut.

My heart pounded, as if I'd been in a battle, and I didn't know why. The soap dispenser and laundry-stealing device hadn't been *that* onerous of opponents.

Sarrlevi was another matter. Once he opened a portal so I could return home, I wouldn't ask him for further help. As he'd pointed out himself, assassins weren't altruistic. Trusting him would be foolish.

15

I WOKE FROM AN UNEXPECTEDLY LURID SEX DREAM WITH MY borrowed nightgown rucked up to my waist and my hand on my chest. Jerking it away, with embarrassment flushing my cheeks, I looked toward the door, hoping I hadn't woken because someone —because *he*—had walked in.

Thankfully, the door was shut. Sunlight streaming through the window of the guest room illuminated a green bird with a spiky crown sitting on the sill. It was, as far as I could tell, the only witness to what I hoped hadn't been a *vocal* lurid dream. I'd fallen asleep irritated as hell with my host, but it had clearly been a mistake to let myself drift off with him on my mind.

"A *normal* girl would have nightmares about all the horrible beings trying to kill her, not dreams about an arrogant assassin." More heat warmed my cheeks as I remembered my antics the night before. As evidence of my lost temper, the soap-dispensing cylinder remained lodged in the wall.

I climbed out of bed, the ceiling-hung frame swaying with the movement, and saw myself in the gilded mirror, the sheer night-gown doing nothing to hide my body. A blast of concern replaced my embarrassment. If that laundry device hadn't returned my clothes, I would have to wander around Sarrlevi's house like this. I might as well have been naked.

"Not that he didn't already see me like that," I growled, yanking off the nightgown.

When I looked around for the equivalent of a hamper, I spotted my clothes, clean, folded, and stacked on a dresser. I started to sag in relief until I wondered when they'd arrived and if the laundry-stealing device had returned them... or Sarrlevi had. Those were the only two options. If he had servants, I hadn't seen evidence of them yet. The thought of him wandering in while I'd been rubbing myself in my sleep mortified me all over again.

Until I snarled in disgust and decided it didn't matter. It wasn't that having sexual interest in a guy or lurid dreams was that big of a deal—given how long it had been since I'd had a partner, it was a wonder I didn't have them every night. It was just that I would prefer *he* not know about them. He was already so arrogant, and that stupid comment he'd made in the pantry burned. As if I'd been about to fling myself at him. Or seduce him with carrot cake and kombucha.

Thoughts of food thankfully prompted my mind to turn to other concerns. Such as breakfast.

As I dressed, with the bird serenading me from the sill, I felt guilty for having had a restful night in a safe place when the police were hunting for me and probably questioning my friends and family. What would my sister say when she heard about the chaos?

I had a plan of action—look up the dwarves in the Polaroids using an image-search app—but didn't know what I would do if they didn't lead to any new clues. Before leaving, I would show the photos and signet ring to Sarrlevi on the off chance that he recognized anything. The engraving on the ring might be a heraldic symbol for a dwarven family. That would be a good clue.

Fully clothed again, with my hammer slung over my shoulder, I ventured out of the room and tried not to think about whether Sarrlevi had seen and judged my pink cotton underwear dotted with blue stars. Had I known someone would see my clothes—or me naked—I would have opted for something sexier, or at least more adult.

None of the seats in the open living area below the walkway were occupied, but a fire burned in a hearth, despite the lack of a chill. My senses told me it was real, rather than magical, so someone had laid it that morning.

My gaze lingered on tall double doors that led outside, windows to either side showing a path winding away through the trees. Before I could wonder if Sarrlevi had left, I sensed him in a room at the end of the living area opposite the fireplace, the door open and a desk visible through it.

His office? Something about imagining an assassin sitting down to pay the bills and work on his taxes seemed ludicrous.

Did the Cosmic Realms *have* taxes? Probably. From what I'd heard, living under the dragons that ruled over all the worlds, even those with kings or queens of their own, was onerous. They probably had *high* taxes.

Inside, Sarrlevi sat at his desk with his legs propped on it and a book in his lap. A magical blue box hummed to one side. A few vials, containers of reagents, and a microscope suggested he'd been working on a science project, not his taxes.

No, I realized, halting in the doorway. He had to be running my blood sample.

"You mentioned you like cheese." Sarrlevi extended a hand toward a large silver platter with a wheel and two blocks of cheese, though they weren't like anything I'd seen before. One was pink, one orange with yellow stripes, and one a deep ocean blue. *Solid* blue, not simply yellow or white with veins of penicillium running through it.

"I did, yes." I was surprised he'd registered that. It had been in the long list of food items I'd rattled off—*burbled* off—when he'd been in the pantry and, I thought, asleep or meditating. "Are those... from cows?"

"Most worlds where intelligent life developed—or was brought in long ago and allowed to evolve—have large herbivores of some kind, but there's nothing exactly like your cows. That cheese is from an *orax,* that from a *tigro*, and that one should call to your blood, or your stomach, since it's from a dwarven *dokdok.* The other races do not domesticate their herbivores, so acquiring the milk to turn into cheese is a dicey proposition. Great warriors usually take on the task, and the scant milk they manage to get is highly prized."

"Is that your way of saying your food is super expensive?" I was suddenly glad I'd brought him stuff from the fancy organic grocery store instead of the dollar market, though I didn't know if he'd tried any of it before the chaos had started.

"I only buy the best."

"And you're going to share it with me?" I'd assumed from his gesture and comment about dwarven cheese that he intended for me to try it, but maybe he had some swill he saved for his mongrel visitors.

"Yes. There are crackers in that box as well and tea in the pitcher on the table." Sarrlevi waved to a tray resting on a small table next to a gaming area with a board for something akin to chess set up and waiting for players. "Go ahead."

I hesitated, my gaze drifting back to the box as I wondered if he'd found something in my blood that indicated he should treat me well. Though I couldn't imagine what that would be.

"Is it not tradition on your world to offer food and beverages to houseguests?" Sarrlevi asked, misinterpreting my hesitation. "Since you brought me provisions when I was injured, I trust you would also offer me refreshments if I showed up on your doorstep."

"Uhm, I would, but you're not going to, right?" I hadn't forgotten that he'd been spying on me as I worked in the project house.

"I have no intention of doing so." He waved again at the cheese, then went back to reading his book.

"Good." I sliced off a piece of each and couldn't keep from smiling happily as I bit into a sample from the blue block, both because I was hungry and had new cheeses to try and because he didn't intend to stalk me in my home. An assassin stalker was nothing to covet.

The smooth tartness of the cheese reminded me of Granny Smith apples and another flavor I couldn't pin to anything, but it was so good that I barely kept from shoving the slice in my mouth whole—and the rest of the block. The other two were different but equally good, so much so that I was tempted to ask if there was anything I could trade in exchange for some to take home. Did elves have a currency? I assumed dollars wouldn't work, not that I had much cash on me.

"These cheeses are amazing," I said. "If you ever want to seduce a dwarf, this would be a sure way to win her heart."

His gaze lifted from the book, eyes glinting as he met mine. "Were that my desire, I doubt the *cheese* would be necessary."

The piece I'd been swallowing stuck in my throat, and my delight vanished as the certainty that he *had* delivered the laundry and *had* witnessed my carnal dreams smacked me like a wet towel. Either that or he was so supremely confident in his sex appeal that he thought he could have any girl with a snap of his fingers. That smug smirk, the same as he'd worn on the walkway the night before, suggested *both.*

I was debating if it would be rude to smash my host in the nose with a fist when Sarrlevi's smirk turned to a frown and he looked out the window. He said something in Elven—it sounded like a curse—and closed his book and rose.

"Stay here. When you're done eating, I'll take you back to your world."

"Wait," I blurted, remembering what I'd intended to ask him. "I have some photos of dwarves and a ring that I found under those stones. Will you look at them and let me know if you recognize any of the dwarves or the ring?"

"Yes. When I'm done with her."

Her?

As Sarrlevi strode out of the office, I sensed someone walking up the pathway toward the house. An elf? Yes, another full-blooded elf with an extremely powerful aura. An equal to Sarrlevi?

It was a woman, I thought, though that was hard to tell from one's aura. Noshing cheese, I looked out the window.

One of the most striking women, if not *the* most striking woman, I'd ever seen glided up the path. Val Thorvald, whom I'd envied for her blonde beauty, would have been plain next to this woman—this elf.

Pointed ears protruded from the silver-blue locks partially swept around her head and partially left to dangle past her shoulders to frame the curves of her chest. Her silky silver wrap dress, with woven green leaves artfully decorating it, made me sigh with longing. I would love to be able to wear something like that, but it would look stupid on me. On her, it was elegant and enhancing, perfect with the green sandals she wore, straps rising like vines to wrap around her slender calves.

She carried a scroll but nothing else, so she hadn't gone on a journey to get here, not in those sandals. As a full-blooded elf, maybe she had the power to create a portal of her own and had arrived at the base of the pathway.

Sarrlevi met her at the home's entrance. Since he hadn't shut the office door, I was tempted to peek out and spy, but as soon as they greeted each other, I realized the conversation would be in Elven. Obviously. And I couldn't understand a word of it. I didn't even know more than a few words of Dwarven and those mostly because of lullabies my mother had sung to me.

The female visitor greeted Sarrlevi with a voice that was more of a sultry purr than I expected from an elegant elf. In contrast, his tone was clipped and formal. Not friends, it said. But then, who was friends with an assassin?

Not his own people if that hint he'd let out about being ostracized was true. Though it was possible I'd made some assumptions about that. The female sounded like she wanted to jump in bed with Sarrlevi, not ostracize him, and I thought of all the sheer gowns in the guest room. This was probably the kind of houseguest Sarrlevi *usually* had.

I chomped on another piece of cheese and examined the magical box humming softly on the table. If my blood sample was inside, I couldn't tell, but the humming implied that it hadn't yet finished its analysis.

A sultry chuckle came from the entryway. My curiosity wouldn't be reined in, and I crept to the door and peeked out. Sarrlevi's tone hadn't changed, so it was hard to believe he'd said something witty. Tone regardless, I hadn't observed much in the way of wit from him, unless one counted his smirk at seeing me naked after attempting to destroy his laundry device.

The female elf stood close to Sarrlevi, her chest almost touching his, and she held the scroll out behind her, smiling coyly and keeping it out of his reach. Unless she was an uber sorceress who could magically prevent him from drawing his weapons, I doubted that would keep him from getting it if he wanted it.

She rested a hand on his chest, fingers curling and her nails digging into his tunic, then tilted her chin toward the walkway—toward Sarrlevi's bedchamber. He said what had to be a no, his eyes focused on the scroll instead of her. Her eyes slitted in irritation, and she said something terse. *Look at me.*

Their body language made it so I could translate some of the words. Sarrlevi's eyes also closed to slits as he considered her. There wasn't the least come-hitherness in that look, but she must have been another elf who assumed everyone would jump into her bed because of her beauty. She leaned in, her lips parting for a kiss, her tongue flicking across her lips.

I curled my own lip and leaned back, not wanting to watch the elves getting frisky. But Sarrlevi stepped back and raised a hand, palm toward her chest. *No.*

A lot more words followed that *no*, but body language wasn't sufficient for me to translate something that complex. Whatever he said, it sparked fury in her eyes. No, more than that. I sensed her aura growing stronger; she was drawing on her magical power. To attack him? To try to force him to have sex with her?

His words from the other night about women manipulating him popped into my mind.

Sarrlevi's aura also grew stronger and more noticeable. Though they never moved, the air crackled with magic as their eyes locked. Had I been fully human, I never would have known they were doing more than staring at each other, but I was sensitive enough to magic to feel it swirling about their bodies and lashing at one another, attempting to strike through each other's defenses.

The female smiled, though her effort kept her eyes tight with tension. Her tongue came out again, slowly running along her bottom lip this time, as if she thought this all foreplay. Maybe something like it had happened before and led to sex? Sarrlevi looked irritated, his jaw clenched, the tendons standing out on the sides of his neck.

When I'd thought they would kiss, I'd intended to back away and give them their privacy, but I couldn't tear my gaze from this.

She was the one to break eye contact first, gasping and stepping back, pressing her fingers to her chest. Sarrlevi's hand darted out. To hit her? No, he snatched the scroll from her grip. She tried to jerk it away, even though she must have come here with the intent of delivering the message. Maybe she'd thought she would give it to him as a reward for a good performance in bed.

Sarrlevi was too fast for her and succeeded in taking it. As soon as he had it, he turned his back on her, on both of us, and opened it as he prowled across the living room toward the fireplace.

As he read, his shoulders were even more tense than they'd been when he'd faced her.

She looked over at me, and I twitched. It wasn't as if I'd thought they would be unaware of me—magical beings could sense other magical beings, after all—but I hadn't intended to watch them for so long or be caught spying.

Her lip curled as she looked me up and down, and I resisted the urge to brush my shirt and make sure I didn't have bits of cheese stuck to it. She asked Sarrlevi a question. It could have been anything, but, based on her dismissive look, my mind filled in: *Did you get a new servant? She's way too homely to fit into your posh house, isn't she?*

I lifted my chin and glared at her. Judging by her squint, that defiance not only surprised her but irked her.

Know your place, mongrel servant.

Somehow, I understood her even though the words she spoke into my mind weren't in English. I wished I hadn't.

In the presence of a princess, she continued, *you should drop to your knees and ask how you can serve, not stare into her eyes like an equal.*

I'm not a servant, I replied, leaning to the side and grabbing my hammer in case she attacked me, though I didn't pull it into her view. I might not be the sharpest tool in the shed, but I was smart enough not to challenge someone powerful to a fight. *I'm an entrepreneur and a warrior.*

You're a mongrel peasant. She squinted at the wall—or maybe *through* the wall, because she was looking right at my hammer. *With a weapon stolen from the dwarven homeland. They will hunt you down for that, and you will get the fate you deserve.* She smirked coldly at me.

Before I could reply, paper crackled, and we both looked at Sarrlevi. He wadded the scroll into a ball and threw it in the fire. It was a brief outburst of violence, but it made me realize I hadn't yet seen him lose his temper.

"Sarrlevi?" the female asked.

He spun and thrust his hand toward the door, the earlier irritation shifting to rage. *Go!*

Not wanting any of that fury turned on me, I backed into the office and out of their sight.

Three beeps came from the blue box. I stared at it. It had completed its analysis of my blood.

16

I WAS LEANING OVER THE DESK, TRYING TO FIGURE OUT HOW TO OPEN the blue box or determine the results, when I sensed the elf female leaving. I was relieved their battle of wills hadn't led to them having sex, in part because I hadn't wanted to be trapped in the office if they got busy in the living room, and in part because she'd been a bitch. Even though Sarrlevi was an arrogant prick, he could do better than that.

Sensing him walking toward the office, I leaned back and clasped my hands behind my back, nobly resisting the urge to grab the box and try to shake information out of it. When he stepped into the doorway, he still looked pissed.

"That bitch isn't really a princess, is she?" I asked.

He blinked. Maybe he hadn't realized we'd communicated. "She told you that?"

"She *thought* it into my head—" I pointed at my temple, "—and I somehow understood her."

"She was a princess. Her family, including the former king and queen, plotted against the dragons and attempted to remove them from power. They successfully assassinated more than one. The dragons weren't pleased, slew the king and queen, and appointed a new ruling family to lead the elves. Slehvyra, her sisters, and a number of their cousins begged forgiveness and, because they weren't found to have personally committed any crimes against the dragons, were permitted to live, but some are still secretly plotting against their kind."

"Are they all as snotty as she is?"

Some of the irritation faded from his face, and his tone grew lighter as he asked, "Do you refer to all elves or all of her kin?"

"I guess my *they* was unspecific, but both. I'd be delighted to meet a non-snotty elf." I thought about amending that statement so that it didn't include him but didn't.

"The current princess is an academic studying goblin engineering, which is about as unlikely a field for our people as you'd think. Judging by your taste in colleagues, you'd like her." His gaze shifted toward the box, and he walked toward it.

Nerves fluttered in my belly. Would Sarrlevi tell me the results of whatever he learned?

He waved his hand over the top, and an image appeared in the air. I guessed shaking the box wouldn't have worked.

A picture of a male dwarf formed, then rose a foot as another picture formed underneath it. A female dwarf.

"That's my mother," I blurted.

Her face was solemn, though she was younger than in the Polaroids. It was as if she had, as a teenager, posed for a portrait and her painter had sternly told her not to enjoy the process.

Sarrlevi looked at me but didn't comment.

The image of my mother slid to the side, and another headshot appeared, another young dwarf female with frizzy red hair, though hers was pulled back in a severe bun, and her snub nose had a haughty tilt. A line formed between the two females and another pointed up toward the male, a dwarf with a thick, curly red beard shot with gray and matching hair, though it was pressed under a metal helmet with golden horns.

"Is that like... my family tree?" I asked.

"It seems you are who you said you are."

"I know *that*. But, uhm, do you know their names?" I waved to the male and other female—my mom's sister?

"I do. You said your mother only gave Roxy as her name?"

"Yeah. My father probably knew her real name, but like I said, I was only four when she died. I really only knew her as Mom."

"Her name was Rodarska."

Roxy sounded better to me. No wonder she'd gone by it.

"Princess Rodarska," Sarrlevi said, watching me.

"Oh, yeah? Like a princess of a king in power or like the elf bitch?" I waved, hoping she'd opened a portal and taken herself back to her own world.

"Elf bitch," he mouthed, and I thought he would be offended, since I was a mongrel and she'd made it clear my place was groveling at her feet instead of meeting her gaze. But his eyes glinted, and he glanced at the hammer now resting on the desk. "I should have had you fight her."

"She seemed powerful. That might have been a bad idea."

"Clobbering a magical soap dispenser is a bad idea too, but that didn't stop you." His eyes were *seriously* glinting now.

"I can hold my own against a soap dispenser. A deposed elf princess with a chip on her shoulder and a lot of power she was trying to flatten you with would be another story."

"The contents are under pressure," Sarrlevi said, and it took me a moment to realize he meant in the soap dispenser. "You might have done all right against her. She primarily uses mental attacks, and you have some of the dwarven ability to resist that. By the time she figured out she would have to do something else, you might have reached her and cracked her on the head with your hammer. She's a powerful magic user but not a warrior. Few elven females study more than archery when it comes to weapons."

"Unless I'm reading you wrong, you look like you would have liked to see me pound her."

"Perhaps."

"Can't *you* crack her on the head? I assume you can kick her ass."

"Of course," he said without hesitation, "but it's more complicated than that. Few on Veleshna Var, the elven home world, speak with me. She's been one of the handful who will deliver messages for me, though I've grown weary of paying her price."

"Sex?"

"It pleases her to irritate her husband by sleeping with me."

"Er, are elves not monogamous when they're married?"

"Usually, they are. Our religious tenets and laws support the concept."

"But rules are made to be broken when you're an elf princess?"

"It was a political marriage, arranged when she was still recognized as a princess and possible future leader of our people. He's cold and rude to her because she's not in line to inherit that rule anymore, but he hasn't left her, because her power and lineage give him more status than his family has, regardless of whether she's an heir or not."

"So they're asses to each other."

"Essentially." Sarrlevi looked back to the floating faces above the box. "You say your mother is dead? You saw her die?"

"Yeah." I closed my eyes, not wanting to think back to that horrific night, but it was impossible not to. The memory had been scorched into my mind and had haunted my dreams all through childhood. "Soldiers attacked our apartment, shooting and throwing incendiary stuff through the windows. My father had a rifle and shot back. My mother had her hammer. They were trying to capture her, I think, but she wouldn't surrender. They wanted her, not me or my sister or my father, and she kept yelling at him to take us and go. The drapes were burning, and bits of the scorched ceiling kept falling down. Penina and I were under the table crying, and I was hugging my teddy bear, as if it could save me or protect me."

I blushed, remembering who I was talking to, and opened my eyes, afraid to see that taunting smirk of his, but he was listening intently and looking not at me but at my mother's portrait.

"They broke down the door and charged in wearing body armor over their camo uniforms, but Mom plowed into them with the hammer. She yelled again at my dad to get us out of there." My voice lowered to a hoarse whisper, more emotion swelling up than I'd thought I still had over the events. "She was buying time for us. To save our lives. But when they shot her twice in the chest, Dad roared in fury and shot back. He hit one in the head. I'm pretty sure the guy died. Even wounded, Mom bellowed and kept fighting, again telling Dad to get us out of there, that there were more coming and they couldn't win. I think he was horrified by what he'd done and what was happening, but he grabbed us and ran out to the balcony. He kept bumping things, the doorjamb, the counter. It was smoky, and he had tears in his eyes and could barely see where he was going. I heard Mom cry out, and he almost ran back toward her, but he looked at us, and... I guess he made a choice. Maybe he knew he couldn't save her, but he could save us. Somehow, with us in his arms, he climbed down from the balcony—it was on the third floor. Then the entire building blew up, and the shockwave threw us to the ground. I remember hitting the pavement in the parking lot and getting scraped up and cut on glass."

As if it would prove my whole story true, I lifted the back of my hand, where an old scar from the incident lingered, faint and pale after thirty years but still visible.

"Penina was crying like a banshee. Dad grabbed us and

hoisted us up only to have a bunch of soldiers come charging out from behind parked cars with rifles pointed at us. They ripped us out of his arms and handcuffed him. That was the last time we saw him. He's been in a maximum-security military prison for my whole life. When I got old enough to learn how to make inquiries about being able to see him, all I was told was that he wasn't allowed to have visitors. I don't even know if he's still alive."

"You didn't actually see your mother die." Sarrlevi looked intently at me.

Irritated that he didn't care about my father at all—or *me*, most likely—I snapped, "Even if two bullets in the chest somehow *weren't* a death sentence, having the building blow up with her in it was, I'm sure."

"Hm," was all he said, ignoring my irritation as if he wasn't even aware of it.

I took a deep breath and tried to smooth my hackles. I was nothing to him, and I knew it. What had I expected from an assassin? Empathy? His only interest in me was my mother, though I still didn't know why.

It felt incomplete not to finish the story, to speak of the long days after that night that I'd spent alone in a room with no windows, separated from my sister. They'd taken away my teddy bear, not even leaving me that comfort. Occasionally, an Army nurse had come in to feed me, bathe me, and check my bandages. Once, a scary Army doctor in uniform had come in to take blood samples from me and run tests, machinery in the room beeping ominously. Everything about that place had been ominous to my four-year-old self.

"Who raised you?" Sarrlevi asked. "The military? Is that where you learned to fight?"

"God, no." I shuddered at the thought. There was a reason I didn't want anything to do with Colonel Willard. "They kept me for a while and ran some tests. Later, when my sister started talking again, she said they did the same to her. I have no idea if they figured out from my blood that I was my mother's daughter and might have some dwarven attributes, or if they cared about that even if they did find out, but two taciturn soldiers eventually showed up and drove us up to Marysville and gave us to my grandparents to raise. My father's parents," I clarified, though that probably wasn't necessary. He knew the dwarven *king* hadn't raised me. "After that, my sister was a quiet and proper girl, never breaking the rules and trying hard not to stand out or get in trouble. I was... more difficult. I had a temper, and I got into a lot of fights at school. Most of them weren't my fault, because I was defending myself from bullies, but since I was stronger than the average human, that was a problem. In third grade, I accidentally broke another kid's arm and got expelled. For a couple of years, my grandparents put me in a special school for, uh, troubled children. That wasn't great, but they also put me in martial arts, figuring that would teach me some discipline as well as how to defend myself without hurting other people. It was helpful, and I stuck with it all through school and into my adult life. I still go when there's time." I thought about mentioning my various degrees of black belt, but someone who'd been a trained killer for however many decades would scoff at the notion of belt tests.

"So," Sarrlevi said, "if you'd visited my home when you were a child, you would have destroyed *all* of my bathing appurtenances?"

"Oh, yeah. And that saucy floating hairbrush that tried to assist me with combing my locks."

"How did you get the hammer?" he asked.

"What?"

"If it was last seen with your mother..." Sarrlevi turned his palm upward.

"Oh." That was a good question and one I'd never considered. All through my childhood, it had been at my grandparents' house.

"Somehow, it made it back to my dad's family. After I'd had several years of martial-arts training, my grandparents agreed to let me have it."

His eyebrows rose. "*Somehow* a priceless magical artifact made it to them."

"The military must not have realized it was more than a metal hammer. Or... someone else intervened." I bit my lip, faced with another unanswered question to ponder.

"You mentioned a ring and photos."

"Yes." I grabbed the chest, opened it, and spread the Polaroids before it occurred to me that he hadn't yet said why my mother was of interest to him.

His gaze went right to the two photos of my mother, and he rested a finger on one. "These are more recent than the events of your childhood?" His eyes were so intense that it was alarming.

"No. They had to have been taken before. Probably before she met my dad and I was born."

"You're certain?"

"Yes, dude. She's dead."

He mouthed, "Dude?"

Not wanting to explain American vernacular, especially when I didn't know if anyone else used that word anymore, I pointed to the other photos. "Do you recognize any of these dwarves? I think this was the renter of the house who was murdered. I know it's a long shot, but if any of the other dwarves are still on Earth, and I could find one to question, I might be able to find out what's under the house and why everyone is after it *without* busting down the magical wall, something you wisely pointed out might not be a good idea to do without any knowledge of it."

I thought he would appreciate being called wise, and might nod in agreement with my assessment, but all he said was, "Yes," as he eyed the other photos. His finger moved to the dwarf in armor. "I recognize this one. He's an engineer in the king's court.

Or was forty years ago. I don't visit that world often, and I believe that's when I last saw him."

"Forty years ago? How old were you?" I looked at him. "How old *are* you?"

Had I underestimated how many years he'd been a killer? Had it been centuries, not decades?

"About three hundred." Sarrlevi rocked his hand in the air. "Elven years are a number of days shorter than your Earth years. It may be more like two-eighty to you."

"So, a young pup."

"Middle-aged."

"For an elf."

"And a dwarf. They live as long as elves. You should live longer than regular humans if you avoid irking soap dispensers."

"Thanks for the tip." I'd been distracted by talk of age. That wasn't important. The dwarves were. "You're sure the guy in armor was an engineer?"

"A respected one, as I recall. Lord... Hennehok. The lords in dwarfdom are somewhat like your nobles in countries that have them. But, among dwarves, most elevated positions in society are won by hard work and the ability to craft things that serve the needs of their people."

"*Thank you* for pointing that out. That's what *I* do. I'm a hard worker and restore houses for people who need them. It's *craftsmanship.*"

He hadn't, I admitted as he gazed blandly at me, said I wasn't a hard worker or a good craftswoman. He'd simply called me a mongrel and a plumber, which was a perfectly respectable profession, but *he'd* said it as if it were beneath him.

"If that's true, I'm certain a dwarf would appreciate you and you would fit into their society."

"What do elves appreciate?"

"Similar things, though they spend a lot more time studying

magic and perfecting its use, finding ways to build upon what their predecessors mastered. Dwarves use it as a means to an end, a way to build more of what they like."

I almost asked what *he* appreciated, or respected in a person, but I didn't care. Why I'd even gotten disgruntled, I didn't know. He made me disgruntled.

"Why do you visit the dwarven world? It's hard to imagine a people who dedicate their lives to crafting being the types to hire assassins." Then again, I had no problem imagining that elf female hiring an assassin, and he'd said elves appreciated similar things to dwarves.

"Most don't. Some do. Politics, and the enemies it inculcates, exist among all of the races."

"So you were there for business?"

He hesitated. "Yes."

I eyed the photos, wondering if the engineer not being seen in the dwarven court for a while implied he was still on Earth. But why would a Lord Something-or-other leave his world for decades? Had he developed a fondness for fast food, cigars, and other delicacies found only on Earth?

"You're sure he's that engineer?" I wondered how well Sarrlevi could tell one bearded dwarf from another. Even in the small sampling of the photos, a lot of them looked similar to my eye. "On my world, engineers usually wear glasses and pocket protectors, not armor."

"It's him. I have a good memory."

I almost called him cocky but thought about *why* he'd developed a good memory—the need to be able to pick out faces after seeing them only once, so he could find and kill his targets—and clamped down on the comment.

"Do you recognize anyone else?" I asked.

"I do not."

Sarrlevi rested a finger on one of the photos of my mother and leaned in close, his chest almost brushing my shoulder. "You're *sure* this was taken before the day you believe she died?"

He looked at me instead of the photo, the intensity back in his eyes, and I felt the whisper of an itch inside my skull. He was trying to read my mind.

I attempted to give him the mental equivalent of the middle finger and almost moved away from him, but I didn't want to give ground, to show any sign that he unnerved me. No, he flustered me. And that was even worse.

"Look, I don't know for *certain*, all right? This type of camera and film were popular for decades. I do know it's not recent, definitely not from the last twenty years. Probably not from the last thirty. But come on. Does that look like the face of someone who's been forcefully separated from her partner and her daughter?" I pointed at the smiling face of my mother.

A pang of regret caught me, sadness that I hadn't known her at that time in her life.

Sarrlevi considered the photo again, and the itch in my mind disappeared. "Perhaps not."

I turned to face him, again resisting the urge to step back. *He* hadn't stepped back, and that left me staring up into his face from six inches away. I studied his blue eyes, needing to know the answer to the question that I should have asked right away, before I'd opened up and told him my life's story.

"Why do you care about my mother? And why," I added, some intuition telling me the events were linked, "were you in the dwarven court forty years ago?"

He gazed back at me, giving me that bland look again, and I didn't think he would answer. Frustration welled up in me. He hadn't been answering me fully from the beginning. Why I expected him to now, I didn't know, but I was already certain I knew the answer to the next question.

"And when you showed up in my backyard, you weren't *really* hunting werewolves, were you? You came looking for me. Or clues to my mother's whereabouts. Look, Sarrlevi. You mentioned honor in battle and understanding that. I'm into honor too. I'm not lying to you. I genuinely believe she died that night thirty years ago."

He exhaled slowly through his nose. "I do *understand* honor and believe in it. If you challenged me to a duel, I would fight you fairly. If someone hired me to kill you, I would walk up openly and challenge you to an honorable battle instead of shooting you in the back. All my life, I've trained so that I'm capable of besting those I'm hired to kill without having to resort to sneak attacks."

"But you won't answer a direct question? That's part of honor, holding yourself to the highest standards of conduct."

I expected him to scoff and tell me I was young and naive and didn't know anything. To him, I *was* young. That elves lived centuries boggled my mind.

"That is correct," he admitted, though the way it came out made me think he didn't want to. "Forty years ago, I was in the dwarven court, where Princess Barothla hired me to assassinate her sister." He nodded toward the female face floating next to my mother's.

17

"You agreed to kill my mother?" The only thing that kept me from grabbing my hammer and challenging him to a duel right there was that I knew he hadn't been responsible for her death. "How—*why*? She was a good person. I thought—"

What had I thought? That he only assassinated despicable people? Some *Grosse Point Blank* version of a hit man?

I stepped back, no longer caring about who gave ground, and gripped the desk with both hands, struggling for control. "Are you still on the *job*? Forty years later? Is she the one who got away, and you're trying to right a glaring deficiency in your otherwise flawless record? Is that why you've been *helping* me? So that I'd lead you to her?"

Of *course* that was why. Why else would an assassin save me from the police, open a portal, and give me a guest bed in his house? He'd even warned me. He'd said it would be foolish to trust an assassin. Assassins weren't altruistic.

"I am hoping you'll lead me to her, but not because I'm still on the job." Sarrlevi spoke with irritating calmness.

I was on the verge of hysteria, and he was calm. Fan-fuckingtastic.

His tone turned dry when he said, "It *was* irritating that she eluded me. Your overpopulated wild world isn't at all where I would have expected a dwarven princess to flee to."

"I'm so sorry that she escaped certain death at your hands and it *irritated* you." I gave him the furious look that his comment deserved. At this point, I didn't care if he grabbed his swords and struck me down.

Not that he looked to be on the verge of attacking. *He* wasn't mad. I was.

"Some time in the past forty years, the king learned what his daughter Barothla had done," Sarrlevi said. "I'm not certain if he confronted her about it or he's trying to find Rodarska in secret. He did search a long time and send dwarves to many worlds to look for her before turning to me out of desperation. He wants me to find her and bring her home, whether she's alive or dead. He would prefer she be alive, but if she's not, he wants her remains brought home for a proper dwarfish burial in the family catacomb."

"That doesn't sound like a job for an assassin." I looked at the desk instead of him, the photo of my mother blurry in my unfocused vision.

"It's not typical for me, no."

"Then why take it? Especially if you were irked that you failed long ago?" Dread crept into my belly, the suspicion that he still wasn't telling me the whole story.

Sarrlevi hesitated, and that seemed to confirm my fear.

"Did the sister ever revoke her offer, or does she still consider you on the clock?" I made myself look at him and try to determine the truth—or lack of it—on his face. I wished I could read his mind and make *his* brain itch.

"She didn't revoke the assignment, no, but I'm not trying to kill your mother now."

It chilled the hell out of me that he'd ever been trying to do so.

"I don't believe you," I whispered.

"That is why I didn't want to tell you."

"Afraid I wouldn't let you tag along with me until you found her?"

"Essentially. I believe you're the key to locating her."

"Fuck you, Sarrlevi." I stepped back farther and jerked a choppy wave at the wall. "Form your portal and send me home." I made myself bite out, "*Please*," though I hated to ask him for anything. If there had been any other way for me to return to Earth, I would have taken it.

Long seconds passed as he gazed silently at me, thinking who knew what, and I worried that he wouldn't do as I asked. That I would be trapped there. Or, worse, that he would decide he'd gotten all from me that he could, and he had no further use for me. No reason to tolerate my lip and keep me alive. If he could take an assignment to hunt down and kill a good-hearted princess, there couldn't be any limit to what he would do—who he would kill.

"Very well," he finally said. "Where do you wish to return to your world? Back in the park?"

Erg, that park. That park near the house, a house that was probably cordoned off by police tape. There might still be police all over the area. I didn't know how long I'd slept or how much time had passed on Earth.

"Are there other places you know in the Seattle area?" I had no idea how portal travel worked.

He hesitated. "I've been to Thorvald's house."

"Dear Lord, don't take me there. She and her colonel are probably looking for me too now. I don't suppose you know where Bellevue Square is? My friend lives near there. I can't go back home, but I don't think anyone would check Zadie's apartment."

Sarrlevi shook his head. "If you show me a map in your mind, I can probably get you close."

"Let you into my head again?" I groaned. I didn't want anything more to do with this bastard, and it irked me that I had to rely on him one more time. "Fine."

Sarrlevi stepped closer and lifted his hand to my temple. "It's easier if I touch you."

Though I wanted to skitter away, I clenched my jaw and made myself stand still. "Fine," I repeated through gritted teeth.

His fingers touched my temple, gentle, almost apologetic. Yeah, right. He'd done nothing to indicate he cared, and I would be a fool to believe otherwise.

I envisioned a Google Earth version of Zadie's neighborhood, then attempted to mentally zoom in on her apartment building.

Sarrlevi nodded and lowered his hand.

As he gazed toward the wall and concentrated on forming a portal, I gathered the photos and the ring—I hadn't gotten a chance to see if he recognized that, but I wouldn't ask him anything else. Not now. After placing the items in the chest, tucking it under my arm, and grabbing my hammer, I impulsively snatched the blue brick of cheese.

I clutched it to my chest and glowered defiantly at Sarrlevi. He was rich from all the people he'd killed. He could get more.

As the portal shimmered in the air behind me, Sarrlevi regarded my mulish stance and purloined cheese, then picked up the wheel and the other brick and placed them in my arms. Then he extended his hand toward the portal in invitation.

When I stepped toward it, he remained by the desk. It took me a moment to realize he wouldn't go first, that he wasn't coming with me. I didn't *want* him to, but I'd expected him to, to keep using me to try to find my mother, but he merely nodded for me to go.

Though I walked through the portal alone, I was positive I hadn't seen the last of him.

18

To my surprise, I came out of Sarrlevi's portal on the rooftop of a building. The sun was setting, sinking over the Olympic Mountains, and traffic roared below, a staccato of honks piercing the evening air.

As the silver portal faded behind me, promising I couldn't return to Sarrlevi's house—not that I wanted to—I crept to the edge to get my bearings. There was a fire escape on the flat roof, but I doubted the door would be unlocked. I might have to climb down the outside. Or get destructive with the door.

Given that Sarrlevi had been going by a map I'd formed in my head, I wouldn't be surprised if he'd missed by a few blocks. As long as I was somewhere in Bellevue but miles from Bridle Trails, that would be fine.

I laughed with realization as I looked down at a familiar street, pedestrians walking into and out of a donut shop that Zadie favored—she always brought celebratory bear claws when we closed a deal. This was her apartment building, just not the way I usually came into it.

It was a five-story drop to the street, with a lot of witnesses below and no handy ladders to climb down. I checked the fire-escape door. As I'd suspected, it was locked.

Fortunately, I had a big hammer. With all the city traffic, including an emergency helicopter roaring past on its way to the hospital, who would hear a few thumps?

After carefully setting my cheese stash and the chest aside, I clobbered the door. I couldn't help but imagine Colonel Willard's face hovering over my shoulder, whispering *vigilante* in my ear. I hit the door harder. Since I hadn't been able to hit Sarrlevi, it would have to do.

I wasn't mad at him for depositing me on the rooftop, but I couldn't forgive him for being an assassin, the assassin that had forced my mother to flee her home world. Had she not done so, I never would have been born, but it didn't matter. He'd taken her sister's money and promised to kill her. My mother. Further, it was possible he'd been lying to me and *still* wanted to kill her. The bastard.

With anger surging through my limbs, the third thump of the hammer not only made the door crumple inward but ripped it from its hinges. It clattered and banged as it flew halfway down the cement stairs. Sadly, it wasn't as satisfying as if *Sarrlevi* had flown down the stairs. And once my temper cooled, I would feel guilty and end up sending an anonymous envelope of cash to the apartment to cover the door.

"This is why it's such a struggle to build wealth in this world," I whispered, relieved the door at the bottom was unlocked.

I straightened my clothes, wished I had a bag for all my goodies, and took the elevator to Zadie's floor. A security camera leering down from the corner made me want to put my hood up.

"Something I should have considered *before* destroying the door," I mumbled.

Sensing a couple of familiar magical beings distracted me from my concerns. Tinja? And Abbas? I hadn't been certain

Zadie would be home; I certainly hadn't expected them to be here.

I jogged to her apartment and knocked on the door with my hammer but only once before it opened.

"I told them I sensed you!" Tinja cried, throwing her arms around me, pliers and wrenches in her pockets banging against my legs.

A brick of cheese slipped out of my arms and almost conked her on the head.

"It's good to see you." I extricated myself from the hug in time to get a thump on the shoulder from Abbas, the living-room ceiling fan threatening to shave his head. "All of you."

Zadie waved from her computer desk, her laptop open. "Just FYI, my commission is going to be four percent now when I sell that house for you."

She rotated the laptop to share a video playing on the screen. A news feed showing police cars and caution tape surrounding a familiar house. The bodies had been taken away and there was no sign of orcs, unless the news reporter pointing and explaining the night's events had a tusked ancestor. But she was a beauty, so it was more likely that an elf had sauntered through her bloodline.

Unbidden, Sarrlevi's smug face came to mind. I grimaced and shoved the image aside. With luck, I wouldn't see him again.

"As long as the other agent accepts two percent." I made myself smile at Zadie.

"No, they'll want four percent too for convincing someone to *buy* this house."

"Is that legal?"

"*You're* not legal."

I wished that were a joke.

"The police are looking for you." Tinja gazed gravely up at me as my face appeared on the news video.

Not surprisingly, no shots of orcs or Sarrlevi appeared. Hadn't any curious neighbors recorded him sword fighting in the street? What a disappointing area that was.

"They came to our home last night and this morning," Tinja added. "I didn't want them to see me—the police don't like goblins even though we are very industrious and create useful things."

"That probably has to do with all the stolen parts that go into your useful things," Abbas said.

"We take what others have no use for."

"You took my tire iron out of my truck."

"You never use it."

"I'll need it if I get a flat."

Tinja returned her attention to me. "I did not tell them *anything*. We know you're not a murderer, Matti."

"Thank you for that. Did they question you? Hurt you?" I hated the thought of my friends being threatened or injured because of me.

"No. They never saw me. I activated my camouflage charm and hid on the roof."

"That must have made it easy not to tell them anything." Zadie watched as I picked up the fallen brick of cheese and set it and the others on the table. "We know you didn't murder anyone, despite the news lady's insinuations, but did you rob a store? Is that cheese? Why is it Smurf blue?"

"It was a gift. It's a long story. But it's good. You should try it."

"We can't eat at a time like this," Tinja proclaimed, but she picked up the cheese and sniffed it curiously.

Judging by the box of crackers and a wine glass by Zadie's laptop, and the remains of a six-pack of root beer that was more to Abbas's taste, they hadn't been fasting while I was away.

"What are you going to do?" Abbas asked. "Do you need money? Help? I went by the project house this morning, but there was still a patrol car there. My mother said they came by to ask me questions but they missed me. I might stay at a friend's tonight."

"Good idea." I rubbed my face, certain the police had questioned my grandparents and sister too. Penina could handle it, but my grandparents were eighty-five. They didn't need extra stress. "And I'm not sure yet, but I want to look up the people in these pictures and see if the internet has any matches." I spread them out and pulled out my phone, only to scowl because the battery had gone dead. "Do you have a charger I can use, Zadie?"

"Yup." She waved at one in the kitchen. "I'll download an app and do a search. Are those dwarves?"

"Yes, including my mother."

She stared at me. "Isn't your mother dead?"

"Yeah. These are old."

"Oh, right." She touched the white frame around one of the Polaroid photos. "Where did you find them?"

"Under the basement in the project house."

"*Under* it?"

"I'll explain more later. Image search, please." I thought about dragging the photos over to check with my phone while it was plugged in, but Zadie had already downloaded an app. "The guy in armor is an engineer in the royal dwarven court—or was forty years ago—so it would be handy if he lives down the street."

Zadie shot me a dark look, either because of how unlikely that was or because she also believed engineers were supposed to wear glasses and pocket protectors, not plate armor.

"Do you know anything about the ring?" Abbas plucked it out of the chest and eyed it in the setting sunlight coming in the window that overlooked the street.

"Nothing except that it's not magic."

"Maybe the design is a key that opens a door. Did you see any locked doors?"

"A brick wall," I said, "but it didn't have a keyhole that I noticed. Or ring hole."

"Maybe it's a *promise* ring," Tinja said around a mouthful of cheese. "Someone in class told me about them. A boy gives it to a girl or vice versa, and they swear to take their relationship seriously, an outward sign of commitment and fidelity to another person. It's so romantic." She touched the cheese to her chest.

Abbas curled his upper lip. "It'd be much cooler if it opened a secret door."

"I thought all your classes were online, Tinja." I watched intently as Zadie scanned the photos. "And that none of your peers knew you were green. When do you chat with them?"

"There's a class Discord server."

"College has changed a lot from when I went," Abbas said.

Since I hadn't gone, I didn't comment. Immigrants without degrees of their own, Grandma and Grandpa had barely had enough money to keep my sister and me clothed and fed. *She'd* gotten scholarships and gone to the University of Washington, but I'd never been a stellar student. There hadn't been scholarships for my talents of martial arts and woodworking, so I'd gone straight to work after high school, helping Grandpa and learning the trades. It was what I enjoyed doing, so it had worked out, but I did sometimes feel inadequate around those who had degrees or, as in my sister's snooty case, *multiple* degrees.

"Engineer dwarf does not have a match," Zadie reported. "Nor that one, that one, or your mother. I guess that makes sense if she died before the internet days."

"Yeah." The old hollowness that I'd often felt in my gut as a kid returned. I'd missed her a lot growing up. By the time I'd reached my twenties, I'd gotten over her loss, or so I'd thought, but having Sarrlevi bring everything up again, along with the implication that she might *not* be dead, left me feeling gutted all over again. If she'd somehow survived and had never come to see me because she didn't care... that would be worse than if she'd died.

"Hello, what have we here?" Zadie asked, pulling me from my

depressing thoughts. "A match on the other female. She's, uh, less bearded now."

"A handy goblin acquaintance of hers probably improved her electric razor." Tinja winked at me.

"Undoubtedly." I leaned in to peer over Zadie's shoulder.

Zadie laughed. "Oh, this figures."

"What?" I resisted the urge to tear the phone from her hands. Barely.

"She owns an axe-throwing business. What a perfectly dwarfy establishment to start."

"Funny. Where is it?"

"Port Townsend. Artie's Axes."

"Artie isn't a very dwarven name," Tinja said.

"She must be blending in with the locals so they don't realize her deep, dark secrets," Abbas said.

"Like that she uses a weed whacker instead of a razor?" Zadie asked.

I punched her in the shoulder. "Do you mind not mocking my heritage? You've never even met a real dwarf. You can't use Dungeons & Dragons as your source material."

"Those pictures suggest otherwise." Zadie smirked and tapped the armor-wearing dwarf.

I sighed. The engineer did look like someone out of a fantasy novel.

"Port Townsend isn't as close as I was hoping," I said, "but it could be a lot worse. Does it list hours? Is there a phone number? Wait, never mind. This is a conversation I need to have with her in person." While showing her the photos, including one of the house, and hoping she was open to having her memory jogged. "There's not much security at the ferry terminal. If I wait until dark, I might be able to get on without being noticed."

"Good luck." Zadie looked pointedly at her laptop, where she'd paused the video, my face frozen on the screen. "Do you have your motorcycle?"

I groaned. "No. It's either still in Bridle Trails or impounded."

"How did you get over here? Walk? You never said where you were last night and all day. You didn't sleep in the park, did you?"

As if that had been an option.

"She was in cheese heaven." Tinja smiled as she caressed the wheel—the now heavily sampled wheel—and held it to her chest. "These are *marvelous*. Is this troll cheese? The stuff that's super rare? I've heard about it, but nobody ever gives such amazing morsels to goblins. Here, taste." She stood on a chair to lift a piece toward Abbas's mouth.

He leaned back. "I'm not sure if that's halal. I can't eat cheese made with bacterial cultures using animal rennet."

Zadie wrinkled her nose. "She's trying to stuff *Smurf blue* food in your mouth, and your religious preferences are your primary concern?"

"Well, they're *a* concern."

Tinja offered the piece to Zadie, who also drew back.

"It's not a *little* blue, like blue cheese," she said. "It's *all* blue. That is so wrong."

"It's good," I offered as I snagged her phone to Google Artie's Axes.

Before I got more than the address, a magical being with an intensely powerful aura registered to my senses.

"Uh oh." Tinja dropped the cheese and peered fearfully toward the window. "That's a dragon."

"A *dragon*? That just happens to be flying by?" Eyes round, Abbas also looked toward the window, the direction the dragon was flying from.

Unease trampled into my gut. That dragon had an aura with such power that it dwarfed Sarrlevi's, and it was heading straight toward us. Toward me?

My instinct was to shake my head in denial—what would a *dragon* care about some human police officers?—but then I remembered who was associated with a dragon and groaned. "Are anyone's senses keen enough to tell if a half-elf woman is riding on its back?"

I looked toward Tinja, the only full-blooded magical being in the room.

"The dragon's aura is *very* strong. It would blot out that of a lesser being, but..." She tilted her head thoughtfully. "Yes, there may be a half-elf with him."

"Shit. That Willard must have sent them. For me. You guys need to hide. I don't want you wrapped up in this." Where could *I* hide? From a *dragon?* He would easily sense me through my magical dwarven blood.

"No, *you* must hide." Tinja thrust her camouflage charm into my hand.

I shook my head and tried to give it back. "If they don't find me, but they find you, they'll question you."

"Dragons do *mind scourings*, don't they?" Abbas touched his head. "I remember my father talking about it. It's horrible. That's why his clan fled when dragons became more frequent visitors to their world."

"I don't know what you all are talking about," Zadie, the one full-blooded human in the room, said, "but I think I should ask you to leave my apartment. Or maybe *I* should leave my apartment."

"I'll go." I tried once more to thrust the charm back into Tinja's hand, but she refused and darted into the hallway ahead of me.

"Abbas, come," she called. "Don't let the dragon sense you or catch you."

"Damn it, you two. Here." I tried to give the camouflage charm to Abbas, but he lifted his hands and ran past.

"Use it on yourself, girl," he called back.

I was about to run out the door after them, having some vague notion of fleeing *somewhere* before the dragon arrived, but I remembered my phone on the charger, swore again, and raced back for it.

"Don't you dare leave that cheese here." Despite her wise words about departing, Zadie hadn't yet. She didn't realize the ramifications of a dragon arriving.

"I'll come back for it later." Not wanting to worry about running with so much in my arms, I sadly abandoned the cheese. I grabbed my phone and the chest of photos, and was about to activate Tinja's charm when a male voice thundered in my mind.

The dwarf mongrel criminal will meet us on the landing pad now. Compulsion laced the words, and I jerked like a puppet toward the door.

"Hell."

19

I WILLED MY FEET TO HALT, TO STOP PROPELLING ME TOWARD THE *landing pad*. Was that the rooftop? It made sense that a dragon would land up there, but I groaned, realizing he would see the mangled door. He'd already called me a criminal. That would only reinforce the notion.

With a jerk and growl, I managed to stop walking. In case it helped, and because Tinja and Abbas had already raced off toward the stairs, I rubbed the camouflage charm.

"Matti?" Zadie asked. "Where'd you go?"

"I'm here, but I'm leaving. Stay inside, and don't answer the door."

"You think?"

As I stepped into the hallway, the dragon landed on the rooftop three stories above. I stared up at the ceiling, able to detect Thorvald's aura now, but his was so overpowering that it was all I could do not to drop to the floor and assume the fetal position.

I went a different way than Abbas and Tinja had, not wanting the dragon to associate them with me, but with a lurch of horror, I realized it was too late. I sensed them in the elevator, going up, not down.

For a hopeful few seconds, I thought they might have decided that hiding on another level was better than running out of the building, but no. They were now out of the elevator and walking at a steady pace toward the rooftop-access stairs that I'd come down, heading toward the dragon.

"No." Skipping the elevator, I charged for the stairs, but they had a head start. "Don't go up there!" I yelled, startling a woman with grocery bags into dropping everything.

She peered around, not seeing me. At least the charm worked.

"Sorry, sorry," I blurted as I rushed past, but that only made her scream and sprint down the hall. "Damn, maybe I *am* a criminal."

When I reached the emergency-exit stairs on the top floor, I sensed Tinja and Abbas already on the roof and right in front of the dragon. The smashed door still lay halfway down the stairs, and I sprang over it to rush outside. Then halted abruptly when I saw the huge black dragon taking up half the rooftop. I backed into the doorway, groping for something to do.

Thorvald stood next to the dragon in the same combat boots, jeans, and duster she'd worn before, nothing but her T-shirt changed. Her sword hilt poked up from behind her shoulder. She hadn't drawn it yet, but it wasn't as if she needed to with that *dragon* standing next to her.

The big black creature looked at her with violet eyes. *This is the appropriate response to a dragon's command.*

He lifted a taloned foot to gesture at Abbas and Tinja who lay prostrate and shaking before him.

"Yeah, but you're being a dick." Thorvald swatted him on the scaled leg.

In this form, that is not possible.

"Trust me, it is. Let them up, please." Her swat turned into a pat. "I do appreciate the help, but these aren't the ones we want."

They are the friends of the mongrel criminal.

So that was where Sarrlevi had gotten that word. Dragons.

I will scour their minds to learn where she went.

"Noooo, Lord Dragon," Tinja cried. "Mind scouring is most painful."

That wrenched my heart, and I strode forward. I didn't think the dragon had done anything to them yet, besides using his powerful magic to compel them to come to him, but I wouldn't forgive myself if he hurt them.

"Can't you compel Puletasi to come up here?" Thorvald asked. "Though I don't sense her anymore. I think she's got a charm."

My dislike of Thorvald diminished an iota since she'd used my name instead of calling me mongrel. Though she was also a half-blood, so that would have been pot-kettle territory.

Dwarves have strong natural mental defenses and are more effective at resisting magical compulsion than many races.

"Must be nice. You two can get up." Thorvald waved for Abbas and Tinja to stand, though they were studying the roof and not looking at her. "But if you know where Puletasi went, you should tell us. It's for her own good."

"I'm right here." I stopped between Tinja and Abbas and spread my hands before realizing I hadn't deactivated the charm.

But I must have gotten close enough that they could detect me through it, because the dragon's violet eyes locked on to me.

Half-dwarf mongrel criminal, he announced into my mind—probably everyone's minds. *You are our prisoner due to heinous crimes you've committed in the human metropolis, and we will take you to the military leader Willard for punishment and rehabilitation.*

Thorvald swatted him again. "We're taking her to be questioned. That's it."

The dragon made something of a *hmmph* sound, then transformed into a handsome male human in a black robe with silver trim.

"Is that true?" I looked at Thorvald, feeling another half-blood might be more honest with me. Since she worked for the military, that was probably a delusional thought.

She hesitated. "Well, Willard will question you *first*. I'm not sure about after that. But you won't go for punishment and rehabilitation. That's a Dragon Justice Court thing."

"Just military prison?"

Thorvald turned her palm skyward. "I guess it depends on if there were any extenuating circumstances?" She raised her eyebrows. "Were there?"

"Yeah, the orcs killed everyone. Not me."

"Ah. Well, you can explain that to Willard."

"I don't suppose that's optional." I looked toward the now-human dragon, who appeared regal in his black robe, though his footwear was startling. Were those yellow Crocs? With charms stuck through the holes? *Meat*-shaped charms?

"It's not," Thorvald said, as I gaped at the collection of ribs, T-bones, and sausages adorning the distractingly vibrant shoes. "But it ought to be better than being captured by the police—who are looking for you, in case you didn't know—and thrown in jail." Thorvald lowered her voice. "Admittedly, Willard might have you thrown in jail *after* your chat."

"Wonderful."

"At least she'll look into orcs if you tell her they were there. The police are still amazingly obtuse when it comes to acknowledging that magical beings exist, less because they haven't seen plenty of weird stuff, I think, and more because their superiors forbid talk about our kind." Thorvald looked at her dragon ally. "What's that Upton Sinclair quote?"

"It will be time to consume supper soon," he said. "We must

complete this task so it will not delay the consumption of the meat cubes in the smoker."

"Meat cubes?" I mouthed.

Thorvald snapped her fingers. "'It is difficult to get a man to understand something when his salary depends upon his not understanding it.' And I told you, they're meat *loaves*."

"They are delicious. We do not wish to delay their consumption."

"Of course not. And it's dinner here on the West Coast, not supper." Thorvald wriggled a finger at him, and he and the Crocs—were there any meat-loaf-shaped charms on them?—blurred as he shifted back into a dragon. "Hop on, Puletasi. We get to skip the traffic and the toll by going over the bridge this way."

I would have preferred to skip the whole journey, but a levitation spell gripped me, lifting me from the rooftop.

Clutching my belongings to my chest, I closed my eyes when the dragon floated me alarmingly close to the edge of the roof. It wasn't a skyscraper, but I didn't care for heights under any circumstances. Another reason I would have passed on flying across the city if I'd had a choice.

"Call if you need help, Matti." Abbas shook his head glumly, as if he doubted he would see me again.

"I'll try. Get to work on the new countertops and cabinets for the kitchen if you get a chance. I'll be back to help as soon as I can." I *hoped* I would be. And that the police couldn't keep the house cordoned off indefinitely.

"I added a few additions to the kitchen island," Tinja said. "Wait until you see my revised blueprints."

"I look forward to it," I said instead of pointing out that one wasn't supposed to make updates *after* the cabinets had already been ordered.

Thorvald and I landed astraddle the big black dragon, her behind me. She put a hand on my shoulder as he sprang into the air. It might have been to offer commiseration or comfort, but she didn't look like the comforting, motherly type. It was probably to keep me from jumping off. Or *falling* off.

As the dragon flew away from the building, only a single person among the pedestrians below noticed and gaped at our passing. Someone with a quarter-elven blood. From what I'd heard, dragons had some natural magical camouflage to their scales and weren't visible to normal humans unless they *wished* to be.

We sailed higher, flying over the buildings of downtown Bellevue and across Lake Washington. Traffic was indeed unmoving on the 520 bridge.

It is a great honor to fly on a dragon's back, our aerial taxi announced. *One I would not usually grant to a criminal or a mongrel of any kind.*

"Isn't Thorvald a mongrel too?" I wasn't even that sure she qualified as not-a-criminal. The myths of the Ruin Bringer or Mythic Murderer, as most of the magical community referred to her, had always painted her as a heinous bitch who mowed down trolls, orcs, and ogres left and right.

Val is my mate and a superior warrior, the dragon replied.

"So... not a mongrel?" I glanced over my shoulder to see if Thorvald was offended, but she seemed amused by the conversation.

She has human blood, but she has worked hard to overcome that handicap.

"Oh, right. I've heard the handicap of being human is great."

It is. She is a hard worker. She also makes me delicious meat and is talented in the nest.

"In the what?"

"It's a dragon expression," Thorvald blurted. "It doesn't translate."

The dragon shared a telepathic image of him in his human

form and Thorvald in bed, naked with the blankets falling on the floor around them, as they—

Hell, I didn't want to see that. I lifted a hand, as if I could shield my mental eyes by blocking my physical ones.

"Zav, haven't we discussed how human social conventions dictate we not talk about private mating habits with others?"

The imagery faded, though a sense of smugness came from the dragon.

You discuss them with your therapist, he said with no hint of apology.

Thorvald had a therapist? I peered at her again, wondering if the Ruin Bringer wasn't quite as badass as the stories suggested.

She grimaced. "Therapists are okay to discuss your sex life with. But strangers on Willard's shit list are not."

Hm. The dragon banked and headed for a block of unassuming office buildings surrounded by grassy lawns.

"The secret to having magical beings from other realms stop calling you a mongrel is feeding them meat and having sex with them?" I asked over my shoulder.

"You should go into a few battles at their side too."

"I don't mind doing that." If Sarrlevi showed up again, maybe I would give him a meat loaf. Though I had a hunch elves were largely vegetarian. Maybe a mushroom loaf would be better. "Is the, uh, sex required?"

Thorvald gave me an unreadable expression, probably not interested in opening up to someone on Willard's *shit list,* as she'd said. Her *dragon* was apparently the one to ask. He seemed quite open.

"That came later for us," she relented in saying.

After our exhilarating night in the water box, the dragon added.

"Zav..." Thorvald groaned.

He landed in the grass in front of one of the buildings, a lawn mower that a maintenance person had left crunching under his backside.

That elicited another groan from Thorvald. "Willard is going to make *me* pay for that."

The dragon's black head turned on his long neck to regard her, and his jaws parted to reveal teeth, though his violet eyes were glinting more with humor than irritation. *I had an itch.*

"Next time, tell me. I'll prong you in the scales with my sword." Thorvald slid to the ground while looking warily toward a landscaping truck parked along the curb. Maybe the staff was on a break, for nobody ran out, hollering about the lawn mower.

Thorvald waved for me to join her. Though I didn't want to, I also didn't want to fly anywhere else with the dragon. When my feet hit the ground, I exhaled in relief, glad the ride hadn't been that harrowing.

I'd had visions of him diving and banking and careening between the Space Needle and skyscrapers of downtown Seattle. The discussion on Thorvald's sex life had been almost equally alarming, but at least it hadn't made me motion sick.

The dragon lifted his head, his eyes focusing on something out toward Puget Sound. *My presence is requested back home. You will not be in danger from this mongrel villain?* The head swung back around to regard me—and my hammer.

"I think I can handle her," Thorvald said dryly.

Even though I didn't plan on making trouble, that irritated me. Why was she so sure she could take me in a fight? Because her elven blood made her agile and fast? Well, my dwarven blood made me strong with the stamina of an ox. And I wagered I'd had as much fighting experience as she had. Maybe not real-world combat experience against deadly enemies, but I wouldn't be a pushover in a skirmish.

"I have more means to defend myself than the average fire-escape door after all," Thorvald said, her eyes closing partway as she tapped the feline-shaped charm on her neck.

Damn, I'd forgotten about her huge magical tiger. That would tip the odds in her favor. And double damn that she'd noticed the door—*and* knew I'd been responsible. The colonel might want to lock me up for that alone. Someday, I would have to learn to better control my temper.

Very well, the dragon said.

"Feel free to stop by the house and grab the meat loaves on the way. Just leave one for me and Dimitri to share."

The meat cubes are already levitating in this direction. With a pleased smile-like parting of his jaws, the dragon sprang into the air and flew off, presumably to intercept his meal before creating a portal.

"It's not clear if he left one for us or not," Thorvald said with a sigh. "I'll tell Dimitri to order a pizza."

I had no idea who that was and didn't care. My stomach was too busy tying itself in knots as Thorvald led me toward the front entrance of a building that said nothing about being a military office. Instead, it promised the IRS worked there.

Deceit. Exactly what I'd expect from the military. I shook my head glumly, certain nothing good would come from this meeting.

20

Thorvald led me down a gleaming hallway that had recently been waxed and buffed, stopping at a closed door with *Colonel Willard* on the name plaque. No sign of her first name.

As Thorvald lifted a hand to open the door without knocking, something thudded against it.

She sighed. "I remember the days when you could visit Willard without wearing armor."

I sensed a magical being inside, a goblin.

Opening the door only partway, Thorvald said, "Put a halt to the siege, will you, Gondo? I've got Willard's prisoner."

Prisoner? What had happened to *we're taking her to be questioned and that's it*?

"Oh, it's not a siege, Ruin Bringer. I'm experimenting with mobile aerial fans for cooling the office during the warm months." Something clunked against the wall near the door. "I understand humans in warmer climates have something called air conditioning, but the colonel says office improvements aren't in the budget. My inventions will make doing paperwork during the summer less burdensome."

"Until the mobile aerial fans hit you in the head?" Thorvald looked inside before committing to entering.

"Once I perfect them, they will not do that. Oh, look out."

Thorvald ducked as something whizzed past, threatening to cut off her braid. When she straightened, she looked back at me. "Maybe I shouldn't have assumed this would be better for you than going with the police."

I would have preferred to avoid both and visit the dwarf in Port Townsend.

"Come in, Thorvald," came Willard's Southern drawl from behind another door.

One had to pass the desk the goblin sat behind—no, sat *on*—to reach it.

"This is her secretary?" Only after looking around for danger did I ease into the outer office.

One floating fan was stuck in a corner, and another whirred in happy circles. If they were doing anything to cool the air, I couldn't tell.

"Gondo." Thorvald waved at the green-skinned goblin, his white hair sticking out as if he'd been electrified recently. Perhaps by a fan. "He's more of an informant than a secretary, though he does answer the phone sometimes."

"I think Tinja might have met him."

One of Gondo's pointed green ears perked. "I have met Tinja. She is not from my clan, but she is a *city* goblin, like me. Our kin sometimes shun us for giving up our rural ways, so she should come visit us and play games at the Coffee Dragon. It is where like-minded and more *cerebral* goblins meet."

"They cerebrally launch dice across the room to the alarm of the other customers," Thorvald said, heading for Willard's door.

She opened it without knocking, pulled her sword scabbard off her back, and plopped down in a chair opposite Willard at her desk. That earned a scowl from the colonel and a glower through the doorway at me before she focused on Thorvald again.

"When I send the MPs to collect someone," Willard said, "they bring the person into my office in cuffs, then stand at attention in front of my desk alongside the prisoner."

"You pay MPs to collect people, don't you? I believe you made this request as a favor. One Zav very nearly objected to since it was almost dinnertime. You know how much he hates to miss meals."

"One wonders how dragons in the wild survive without a mate at home running a meat smoker around the clock."

"It is a mystery. If Puletasi tries to run, I could call roots up from the floor and entangle her. I've been working on perfecting that bit of magic."

"Yes, I want roots thrusting out of my recently polished floors." Willard pointed at me. "Get in here, Puletasi."

I bristled. *I* wasn't in the military and didn't need to stand at attention for anyone.

But a fan whizzed past, threatening to gouge the back of my head, so I hustled in. There wasn't a chair for me, but nobody had handcuffed me yet, so it could have been worse. I wondered if the supposed IRS building had a block of prison cells in the basement.

"Did you *really* escalate from side kicking thieves into soda refrigerators to killing police officers?" Willard asked without preamble.

"No, ma'am." I decided to be polite, especially since it sounded like she might not have made up her mind about that yet.

"She side-kicked a metal fire door," Thorvald said before I could explain what had happened. "Knocked it halfway down the steps."

"I used my hammer for that," I said before realizing I shouldn't have. Unless there'd been a camera I hadn't seen on the rooftop, there wasn't any proof that I'd been responsible. Though the hammer dents might serve as evidence. Since I couldn't retract the words, I clarified with, "It was an emergency. An elf opened a portal and left me on the rooftop and locked out of the building."

They looked blankly at me. Hadn't *anyone* known Sarrlevi was there for the fight with the orcs? And the werewolves? How had I gotten all the blame? Did they know about the monster in the park?

"I'm not an elf. I can't shimmy down drainpipes. I have mass. They bend." I pantomimed a drainpipe tilting away from a wall, then gave up and launched into the story. Or started to. Before I'd gotten past the werewolves and the quirkiness of the house, Thorvald stood up and lifted a finger.

"I need to step out. Someone is speaking to me." She touched her temple.

Willard lifted her eyes toward the ceiling. "Can't your mate enjoy his evening without you feeding or boinking him? This will only take an hour."

"It's not Zav. He had to go home. And I'm positive this person doesn't want me to boink him." Thorvald gave me an odd look, then walked out without waiting to be dismissed. She ducked a fan ricocheting off a wall and headed outside.

"She was in the Army for ten years, if you can believe it," Willard said.

"Huh," was all I said, not surprised. I'd figured the military types stuck together.

"Continue with your tale."

"It's what happened, not a *tale*." Maybe she wasn't as opened-minded as I'd hoped. Or maybe she didn't believe that something was under the house. Well, that part would be easy enough to verify. The giant hole in the floor of the laundry room wouldn't have gone away. "Oh," I blurted, recalling the bullet I'd found and fished in my pockets. Then I remembered that Sarrlevi's laundry device had washed my clothes. I almost stopped hunting, figuring it would have fallen out, but I did find the casing wedged in the bottom of the pocket. I set it on Willard's desk. "There are bullets embedded in the foyer wall by the front door, and I bet they match this. Those that were lodged in the body of the renter presumably match too."

"I'm more concerned about the dead police officers," Willard said, though she did scribble *renter* and a couple of notes on a pad, then looked at the bullet. "That could be a round from an M4 carbine."

"That's the standard Army rifle, right?"

"It's used by many forces worldwide."

I took that as a *yes*.

"Continue," she prompted.

Though the suggestion that the *military* might have been in my house shooting dwarves disturbed me, I told her what I'd seen. Since I hadn't been an eyewitness to the deaths of the police officers, I had to admit someone besides the orcs might have been responsible. But not Sarrlevi. Not with a blunt weapon. He only had those two swords and some daggers.

Thorvald returned to catch the tail end of the story.

"What happened to the assassin after you ran?" Willard asked.

"He met me in the park and, uhm, helped me avoid being arrested. He made a portal."

"Like a *getaway* portal?" Willard arched her eyebrows. "Why is he helping you?"

I shrugged, wondering if I should have left that part out. Should I tell them about Sarrlevi's link to my mother? I was reluctant to give them anything more than I had to, but the story might be less believable without all the details.

"Sarrlevi is who was talking telepathically to me," Thorvald said. "He wants us to know that he was with Puletasi and that she didn't have anything to do with the deaths. She was digging a hole under her house when the fighting was going on outside."

"Digging a hole?" Willard asked. "While the police swarmed the neighborhood?"

"Well, she is half dwarf. Tunneling is in their nature."

"Hilarious." Willard pressed the heel of her hand to her forehead.

"That means she finds you trying," Thorvald told me, smiling for the first time. "It's a gesture she uses a *lot* with me."

Willard looked toward her window without commenting. Twilight had come outside. It was probably past the hour that colonels were supposed to be in the office.

My stomach rumbled, reminding me that I hadn't had anything except cheese to eat that day.

"As I recall, Thorvald," Willard said, "you first encountered the elf assassin because he was trying to kill you."

"That's right."

I blinked in surprise.

"And now you consider him a reliable and trusted resource?"

"Well." Thorvald paused as a whack came from the outer office. "Maybe not as reliable as *Gondo*—"

Willard grunted.

"—but I don't know why he would lie about this. He's honorable. There were a couple of times when he could have killed me, but he wanted a fair duel instead of sniping me from a distance or taking advantage when I was wiping sweat out of my eyes. I should be glad about that because he's a better fighter than I am. I got lucky in the end. I figured out how to use Storm's magic better, and the fae realm where we were dueling was an easy place to pop those elven roots out of the ground." Thorvald hesitated. "I think he may also have been a little worn out from chasing me all over the place and banging the fae queen. She seems like she'd be demanding in the sack."

"I was about to compliment you on your uncharacteristic

modesty," Willard said, "and then you gave me details I really did not want to know."

I hadn't wanted to know them either, especially since they prompted me to imagine this fae queen in Sarrlevi's guest room in one of those sheer nightgowns.

"My point is that he's honorable," Thorvald said.

"And irresistible to females, apparently."

"I wouldn't know about that. I was busy not resisting a certain dragon at the time. Anyway, Zav mangled the dragon who hired Sarrlevi and convinced him to cancel his contract on me. Sarrlevi also owes me a favor, so I don't have any reason to believe he's lying to me."

"Favor?" Willard asked.

I couldn't keep from raising my eyebrows in curiosity too. Thorvald's assertion that Sarrlevi was honorable made me wonder if I'd been too quick to assume he was lying to me. I didn't believe I was wrong for being huffy that he'd once taken an assignment to kill my mother, but maybe he truly did want to help her now. Or he was, perhaps more accurately, more interested in the king's pay than the sister's pay.

"I hooked him up with a supplier of fine chocolates, which he took to the fae queen as a bribe or payment," Thorvald said. "I'm not quite sure on all the details, but she was apparently in such a huff when he refused to keep having sex with her that she was telling people all over the realms that he's inadequate. An assassin doesn't want *that* rumor getting around, whether it's referring to weapons prowess or bedroom prowess."

"I'm sorry I asked," Willard grumbled.

"I gather he's now back in her good graces and she's trying to woo him into the sack again. Nobody else will do."

"I suppose if you can't have a dragon..." Willard gripped her chin and looked at me. "Why is Sarrlevi spending time with *you*?"

I wasn't sure if she was implying I was chopped liver next to a fae queen or that I was, as Sarrlevi himself had said, too insignificant for anyone important to pay attention to. He'd been talking about the people who hired him, not himself, but I assumed he considered himself significant too.

"My allure," I said, because they were both looking at me now, and I hadn't decided if I should divulge that my mother was a lost dwarven princess. These people were military, and the military had been responsible for her death. My shoulders rucked up, and I didn't say anything else.

"Uh huh," Willard said. "Is that allure enhanced or diminished by the fact that you need an electric razor capable of trimming hedges?"

Heat scorched my cheeks. Even if *I'd* told her about that, I didn't appreciate the insinuation that I was hideous—or hairy. Especially not from some graying Army officer closer to fifty than forty.

Thorvald snorted. "Come on, Willard. She's pretty. And stacked." She grinned and waved at my chest. "Elf guys don't see that a lot. Their women are all slim and stickish. Maybe he's intrigued."

"We're not having sex," I blurted, almost as horrified by her assessment as by Willard's. "He's on a mission looking for a dwarf and thought I might be able to help. That's it."

Willard frowned. "Not a dwarf to *kill,* I hope." She looked at Thorvald. "Did your instructor go back to his home world? Lord Chasmmoor, wasn't it?"

"Yes, he did," Thorvald said. "Though he visits Dimitri from time to time. He fawns appropriately over Chasmmoor's abilities as an enchanter."

"I don't know who that is, but that's not the dwarf that Sarrlevi is looking for." Not wanting to say who he *was* looking for, I changed the subject. "Look, if you believe him and that I'm not responsible, can you get the police off my back? I'm sure the orcs framed me. They want me out of the picture so they can get in the house and find an artifact, the same as the werewolves."

"Orcs *framed* you?" Willard asked. "That sounds sophisticated for their kind."

"Sarrlevi said there was a shaman," Thorvald said.

"Who is thus a genius?"

Thorvald shrugged. "I think the shamans read scrolls and books."

"*You* read books." Willard's smirk made it clear she didn't think Thorvald was a genius. At least they ragged on each other as much as they had me. Thorvald had even been vaguely supportive, if pointing at my chest and calling me stacked could be considered support. "Admittedly smutty books about dragons." Her smirk broadened.

Thorvald rolled her eyes. "*Lord of the Rings* isn't smutty."

Willard rested her forearms on her desk and threaded her fingers together as she regarded me again. "Here's the offer, Puletasi. I'll investigate the situation more thoroughly and see if my people can find the orcs responsible and deal with the werewolves and this creature in the park. I'll also send Thorvald back to your house with you to help find whatever artifact is luring legions of magical beings to the grounds. In exchange, assuming you survive the week, you'll come work for me."

I slumped. It was better than prison, but I *had* a job, damn it.

"I like how you say your *people*, Willard," Thorvald said, "as if you're not going to send me to handle all that."

"Well, if Puletasi here gets her house in order, she can help. As my new government contractor, it'll be her honor to do so." Her dark eyes glinted.

"It'll be her honor to serve you? Zav is starting to rub off on you."

"I'm a wonderful employer, Thorvald. You know that."

"Make sure you negotiate your pay in advance and insist on combat bonuses," Thorvald advised me.

I pushed a hand through my hair. "If you can get the police to leave me alone and clear any suspicion from my name, I will help Thorvald with the orcs, werewolves, and *brysarrusi.* We can negotiate my further services after my house isn't more exciting to break into than Fort Knox."

"I have a feeling whatever is down there is more interesting than gold," Thorvald said.

"I honestly have no idea." I spread a hand, watching Willard's face and hoping she didn't push for me to accept her version of the offer. I loved my work and didn't want to become a professional bruiser. Yes, stopping crime and taking out aggressions on bad guys from time to time was appealing, but so was taking dumpy old houses and turning them into beautiful places for people to live.

"Get whatever it is out of that house," Willard said, "so that neighborhood can go back to normal."

"You want me to bring it back and put it in your artifact room in the basement?" Thorvald asked.

"So the weirdos will break in *here* instead?"

Another thwack came from the outer office.

"I've got news for you, Willard," Thorvald said. "The weirdos are already here."

21

THE INSIDE OF THORVALD'S BLACK JEEP SMELLED LIKE CATS—OR WAS that tiger?—and gun oil. A yellow tree-shaped car freshener dangling from the rearview mirror did little to mask the scents. Silver fur proliferated.

"Am I in your tiger's seat?" I asked as she started the Jeep.

"Nah, he sits in the back. That's why the seats are always down. He's a big fella."

"How often does he visit?" I had no idea what to talk about to the woman who was my putative jail keeper.

Willard hadn't suggested that I had an option about working with Thorvald. At least we all seemed to want the same thing. For now. I was sure the Army didn't care if the house I'd bought to renovate was demolished, but they wanted that neighborhood safe and for police officers not to die. I did too.

"Whenever I summon him, but he can only stay on Earth for about six hours, so I usually save him for battles. He likes battles. He makes snarky comments and threatens to gnaw off my foot when I bring him for less stimulating reasons."

"I never envisioned tigers as being snarky."

"He's an ambassador from the Tangled Tundra Nation on Del'noth, not just a tiger."

"I've never heard of that."

"Yeah, nobody has. Except the dragons. They were partially responsible for creating it and linking some tigers to the charms."

"How'd you get one?"

"Killed an ogre wizard who was making Sindari do vile things. Where'd you get your hammer?" Thorvald asked it casually, but she eyed me sidelong, and I had a feeling Willard was the one who wanted to know. Before we'd left, she'd pulled Thorvald aside for a private conversation.

"My mom brought it from her homeland. Home *world*." When I'd been little, she hadn't spoken of other worlds, instead leading me to believe she had come from some other exotic country on Earth. That had probably been to keep me from blabbing her secrets to other children, not because she never wanted me to know. "Would you mind stopping at Port Townsend on the way to Bellevue?"

Thorvald had been about to pull out onto a busy street, but she halted and stared at me. "On the *way*? Port Townsend is across Puget Sound. I don't know if you've looked at a map lately, but that isn't on the way to Bellevue from Seattle. Or anywhere."

"I know, but I have a lead. I was doing some research when you and your dragon showed up. Oh, can I use your phone charger? Sarrlevi didn't have one at his house, if you can imagine that."

She kept staring at me. "Look, Puletasi. Willard doesn't trust you, and I… I haven't made up my mind yet. I know what it's like to fight these guys, and that shit happens sometimes, but if you're trying to figure out a way to sneak out of town on me, I'll kick your ass. Don't think you can get away from me. Sindari is an excellent tracker."

"I'm not sneaking anywhere. I have a house and a business and friends here. My grandparents live in Marysville. I want my name cleared. Trust me."

"Then what's in Port Townsend?"

I fished in the chest while turning on the overhead light so she could see the photos. "This dwarf, I'm hoping. She runs an axe-throwing club there. She's the only one of several dwarves that—" That what? Were in the pictures? That was all I knew about the group. And that they knew my mother. "I think they have something to do with what's under the house. At the least, my mom was hanging out with them back before I was born, and I found this chest in that house. There's an enchanted wall that we have to get through to find out what the orcs and werewolves are after, and Sarrlevi pointed out that it might not be a good idea to break down a wall when we don't know why it was built."

"It's already after dark. The police aren't going to be staking that place out again tonight. Aren't you worried about the werewolves and orcs getting in if you're not there?"

I hesitated. I *was* worried about not being there to keep an eye on the house, but... "Sarrlevi put some wards around it. It didn't keep dead bodies from being hurled onto the lawn, so I'm not sure exactly what they do, but I *think* they were keeping the orc shaman on the perimeter."

Thorvald rubbed her face. "What's your deal with Sarrlevi? Why is he even here on Earth? Now that he knows where the chocolate factory is, I wouldn't expect him to hang around." She glanced at my chest, as if contemplating her earlier joke that a short stout dwarf might be a nice change from elven females.

I shook my head. "It's not about me. I mean, it loosely is. He wants to *use* me. He's trying to find my mother. I keep telling him she's dead, but he either doesn't believe me or he insists on being thorough and making *sure* she's dead."

"He is the thorough type. Who was your mother?"

"According to him—and a blood test gizmo he has—one of

two daughters of the dwarven king in, ah, the place where they live."

"Dun Kroth," Thorvald said, then smacked her hand on the armrest between us. "He's not here to *kill* her, is he? I'll choke the bastard."

"He says he's looking for her at the king's behest. At first, I didn't trust him… because he said he *did* take a gig to kill her forty years ago, and that's presumably why she had to flee to Earth. But if what you said is true, and he's honorable and wouldn't lie to me…" I raised my eyebrows, not sure how much stock to put in Thorvald as a judge of character. I barely knew her.

"He's honorable in battle, but if you're his target or he needs something from you, I wouldn't guarantee he wouldn't lie. He's crafty, the kind to set traps. He did that to me." Thorvald grimaced and touched her sword scabbard.

That did not reassure me.

"I thought assassinations were his thing, not bounty hunting or finding lost princesses," Thorvald continued. "That seems like something he would consider beneath him. Unless it's really challenging or something. Maybe that's it. He's the kind of guy to like a challenge."

"Well, I'm pretty sure she's dead, so that's going to make it difficult to find her."

Thorvald pulled out her phone to look something up. "Go ahead and use the charger."

"What are you checking?" I hoped it was the axe-throwing place.

"The ferry schedule to see if we can even get there before it closes. Without Zav, we're stuck traveling the old-fashioned way. And Port Townsend isn't exactly a carousing bars-open-all-night kind of place."

"There are a few pubs," I said, though I hadn't visited in years. "And a Mexican restaurant."

"It's a real rip-roaring town, yeah. Looks like your axe-throwing place is open until eleven. Have you called the dwarf? Do you know if she works there or just owns it?"

"No. I figured I would need to show her the photos to get her to talk. Dwarves are kind of recalcitrant by nature." Admittedly, I hadn't met many dwarves—*no* full-blooded dwarves—but *I* was recalcitrant. It had to come from somewhere.

"No kidding." Maybe Thorvald had met some dwarves. "Dimitri is one-quarter dwarf, and he's a grump most of the time." She dropped her phone in the drink holder and took off.

"Who is that?"

She'd mentioned him a few times.

"My roommate. Originally, he was my mother's roommate, but he preferred a house to living in a van in her driveway. Oddly. There's also a vampire in the basement. And occasionally my elf half-sister when she's visiting."

"That's a lot of roommates. Aren't you and, uh, the dragon... a couple?"

"Lord Zavryd'nokquetal. We're mated in the dragon way and married in the human way, as he says it, yes." Thorvald spread her fingers to show off engagement and wedding rings—they looked like the kind of jewelry one won in a World of Warcraft quest rather than anything picked up at Tiffany's. "My roommates have to stick cotton balls in their ears if they don't want to listen to us enjoying the married life." Thorvald gave me a wicked grin, promptly making me glad that Tinja had never brought a man—or male goblin—home. "It's a big house," she added. "Just to reiterate, if you try to sneak away from me at any point in our adventure, I'm sending my tiger after you."

"And kicking my ass, I know."

"That's right." Thorvald eyed me sidelong again. "Willard says your father is in jail."

"A military prison, yes. He's not allowed to have visitors. I haven't seen him since I was four." Since the night Mom had died, and my sister and I had been ripped from his arms...

"She also says you got in trouble a lot in school."

It continued to creep me out that the military was paying that much attention to me. How *long* had they been watching?

"*Some* trouble. Not a *lot* of trouble. Yes, I have a temper, but I'm not..." I scowled at the dashboard, hating to have to defend myself to a near stranger. What the hell had happened this week that I'd become someone considered dangerous and suspicious in the eyes of the law? And the damn military? "I'm not a bad guy, all right? I *help* people."

"We'll see."

I was more worried about solving the house problem and figuring out the connection to my mother than proving myself to Thorvald or her colonel, but a part of me couldn't help but wonder what would happen if someone else tried to frame me or I royally screwed up. Would I end up in prison after all?

22

Thorvald pulled into a parking spot in front of Artie's Axes, one of several available. According to the internet, the establishment would be open for two more hours, but people had either cleared out early, or it wasn't the hip and happening weapon-hurling business that one might expect.

"Probably because they don't serve alcohol," I muttered.

A banner on the website had mentioned snacks, sodas, and carbonated waters for sale.

Thorvald looked at me, and I started to explain, but she must have understood, for she said, "If the fantasy novels I've read are any indication, it's not a good idea to mix alcohol with weapons throwing. It's a wonder any of those pub proprietors stay in business."

"You read fantasy novels?" I thought she'd been joking when she'd defended *Lord of the Rings* to Willard.

"Don't you?"

"I like rom-coms." I decided not to mention that the utter lack of romance in my own life might be a driver there.

"Without dragons, fae, or elves in them?"

"Definitely not elves." After grabbing my hammer, I hopped down from the Jeep, glad it didn't have huge tires that jacked it up higher than normal. I already felt like a toddler next to Thorvald.

When we walked into the cedar-sided building near the waterfront, our boots kicking up sawdust on the floor, a few men looked at her. The same men didn't notice me at all, but that was fine. I hadn't come for a date.

Unfortunately, I didn't sense anyone with full-dwarven blood, not unless they were camouflaging themselves the way Sarrlevi had. A surly teenage boy handing out sodas and trios of throwing axes at the bar did, however, have an aura similar to mine. Could Artie have a son? Or maybe she preferred hiring sturdy individuals who could stop a brawl if people arguing about the score got physical.

"You have a reservation?" he asked me while he looked at Thorvald.

"No." I eyed the caged axe-throwing lanes, six out of the eight empty. "Is Artie here? She was a friend of my mother's, and I'm hoping to speak with her."

The boy squinted at me, giving me his full attention. "She's still recovering from the *last* person who came to talk to her."

"What do you mean?"

"She's not here. Even if she were, she wouldn't want any more visitors." He jerked his thumb toward an open office at the end of a short hallway behind the bar. Was that axe embedded in the door decorative or an indication that there'd been trouble earlier?

Thorvald walked around the bar and strode toward it.

The teenager hopped off a box—I'd thought he'd been tall for someone with dwarven blood—and planted himself in front of her. "She's not here, and nobody else is going to bother her."

"Who bothered her before?" As I glanced again at the axe in the door, unease crept into my gut. Had someone beaten us here?

To question her about the house and what was underneath it? But who else would have known about her?

Before the teen answered, I gripped the edge of the bar as realization struck me like a mallet. Sarrlevi. I'd shown him the photos.

He hadn't been in Zadie's apartment when we'd looked up this place, but that didn't mean he didn't have other ways to find people. He'd found *me*, after all.

"A stuck-up blond guy that I wanted to punch before he opened his mouth. And even more after he did. He was an elf, I think. He had a hood up, but I could tell. I wish I *had* punched him. Then she wouldn't have— Never mind." He scowled at us.

"He hurt her?" I balled a hand into a fist, angry all over again with Sarrlevi. If he was tormenting people to get information about my mother, I'd shove one of his blocks of cheese up his ass the next time I ran into him.

"Roughed her up. She's real tough, but she looked scared when I went back to check on the noise. He had his hand around her neck. I wanted to stop him, but Artie said to stay back, that he was too dangerous to fight."

"Did they leave together?" Thorvald asked.

"No. He left first, and then she said she was going to warn someone about him and for me to lock up tonight. I called her house a little bit later, but she didn't answer. She's old school and doesn't have a cell phone."

"What's her address?" Thorvald asked.

"I'm not telling you. You look like someone who'd be with *him*." The teen looked at her ears, though they were rounded instead of pointed. Like me, Thorvald looked fully human, but if he had half-magical blood, he would be able to sense that we did too.

"Trust me, I'm not." Thorvald looked at me. "You think it was Sarrlevi?"

"I don't know anyone else who fits that description."

"Stuck-up blond guy? That's a lot of elves." She gave a quick smile. "Most of them."

"I don't know anyone else," I clarified, "who fits that description who might be researching my mom."

"Right." Thorvald slipped past the teenager, seeming to melt away from a snatch he made for her arm, and strode back to the office.

"We'll just be a minute." I lifted a hand to intercept him when he tried to follow her. "If she's in trouble with the assassin, we might be able to help."

"Assassin?" he mouthed, halting. "No wonder Artie said he was dangerous. He did have that vibe. I thought he was in a gang or something."

"If only he were that benign." I stopped in the doorway, ducking to avoid the haft of the axe jutting from the wood planks, and watched as Thorvald looked around. The accounting books, papers, and thirty-year-old calculator on the desk hadn't been disturbed, and nothing had been knocked to the floor.

A couple of dark splotches of liquid under the axe drew my eye. There wasn't any sawdust covering the wooden floorboards back here, and I crouched to touch one. It had mostly dried, but a hint of red came away on my finger. Blood.

"I'm beginning to think I got lucky," I whispered, belatedly deciding that spending the night in an assassin's guest room had been a bad idea.

Thorvald looked at my finger and pointed to a back door. "Let's check her house. I think it's down the street a block or two."

"How do you know?"

"I sort of saw it in the kid's mind."

I stared at her as I wiped my finger and stood. "You can read minds?"

"Not very well, and my telepathic powers are limited, but my half-sister has been teaching me about my elven magic this past year, and I've picked up a few things."

"Sounds handy."

"Picking up magic or having an elven half-sister?"

"Both. All my half-sister does is try to hook me up with accountants and send me pictures of dresses from catalogs in the hope that I'll buy them and wear them when I meet the accountants."

"And you're not into dresses?" Thorvald nodded as she held the door open for me, as if she understood perfectly.

"I like them fine, but not the ones my sister picks out. They don't have enough personality." I followed her into a well-kept alley without anyone sleeping in it or rooting through the dumpster.

"Personality?" Without hesitating, Thorvald headed toward a street.

"You know, color or lace or ruffles or anything fun. My sister thinks I should wear *business casual.* I don't even know what that means, but, judging from her wardrobe, drab colors are required, preferably navy and gray. Especially navy-and-gray pinstripes."

"Elven sisters do have personality, I'll give you that. Freysha has never commented on my attire, though I'm sure she'd like my jacket to be trimmed in vines and flowers." Thorvald pointed to a cute blue house that managed to appear bright and perky even at night. A streetlamp at the corner provided enough light to see metal artwork in the beds, sunflowers and tulips made from copper and aluminum thrusting from the mulch. "A dwarf *must* live here."

I sensed something magical inside but not the aura of a living person. More like an artifact.

As she headed to the door, Thorvald eyed the lawn to either side of the walkway, as if she were looking for something. She knocked, but nobody answered. I was beginning to suspect this side trip to Port Townsend had been a waste of our time. Sarrlevi might be long gone with what he'd learned.

Thorvald tried the knob, found it locked, and pushed open a window to slither inside with impressive ease for someone six feet tall with a sword scabbard on her back.

"Be careful," I said. "Whatever we sense in there could be an alarm system."

"It's coming from the bedroom," Thorvald called softly back.

"Maybe she doesn't want anyone molesting her goose down."

Not answering, Thorvald padded around in the house without making a sound. Only her aura allowed me to track her as she headed for the back. Since she hadn't unlocked the door, I thought about replicating her window entrance, but she soon returned, letting herself out the front door. She held something in her hand, shining her phone screen toward it so I could see.

"A little coin?" I asked as she flipped it over, showing a leaf on one side and a sword on the other.

"It's Sarrlevi's calling card. In case there was any doubt that he was the one harassing dwarves."

I sank into a crouch. "You don't think he would have killed Artie, do you? If she didn't tell him what he wanted to know?"

Was he that twisted that he believed he could kill those who'd been friends with my mother in his quest to find her? The dwarven king wouldn't approve of that. He *couldn't*.

"Not necessarily," Thorvald said. "He left one of these near my mother's house when he was researching me."

"When he intended to kill you?"

"Yeah."

"Did he threaten her?"

"As far as I know, he only spied on her."

I scowled. "He's good at that."

"Assassins like to study their prey, including friends and relatives who might get in the way, before springing."

"According to him, he's supposed to be *helping* my mother, if she's alive, which she isn't."

"Are you sure?"

"Yes, but *he's* not. He said that even if she's dead, her father wants to know for certain. Maybe he's supposed to dig up her grave and bring the remains." Disturbed by the image, I rubbed my face, hiding a quick wipe of my eyes as emotions bubbled to the surface again.

Would my mother have been buried in a grave? Or would the military have left her to burn to ash in our apartment building?

"You may want to see the spot where I found this." Thorvald tilted her head toward the door.

"Does your boss approve of you breaking and entering random people's houses?" I asked, glad for the topic change.

"I didn't break anything. The window was open."

"You did enter."

"Yes, and you're going to, too." Thorvald gripped my arm and led me through a living room where every piece of furniture was covered in a hand-knitted afghan, the decorating style not at all what I'd expected based on the metal-flower garden or axe-throwing business.

"You're a bad influence." Despite the words, I let her lead me to a hallway where framed pictures hung on the wall. Most were illustrations of landscapes, specifically snow-capped mountains, with a few of caves and underground pools. One was quite beautiful, a great subterranean lake with stalactites dripping water in front of veins of silver gleaming from a rock wall. The artwork seemed more in line with dwarf tastes than the afghans.

"I've heard that before." Thorvald's phone buzzed, and she tugged it out as she pointed at the sole picture featuring people. "Hey, Amber."

My breath caught as I focused on a familiar dwarf woman with frizzy red hair. She stood between the dwarven engineer from the

Polaroids—this time wearing overalls and carrying a toolbox—and Artie, who had a fist propped on her hip and glowered as she stood defensively beside my mother. Protecting her? Mom had her hammer slung over her shoulder and looked like she could protect herself. Their closeness made me suspect the two dwarves with her were good friends.

It was an illustration rather than a photo, and I searched for evidence of the artist, not that any painter's signature was ever legible. There was none.

"The assassin's calling-card coin was resting on the lip of that painting," Thorvald told me before switching back to her phone conversation. "Yeah, we can do our practice later tomorrow. I'm on a special project that might keep me up all night."

I touched Mom's face in the painting, then studied Artie, wishing more than ever to speak with her. Would she be back tonight? Was it worth staying? Or had Sarrlevi scared her out of town? Or—my gut twisted—had he done something to her? No, the teen had said she'd gone to warn someone.

"No, I'm not talking about having sex with Zav," Thorvald replied to whatever the caller was saying. Whoever it was sounded young, but I wasn't paying that much attention. "You're almost an adult now; I don't feel the need to use innuendos with you. If I'm going to get jiggy with my mate, I'll let you know."

"Ew, *gross,* Val." The voice was impossible to miss there. "And nobody says *get jiggy with* anymore."

"No? What's it called now?"

"Watching Netflix and chilling."

"Neither activity excites Zav. He prefers hunting to television and the hot tub or the sauna to anything that might *chill* him."

"Just say *having sex*, Val. But not to me. I don't want to hear about it. I just wanted to say I can't start so early tomorrow, because... well, reasons."

Thorvald wandered back into the living room to finish the conversation.

I took a photo of the illustration. The background was a simple bluish gray with no details of a location, nor did anything about their clothing or gear give me any clues about when the painting had been done. I just wanted a photo of it because I had few mementos of my mother.

My phone rang as I joined Thorvald back in the living room and looked around one more time in the vain hope that the homeowner would appear. Should I leave her a note?

Not recognizing the number, I almost let it go to voice mail—I didn't yet know if Willard had gotten the police off my back—but with Sarrlevi wandering around questioning people with his hand to their throats, Zadie, Abbas, and Tinja might be in trouble.

"Hello?" I answered.

"*Matti*," Tinja whisper-squeaked. "Someone's in our house."

"Where are you? On the roof again?" I tapped Thorvald's shoulder, pointed in the direction of her Jeep, and mouthed, "We need to go."

"On Mrs. Ming's roof," Tinja whispered even more softly. "This is her phone. But I'm not safe up here. It's not the police this time. I think he can sense me. I—" She broke off, and clunks sounded, followed by a thud.

The phone dropping? *Tinja* dropping?

"Tinja?" I looked down at the phone to see if the line was still open. It was, but only the whine of a mosquito came over the line. And... was that the sound of footsteps? "*Tinja*."

The line went dead.

23

"I'M LOOKING AT YOUR HOUSE NOW," ABBAS SAID. "DO YOU WANT the good news or the bad news first?"

"I want to know if Tinja's there and alive." I was shouting at the phone, and Thorvald kept glancing at me from the driver's seat, but I couldn't calm down. My friends had been in danger all week, and it was my fault. Sarrlevi was looking for my mother, and he apparently didn't care who he hurt or threatened as a part of his mission.

Maybe I hadn't picked out the project house and couldn't be held responsible for the strange artifact bricked in under the basement, but it was hard not to feel that even that was at least partially my fault. I still didn't know how or why, but it was tied to my mother.

"Uhm," Abbas said.

What did *that* mean? I imagined Tinja's little goblin body mutilated and left on the lawn where she'd fallen off the roof—or the damn assassin had broken her neck and shoved her off the roof.

"I don't sense her, but I'll check around," he said.

"Check the neighbor's yard too. She said she was calling from Mrs. Ming's roof."

"Okay. Do you want me to try to fix your door enough to shut it?"

"What's wrong with my *door*?"

"That's some of the bad news. Someone kicked it in and ransacked the place. The good news is that your TV is still there, so I don't think it was a robbery."

"I'm sure robbers would have been disappointed with the thirteen-inch tube TV in the corner of the living room."

"It was definitely ransacked though. Your furniture is all knocked over."

"I'm going to kill that bastard." I envisioned Sarrlevi's face turning red because my hands were wrapped around his neck and squeezing. "Can't you make this boat go any faster?" I barked at Thorvald and waved in frustration at the cars lined up around us as the ferry trundled sedately across Puget Sound toward Edmonds.

What I really wanted to yell was for her to stop glancing over at me. She was probably sympathetic to my plight rather than judgmental, but I didn't care. I didn't want anyone to witness me falling apart over the roommate and architecture student I'd never thought I'd wanted in my life but who had, over the last year, become a friend.

"That's not among the magical spells Freysha has taught me, no," Thorvald said. "And I'm afraid Zav hasn't returned to Earth yet."

"You're probably not allowed to leave your car on the ferry while you fly off on a dragon anyway," I muttered, glowering at the phone and waiting for an update from Abbas.

"No, but Zav can lift a Jeep off the ground. I know that for a fact. Trust me." Thorvald tried smiling at me.

I wasn't in the mood for it.

"I don't know if it helps, but it probably wasn't Sarrlevi," she added.

"What? Who broke into my house and took my friend?"

Thorvald hesitated. "I don't know about your friend, but I can't imagine Sarrlevi knocking over furniture. He seems like the type who would leave your house tidier than he found it if he broke in and rifled through everything."

That was possibly true. His house on whatever that world had been was immaculate. The magical cleaning devices might have been responsible for that, but Artie's house hadn't been ransacked either.

"She's not here," Abbas said. "I'll go check the project house."

"*No,*" I said more harshly than I intended. I made myself take a breath, blow it out, and say, "No, Abbas," more calmly. "I don't want you to be hurt too. I… I'm sorry you guys are mixed up in this."

"What exactly *is* this, Matti? Do you know?"

"It's a couple of things, but somehow it's all tied in with my mom."

"I thought your mother was dead."

"She is."

After a pause, he said, "Tinja is my friend too. I want to go look for her."

"We will. Just wait for me, okay? I'm on my way back, and I've got some muscles to help."

"We've *both* got muscles, Matti."

"I mean some in addition to mine. A half-elf and a tiger."

"I guess they could be useful."

Thorvald arched her eyebrows.

"The tiger especially," Abbas said.

"Sindari would be whuffing with pride if he were here to hear that," Thorvald said.

A reverberation went through the deck as the ferry came into dock.

"We'll be there soon, Abbas," I said. "Wait for us."

"There's nothing left at your house. I'll meet you at the project house."

"Don't go in."

"I'm not going to take your cheese stash."

"I know *that*. I meant that an assassin or who knows what could be in there." Earlier, I'd been thinking that the house might be decently protected because Sarrlevi had put up those wards, but he might have been working against me the whole time. He'd vouched for me to Thorvald and Willard, but then he'd used my intel to stalk down that poor dwarf woman. I didn't know *what* to think about him.

Abbas sighed. "I know. I was joking. I won't do anything unless I see Tinja. And then, I've got to nobly rescue her, Matti. She's just a little squirt, you know. She needs big guys to protect her."

"I know, but wait for me if you can. We're on the way." I tried not to think about how long it would take for the ferry to unload the cars and us to drive over to Bellevue.

Abbas hung up without confirming that he would wait. Damn it.

The fear that all of my friends would be killed tonight plagued my mind.

As we waited, the engine idling, for the unloading to start, Thorvald's phone buzzed again.

"Hey, Willard," she answered. "We took a detour, but we're on our way to Bellevue now."

"Good." It was quiet enough that I had no trouble hearing Willard's drawl. "When you're done investigating the trouble under Puletasi's house, I might need you to check out Bridle Trails. A woman went missing in the park—her dog came back from a walk without her—and there have been sightings of a sasquatch-like creature over there."

"It's not a sasquatch," I said. "Sarrlevi called it a *brysarrusi*. It's from the shifter home world."

"You hear that Willard?" Thorvald asked.

"Yes. She mentioned it when she was in my office. I'll check our compendiums on the Cosmic Realms for more information on it."

"Sarrlevi said they regenerate fast and are hard to kill," I said.

"I may need you to prioritize hunting it down tonight, Thorvald," Willard said. "Sorry, I know Saturday mornings are for sword fighting with your daughter, but this may take a while."

"I already told Amber," Thorvald said. "She canceled on me first, anyway. Said she had a concert tonight and would be too wiped in the morning for working out."

"It's hard being a mom."

"Something you know all about as a cat owner?"

"You've met my cat," Willard said. "She can be trying."

"That's an understatement. I'll check on the park after... everything else." Thorvald waved her phone in an expansive gesture that implied *everything else* was daunting.

I decided not to tell her that the creature was challenging enough to fight that Sarrlevi hadn't managed to kill it. Maybe he would have if he hadn't had to deal with werewolves shooting magical bullets at him at the same time.

My phone rang, a familiar number popping up.

"Hey, Zadie. Have you seen Tinja? Please tell me she came back to your apartment and is happily devouring everything in your pantry."

"No. She's missing?"

"Someone snatched her."

"I called to warn you that someone tried to snatch *me*."

I slumped back in the seat, any relief I might have felt that the Jeep was finally moving quashed by Zadie's words. "Sarrlevi?"

"Who?"

"A stuck-up blond elf."

"No, he's the one who kept me from being snatched."

"Give me the whole story, please."

"There was this big hairy brute with tusks that forced his way into my apartment. His head kept hitting the ceiling when he tried to grab me. And there was another one in the hallway with a hood up, muttering under his breath as his buddy chased me around my sofa. That was *after* they smashed in my door." Zadie was speaking rapidly, the words tumbling out. "My door, Matti! What's my landlord going to say?"

"Generally," Thorvald said, "they'll pay for the first or second door replacement. After that, you're on your own."

"They sound like orcs," I told Zadie. "You're lucky to be alive."

"I was on the verge of jumping out the window to escape them. I don't know if you noticed, but I don't live on the first floor."

"I noticed. You said Sarrlevi showed up?"

"Yeah. Loud clangs came from the hallway—a sword fight, I realized eventually—and he sprang inside. I glimpsed the hooded one limping away and grabbing his side, with blood all over his hand. There's still blood all over the hallway floor." Her voice went up an octave as she demanded, "What am I supposed to do about the *blood,* Matti?"

I looked at Thorvald, more because she might have advice on how to talk a terrified friend down from a ledge than because I wanted her opinion on the blood.

"If they're hard floors, a mix of water and dishwasher detergent usually works," Thorvald said, "though it's easiest if you deal with it before it dries. For carpets, it's tougher. The stuff for getting pet stains and odors out works pretty good."

If she hadn't been driving us off the ferry and toward the freeway, I might have punched her.

"I'm sorry you had to deal with that, Zadie." I understood her fear and regretted that she'd been targeted, but I also wanted to know the rest of what had happened. "Uhm, Sarrlevi? What did he do after that?"

"He came in and drove the other one off. And by drove off, I mean he lopped his pointed, blue-tinted ear off and cussed him out in a foreign language. Matti, there's an *ear* on my floor. Between my coffee table and sofa. What do I do with an *ear*?'

I thought Thorvald might have advice on ear disposal, but she merely touched hers and grimaced.

"Maybe you can compost it," I said. "Did Sarrlevi say anything afterward? Do you know where he went?"

"I don't think you're supposed to compost meat," Thorvald said.

"Does an ear count as meat?" I asked, though I was waiting to hear answers to my other questions. "It's mostly cartilage, isn't it?"

"I don't think you're supposed to compost cartilage."

"Fair."

The whoosh of a toilet flushing came over the phone.

"Are you... in the bathroom, Zadie?"

She hadn't been so distressed that she threw up, had she? I hadn't heard anything like that.

"I flushed it," she said.

"The ear?"

"Yeah."

"Now that you've handled that, uhm—"

"Yeah, yeah, the stuck-up blond guy with the swords. He asked what I knew about you and your mother. Matti, I didn't even know you had a mother."

"I don't. Not anymore."

"That's what I thought and I told him, but..." Zadie hesitated, such a long hesitation that I checked to make sure the call hadn't dropped. "It got kind of fuzzy. I can't remember everything he asked or what I said."

"That sounds like when dragons question people." Thorvald frowned. "They use magic to hold them still, lower their defenses, and read their minds."

"Can *elves* do it?"

"Freysha hasn't mentioned it, but she's kind of a goodly elf. I don't think she studies magic like that. If you want to grow forsythias from a pot to your ceiling in four days, she's your elf."

"Great, I'll call her for landscaping jobs."

"I wouldn't be surprised if Sarrlevi can use magic to read minds," Thorvald admitted.

I grimaced. He'd already tried to read mine. Zadie wasn't protected by whatever dwarven mental defenses I supposedly had. Maybe it was just dwarven stubbornness.

"I don't think I told him anything important about you." Zadie sounded apologetic, as if this were *her* fault. No way. It was all Sarrlevi. "I don't even know you that well. All I do is sell your houses. That's what I told him. And that you're popular at the Rose and Lily."

"Oh, great."

That earned a glance from Thorvald, though she was driving us along the curving on-ramp to the freeway. "If that's the way your tastes run, Sarrlevi will be disappointed."

"It's not, and he's not interested in me. Even if he were, he's making the lives of my friends—and apparently my mother's old friends—hell. I wouldn't kiss him if he gave me chocolates, flowers, and massaged my ass."

Thorvald didn't answer right away, either because I'd stunned her with the visual or because she was concentrating on traffic. Thanks to construction that had two lanes closed, and rain that had met us as we drove off the ferry, it was more gnarly than it should have been that late at night.

"Is the ass the preferred erogenous zone for dwarves?" she finally asked.

"It's all right. Did you know you're obnoxious to work with?"

"Willard tells me that frequently. Her precise term is *pain in the ass*."

"So... that must not be an erogenous zone for her."

Thorvald smirked at me. "I guess not. We'd have to ask her Australian shifter doctor friend."

"Why does she hire you if she finds you obnoxious?"

"I get the job done."

"Matti?" Zadie asked quietly.

"Yes?" I didn't know how much of the conversation with Thorvald she'd heard but apologized for being distracted.

"It's all right. I'm still in the bathroom, looking at the toilet. I feel like my world just got really weird, and I'm not sure what to do about it."

"Have some wine and pretend it didn't happen. Sarrlevi didn't do anything else, did he?" As if the mind reading wasn't bad enough.

"No. He bowed to me, suggested I hire a bodyguard to ensure intruder orcs can't enter my apartment building, and stepped over the broken door and left."

"Oh yeah, I'm sure bodyguards are in the budget for real-estate agents. I need to find Tinja and make sure Abbas isn't getting himself killed, but I'll call back to check on you later."

Wishing I'd been joking, I said goodbye and stared bleakly out the window. Not for the first time, I wished my mother were still alive and that I could ask her about the strange legacy she'd left me.

24

"You still don't know what it is these orcs, werewolves, and the *brysarrusi* are looking for under your house?" Thorvald asked, exiting the freeway.

"No." My nerves jittered as we headed toward Bridle Trails and the project house. "The recently bricked wall I told Willard about has, according to Sarrlevi, a gnomish enchantment on it. I was going to try to break through it with my hammer, but Sarrlevi pointed out that might be unwise."

"And you listened to him?"

"I agreed with him that it would be smart to take precautions. He's three hundred years old. He's probably done a lot of unwise things in his life and knows how to recognize them now."

"He's probably killed a lot of people who did unwise things."

"Resulting in bounties being put on their heads?"

"Yeah."

I shrugged, not wanting to lump my mother into that category. I couldn't believe she'd deserved to have an assassin sent after her. Her *sister* might deserve it, for having hired Sarrlevi in the first place.

"Anyway," I said, "we were interrupted by orcs attacking the house before I had time to study the wall. All I managed to get before running were the photos of dwarves, including my mother, and a ring."

"Everything about this secret seems to be related to dwarves, right?" Thorvald turned into the neighborhood, and the first hint of magic tickled my senses. Not surprisingly, it came from the direction of the house.

"So far, yes."

"Then why would a *gnomish* enchantment be on the wall?"

That made me shrug again. "I wondered about that. Gnomes and dwarves are often allies, right? Both species enjoy building and crafting. Maybe the dwarves called a gnomish enchanter in for help."

"Dwarves have good enchanters of their own. I sense magic." Thorvald frowned through the windshield. "A lot of it. And a lot of magical beings, including one with a very powerful aura. Not dragon powerful but... nothing I'd voluntarily jump into a fight with."

"It's the *brysarrusi*." My senses suggested it was still in the park, but right at the edge, maybe peering out toward the house and telepathically commanding its werewolf minions. I sensed a number of them. Ten? Twelve? At least as many as had been in the park the other night.

Most were near the property, though some were in the streets. Guarding the way to the house? Because they expected me?

"There are werewolves all over the place," Thorvald grumbled, slowing her Jeep.

"I know."

"We better park here and walk in. We can share my camouflaging charm if you don't have one of your own."

"I still have Tinja's." I winced, regretting that I hadn't forced her to take it back. Maybe if I had, she wouldn't have been caught.

As Thorvald pulled over and parked, I held it up, the dash lights glowing enough to highlight how ugly it was. She snorted, took the key from the ignition, and held it aloft. A similarly ugly charm dangled next to her fob, soda-can tabs, gum wrappers, and paperclips formed into a sphere.

"Yours must be of goblin make too," she said.

"Yes."

"I refused to put it on my thong and wear it around my neck. As handy as it is, a girl has to have some standards." Thorvald touched the attractive feline charm dangling in the center of her collection. "Sindari, I'm going to need your help tonight. We've driven into a bad neighborhood."

"Said no real-estate agent ever about Bridle Trails."

As silver mist formed in the back of the Jeep, Thorvald said, "Let's hope we're able to fix the problem so the real-estate agents of the East Side won't have to amend their descriptions of the area."

Her large silver tiger solidified from the mist, his head pressed against the top of the Jeep, and he gazed at Thorvald with forest-green eyes. He swished his tail and sniffed toward an open window.

I smell werewolves and a brysarrusi. *Tonight should prove to be most stimulating.*

Stimulating or terrifying?

"Sindari is excited to go into battle," Thorvald informed me.

"I wish I was." I rubbed the goblin charm, grabbed my hammer, and got out of the Jeep. If the creature remained in the park, and all we had to deal with were the werewolves, that might be doable. With two of us—three of us—and twelve of them, the odds weren't in our favor, but maybe they would kindly remain spread apart and not all attack at once.

Somehow opening the door with his paw—or his magic—Sindari let himself out of the Jeep and tested the air.

"Does he smell any goblins, by chance?" I asked. "Or a half-troll?"

The half-troll has been in the area. If there is a goblin, I do not yet smell it.

"Her," I said, grimacing at the demotion of Tinja to an *it.*

Sindari sniffed a fern, one of many creating privacy for a house set far back on its lot. *An elf has also been in the area. A familiar elf. Has Varlesh Sarrlevi changed his mind about assassinating you, Val? Lord Zavryd would be most displeased.*

"He's loitering around because of his interest in Puletasi here."

The tiger looked at me. We were close enough that he didn't seem to have any trouble seeing me through the charm's magic. I reminded myself that it would only be effective if I kept my distance from my enemies.

"You can call me Matti," I told him.

Half-dwarves are not common in this world.

"Are they common elsewhere?" I asked as Thorvald activated her own charm and started walking in the direction of the house.

They are rare and, of course, the dwarf blood is not mingled with human blood on other worlds. I once encountered a half-dwarf-orc that was quite ferocious.

"Did it have tusks?" Though such contemplations were far from my primary concern, I couldn't help but wonder which species' blood ended up being dominant in such a pairing.

She did have tusks. And a voluminous beard.

So, a mix of traits. Unless female orcs were more inclined toward hirsutism than I'd observed before.

Sindari continued to walk beside Thorvald but faded from my senses. He must have had an innate ability to camouflage himself, no goblin charms required.

Speak telepathically from here on out, Thorvald spoke into my mind, waving toward the road ahead.

The first werewolf hadn't yet come into view, but I sensed one to the right at the next intersection.

I don't know how to do that, I replied in my mind, envying Val for having an elven half-sister tutoring her. If my mother had lived, she presumably would have taught *me* magic. She would have taught me many things. *Can you hear me?*

As long as we're close, yes, Thorvald replied.

Even though I sensed our enemies and expected them, the huge gray wolf standing in the next street gave me a start. He was looking right at us.

Thorvald had already drawn her sword, and she started to lift it before pausing. Even though the wolf stared in our direction, he hadn't focused on us. The charms were working.

I pointed toward the backyard of the house on the corner. When I'd been fleeing the police, I'd crossed through it and another instead of going out on the street. Even with the charms, that route seemed safer.

Thorvald nodded and gestured for me to lead.

Careful not to rustle leaves or step on branches, I eased past rhododendrons and ferns, then padded across the grassy yard. A security camera mounted near the house's back door caught my eye and made me question this choice. Did magical charms fool technology?

I don't suppose you know if your boss convinced the police not to keep looking for me? I asked silently.

I'm not sure, Thorvald replied. *She may be waiting to see how things pan out.*

To see if we're able to deal with the problem? Or if I go rogue, kill a bunch of good guys, and flee to Canada?

Both of those things, yes.

As we slid through shrubs and climbed a fence to get into the yard next door, Sindari, who easily sprang over the fence, said, *A domesticated canine marks this yard frequently.*

I eyed the house, a doggie door visible in the back, and hurried between garden beds. *It's only two houses until we reach the one we want.*

My experience with the charms is that they mask one's aura and one's scent, Thorvald said. *As long as we don't make noise, we should be all right. This late, the dog ought to be sleeping.*

With werewolves all over the neighborhood? I asked. *It might not be sleeping* well.

I wouldn't.

Sindari! Thorvald spun and jerked her arm in a come-here wave. *This is not the time.*

Her magnificent silver tiger had backed up to a tree and was squirting urine at it.

It is always the time to inform an inferior predator that a superior predator has been in the area. The tiger sashayed to another tree.

Not when the dog might wake up and alert the world to our presence. Exasperated, Thorvald jogged to the next fence and sprang over it, as if running from the tiger would prompt him to hurry after her.

He appeared disinclined to do so and only slowly ambled in that direction.

A little tip for you, Thorvald told me as I climbed over the fence. *Every powerful item you acquire will have an up side and a down side. Nobody gets Superman powers without some kryptonite.*

I wondered if that applied to my hammer as well as territorial tigers.

Yapping came from the house. It belonged to a small dog, but that didn't mean it couldn't wake up everyone in the neighborhood.

I groaned inwardly. Though it had been inevitable with all these werewolves roaming about, I'd hoped in vain that everyone living in the area would remain oblivious and stay inside asleep where they would hopefully be safe.

As Sindari sprang over the fence to join us in the backyard adjacent to mine, a white dog with curly fur shot through the pet door behind us. The barking grew louder, ringing from the trees.

Thanks so much, Sindari. Thorvald shot him a dark look.

You don't know that I caused that. There are werewolves nearby. Many of them.

The dog ran straight to the first tree you marked. I doubt the wolves were back there whizzing in its yard.

Ignoring her, Sindari padded toward the property line. Through the trees, I could see the project house and grimaced. The lights were on. I hadn't left them on.

Someone must have gotten past the wards. I stopped between the trees and pointed.

Thorvald gazed at the kitchen window. *I sense two or three beings inside... I think they're orcs.*

There's a shaman. Maybe he was able to get through Sarrlevi's wards? He was examining them the other night, I think.

I sense and smell your goblin, Sindari said, his back to the dog that was now yapping at the fence behind us. *She is inside.*

We might as well have sounded an air horn. The werewolves in the street were gathering in front of the house. Near the mossy patio behind the project house, one stood in human form with his arms crossed.

She's alive, right? I struggled to sense her, though I could detect the orcs now. One was notably more powerful than the others. The shaman. *Being held captive?*

She is alive, Sindari said.

That's something anyway. But why did they bring her here? She knows even less than I do.

They don't have you, Thorvald pointed out.

Not yet. I frowned back at the dog, wishing I had something with which to shoo it away.

Abruptly, it stopped barking, sprinted back to the house, and disappeared through the dog door.

I expected you to come eventually, a familiar voice spoke telepathically from beside us. Sarrlevi. *I did not expect your arrival to be so blatant.*

I'm a blatant kind of girl. Thorvald frowned back at the bushes.

Though I believed he was close, I could only hear Sarrlevi's telepathic voice, not sense or see him.

You are, Sarrlevi agreed. *And I know the mongrel dwarf is, so I do not know why I expected stealth from either of you.*

I ground my teeth. *It's Matti. I spent the night in your bed. You'd think you could remember my name.*

In the dark, I didn't *see* Thorvald's eyebrows fly upward, but I sensed her reaction.

In his guest bed, I amended quickly.

A wolf howled from the street, making the hair rise on the back of my neck. The human-form shifter near the patio prowled toward the back of the house. He halted, waved his hand at the air in front of him, then jerked it back as he encountered Sarrlevi's magic.

What did you do to the dog? Thorvald asked him.

Convinced it a wolf was about to jump out and eat it, Sarrlevi replied. *Even though the wolves are far more interested in attacking us.*

What did you do to Artie the dwarf? I glared in the direction where I thought he stood, more concerned about *that*. The dog might have been scared, but it had seemed fine.

Questioned her, he said without hesitation.

With your hand around her neck? The kid out front said you attacked her. I didn't show you those photos so you could stalk those poor dwarves and threaten them.

I did not threaten her, and she attacked me. *I merely defended myself.*

By wrapping a hand around her throat.

To stop her from throwing another axe at me? Yes.

You must have threatened her if she hurled weapons at you. Dwarves aren't homicidal.

Perhaps not, but some have a short temper. He was glaring at me now. I couldn't see it, but I could *feel* it. *She did recognize me. That's likely what prompted the visceral reaction.*

Do most people who recognize you throw blades at you?

Most run in the other direction, he said coolly.

Uh, guys? Thorvald held up her hand.

Sindari was crouching, poised to spring as two werewolves in human form came around the side of the house. They pointed at the one on the patio and then into the bushes. *Our* bushes.

The charms might have kept them from sensing us, but thanks to the dog alarm going off, they had a good idea that *someone* was in the area.

Maybe you can discuss that later, Thorvald added. *We need to deal with the werewolves, or they're going to figure out where we are and try to deal with* us.

They can try, Sarrlevi said, his telepathic tone still cool, as if he was irked with me.

Well, I was irked with him for threatening that dwarf woman. I didn't believe she'd tried to kill him first without provocation. Unless...

I rocked back with a realization. Artie must have recognized him because she'd been with my mother all those years ago. As I'd considered before, the dwarves in those Polaroids could have been my mother's friends or protectors. Or both. If she'd been a princess, it made sense that she might have had people from her father's court who'd sworn to protect her. Maybe even accompany her to a wild world to ensure an assassin didn't find her?

The shifters are not strong enough to pass through my wards, Sarrlevi said. *Thorvald, here. I will make it so you can go through them. The three of us can step inside then and will only need to focus on orcs in the house.*

Right, Thorvald said. *Good.*

Unless you wish to retrieve your half-troll acquaintance first, he added.

Abbas? Where is he? I hadn't sensed him yet, though Sindari had said he smelled him.

The brysarrusi *has him in the park,* Sarrlevi said.

My fist clenched. I wanted to punch something. *Why?*

To lure you away from the house, I assume.

A new voice spoke into my mind, one I didn't recognize. *We have your friend.* The speaker—the orc shaman?—popped an image into my mind of Tinja, tied, gagged, and scared. She knelt on the packed dirt floor with that brick wall behind her. Two hulking orcs stood to either side of her, axes pointed at her neck. *Come inside, remove the enchantment, and knock down this wall, or we will kill her.*

Frustration boiled inside me, and I wanted to scream with rage. How was I supposed to pick which friend to go after first? Would Sarrlevi and Thorvald split up to help them both? Unfortunately, my friends didn't mean anything to them. I doubted *I* meant anything to them either.

I looked at Thorvald to check if she'd heard the shaman, but she was looking in Sarrlevi's direction, not at the house or the werewolves arguing in the backyard and pointing toward our bushes. Any second, they were going to head toward us.

Guys, I said, hoping Thorvald and Sarrlevi were still listening to my thoughts, *we need to—*

Intense pain erupted inside my brain. If not for the werewolves nearby, I would have cried out. I almost did anyway. Ten times worse than any headache I'd ever experienced, it was as if someone had driven a stake into my skull.

My knees weakened, and I couldn't keep from crumpling to

the ground. I managed to keep hold of my hammer, though I wanted to grab my head, to find some way to stop the pain.

A hand rested on my back. Thorvald's? Sarrlevi's? I couldn't focus through the pain to figure that out.

Come inside, the shaman ordered, and I was certain he was responsible for the mental attack. *Now. The artifact has been guarded for long enough. Our people deserve it. Your green friend will experience everything you feel and more. The only way to stop that torment is for you to come inside.*

Why can't you knock down the wall yourself? I demanded, struggling not to pant, not to make noise and give away our position.

I am not a dwarf or a gnome.

What kind of answer was that? I wasn't either of those things either, not fully.

Despite my efforts to keep from rolling around on the ground and crying out, I must have gasped, for Thorvald said, *They heard her. Damn it.*

Deal with the werewolves, Sarrlevi said. *I'll help her.*

I hissed, not wanting to be left alone with the guy who tormented dwarves for a side gig.

But as the two werewolves—no, all three—headed in our direction, there wasn't time to debate. Thorvald raised her weapon and sprang into the yard. Her tiger companion leaped out ahead of her, charging our enemies.

Another howl came from the street. A call for reinforcements?

The pain in my head intensified, and black dots floated across my vision. I tried to will the attack away, to somehow mentally brick off my mind, but the shaman was too strong. He only punished me further for my attempt to push him away.

Tears leaked from my eyes as I gasped for air and struggled not to pass out. If I did, Tinja and Abbas might not survive the night. Hell, *I* might not survive the night.

25

A WALL SEEMED TO FORM AROUND MY HEAD, AND THE STABS OF PAIN assailing my mind lessened. I grew aware of the clang of metal against fang and the roars of a tiger. Also of the hand on my back. It belonged to Sarrlevi. He stood at my side, his magic strengthening, pushing back the orc shaman's attack until it disappeared completely.

My relief was so intense that I slumped to the side, leaning against a tree. No, that was his leg.

Crouched beside me, Sarrlevi was visible now, his magic protecting me as he watched the battle between Sindari and Thorvald and three shifters, two in human form and one a great shaggy wolf. I sensed more of their kind heading toward the backyard.

"Go help her," I rasped, my body shaky after the attack. "I'll join in as soon as I can stand."

My hand was still wrapped around the haft of my hammer. Good. It was bad enough I'd slumped against Sarrlevi; I didn't want him to think I was so pathetic that I couldn't keep a grip on my weapon. So much for me having some dwarven resistance to mental intrusions.

"Or, if you can, help my friend in the park. The half-troll. Please." I hated to ask him for anything, but it was better than letting Abbas die.

I would have a hard time fighting and protecting you at the same time, Sarrlevi said. *It's likely the shaman will resume his attack as soon as I am distracted.*

I'll be fine.

You weren't fine a minute ago.

I'll survive, damn it. Just don't let anyone die. Though I was most worried about my friends, it occurred to me that if Thorvald died, Willard might hold me responsible and unleash the power of the entire military against me. This week kept getting worse and worse.

Stay here. As two more wolves loped into view, Sarrlevi rose and drew his twin long swords. *Do not let the shaman coerce you into the house. It's clearly a trap.*

"No shit," I said.

But, as he sprang out to help Thorvald, I accepted that I would have to walk into that trap. I couldn't leave Tinja to be tormented, and I didn't know how to get her out without going in myself.

Gunshots fired. Thorvald had a firearm, but the shooter was one of the werewolves, one lurking by the corner of the house, and trying to pick off his enemies without engaging them physically.

Sarrlevi, after being injured in the park, must have found a new charm or enhancement to his armor, for the bullets struck something invisible around him and pinged off into the woods. One slammed into a tree above my head. Another lodged in the siding of the house.

Though it should have been the last thing on my mind, I couldn't help but think that was one more thing I would have to fix before I could sell the place.

Grunting, I used my hammer as a crutch to push to my feet. My knees were still weak, and I wobbled, stubbed my toe on a rock, and almost lurched into the bushes. Though worried I would be a liability instead of an ally until I recovered, I locked my joints and refused to slump back down. Thorvald and Sarrlevi were accomplished fighters, but they were outnumbered.

I almost shouted for them to run through the wards, as we'd talked about before, but I didn't know if Sarrlevi had been given enough time to make it so Thorvald could pass.

After firing again at Sarrlevi and failing to get past his defenses, the werewolf sniper shifted his aim toward Thorvald.

"No, you don't," I growled and grabbed the rock.

My arms were as weak as my legs, but a jolt of adrenaline gave me the strength to hurl it. It slammed into his chest, and I propelled my wobbly legs into motion and charged at him.

The werewolf had been about to fire again, but when the rock struck him, it disrupted his aim. His shot went wide. Unfortunately, he wasn't so injured that he dropped the weapon. Snarling, he shifted the gun toward me.

Still ten feet away, I wouldn't get to him in time. But his gun jammed. My first bit of luck all week.

Before he could clear the round, I dove toward his legs. Rolling hard across the grass, like a dwarven bowling ball aimed at a pin, I swung my hammer as I approached. He cursed and tried to scramble out of the way. My hammer gave me the reach to clip him, the head colliding with his knee.

That time, he dropped the firearm. I pushed myself to my feet, swinging again as his weapon landed in the grass. He sprang back, but I must have been faster than I looked, for he didn't move quickly enough. The hammer crunched into his ribs.

With a roar, he backed away, blurring as he attempted to shift into wolf form. Relentless, I followed him, bashing him again before he could make the change.

The magic of the hammer, or maybe simply receiving a thud to the chest, made his transformation falter. He turned back into a human in time for me to club him in the side of the head. Had the circumstances been less dire, I wouldn't have aimed for such a lethal target, but I was beyond caring if I killed these guys. Their greed to get whatever *artifact* was buried down there was pissing me the hell off.

The blow sent the werewolf tumbling into the side of the house. He hit the siding, crumpled to the ground, and didn't stir again.

The clangs of other battles continued in the backyard. Thorvald and Sarrlevi fought back-to-back, their weapons a blur as they defended against and took down their enemies. The original three werewolves were on the ground around them, dead or unconscious, but more had arrived.

Even though I sensed two more running in from the street, I couldn't help but watch elf and half-elf for a moment. Their grace and beauty in battle, especially Sarrlevi's, was amazing to behold, like the most elite Olympic athletes performing feats the rest of humanity found impossible to match. And they complemented each other well, each defending their half of the circle they battled within, two people with elven blood, born to fight together.

A stab of envy prodded me, a sad certainty that my stubby half-dwarven legs and arms would never mesh with the fighting styles of the tall agile elves. If we tried to go into battle together like that, they would probably trip over me.

Frustrated by the thought that I wasn't good enough, I pushed aside my earlier weakness and sprang into the path of the two wolves rushing to join the battle.

It might not have been as elegant, but my hammer did some blurring of its own. Instead of waiting for the wolves to reach me, I sprang at the one on the left, swinging the hammer toward his furry head while angling to land beside him, so he would be in the way if his buddy attacked me.

With the preternatural speed of their kind, he ducked below

the hammer, jaws snapping toward me. But I'd landed out of reach of his fangs and was already sending a low kick around to sweep his hind legs out from under him. The attack would have knocked down a human, but he lurched forward and recovered, taking his weight on his forelegs until he found his balance.

The other wolf did indeed turn to attack me. When he couldn't plow through his buddy, he sprang over him.

Though surprised, I had time to jab the hammer toward his face. The top smacked into his snout, halting his airborne assault in midair.

The lower wolf had recovered and twisted toward me, attempting to bite me again. My foot came up in a straight kick, and his jaws clattered as I struck him in the chin.

The other wolf, blood dripping from his squashed snout, landed on his buddy's back instead of clearing him. I didn't pause, instead swinging again while they were discombobulated. I connected solidly with one, hammer cracking into ribs, and knocked him into the bushes. Branches shuddered and snapped under his weight.

The remaining wolf snarled but regarded me more warily now that he was alone and injured. Semi alone. I could sense others in the area and, knowing more threats would come, didn't hesitate to spring for this one. He lunged first, trying to surprise me. His jaws opened, fangs white against night's darkness, and went for my shin.

That shin had barely recovered from my *last* encounter with werewolf teeth. I struck him in the face with the hammer before his jaws could close around my leg. He tumbled toward the house but yelped before hitting it, then found his feet and ran off toward the street. Maybe he'd struck the wards. I didn't know exactly where they were myself, only that they didn't keep bullets or bodies from getting through.

A rustle came from behind me, and I whirled with my

hammer raised and what had to be fury—or maybe blood lust—in my eyes.

"Easy, killer." Thorvald still had her sword out, but she lifted her free hand and smiled. "We're on the same side."

Sarrlevi, his swords in hand but lowered, smirked at me, that all-too-knowing smirk that made me crazy.

I hoped I'd looked competent as I'd battled the shifters, but I'd been pissed, and my reflexes had taken over. I'd probably looked like a maniac. At the least, I was dripping sweat and grimaced as I dragged a sleeve across my brow. Sarrlevi wasn't sweating. Elves probably didn't do that. Too inelegant.

Sindari, his silver fur spattered with blood that didn't appear to be his, was swishing his tail as he looked toward the street. I sensed three or four more werewolves out there, but they weren't moving. A lot of their comrades were unconscious—or dead. With luck, they had decided not to test us further, but I worried they might have called for more reinforcements. Or be communicating with the creature in the park.

"What's the plan for dealing with the orcs?" Thorvald tilted her head toward the house.

I grimaced, relieved the shaman hadn't attacked me again while I'd been fighting. That pain had been crippling, and, if I'd crumpled, the werewolves would have taken advantage and killed me. I had no doubt.

"Not walking into a trap." Sarrlevi held my gaze.

"Always a good idea," Thorvald said, not aware of our earlier conversation.

"When your friend is being tormented and used as bait," I said, glaring back at Sarrlevi, "sometimes you don't have an option."

Thorvald grimaced but nodded. "The shaman probably used his magic to observe us fighting. He'll know exactly what to expect."

"I can handle a shaman," Sarrlevi said.

"I'd rather you handle the monster in the park," I said. "Will you? And help my half-troll friend? While I get Tinja?"

Sarrlevi considered me. I wanted to shake him and *make* him help, but there was little else I could offer him.

"What are you doing here, anyway, Sarrlevi?" Thorvald asked, looking from him to me, as if I might know.

But I still hadn't figured him out. He kept showing up and helping me, but he was also harassing the people around me.

"This isn't your fight, is it?" Thorvald added.

"Unless you think whatever is under the house will lead you to my mother," I said. "My mother's *remains*."

"It may," Sarrlevi said.

"Do you have any idea what this artifact is?" Thorvald asked him. "Willard doesn't know."

"I've heard the shifters refer to it as the dwarven artifact." Sarrlevi shrugged. "That's all."

"How has it been down there for forty years, and everyone is just *now* trying to get it?" Thorvald asked.

"Up until recently, I think the renter was always guarding it." I shifted my weight from foot to foot, impatient. Couldn't we have this discussion later? Whether Sarrlevi would help or not, I had to try to get my friends.

"If he was a full-blooded dwarf and had magic, he could have been powerful, I suppose," Thorvald said.

"A match for an orc shaman, yes." Sarrlevi lifted his chin. "As am I."

"You're still cocky, I see," Thorvald said.

His eyelids closed halfway as he regarded her. "I will duel you again any time you wish to test yourself. I'd like a rematch."

"I bet you would." She grinned at him. "It's got to make you crazy that I beat you. Not many of your targets do, I'll wager."

"No. I would not be alive if I was bested often. I went from overestimating you and your knowledge of your dragon blade in our first encounter to underestimating how much you could quickly learn in our second."

"I know. It was awesome." Thorvald slapped him on the shoulder.

That should have irritated some of the smugness off his face, but he didn't acknowledge her, instead spinning and looking toward the side yard. Or... in the direction of the park?

The brysarrusi *is coming,* Sindari warned us.

Thorvald's grin dropped.

"Is my friend with it?" I asked.

"No," Sarrlevi said.

What did *that* mean? That Abbas had been left behind? Left for *dead*?

Sarrlevi looked at me. "I will deal with it. You and Thorvald will have to fight the shaman."

"Always a good time," she muttered.

I hesitated. I'd *wanted* Sarrlevi to confront the *brysarrusi* and find Abbas, but now that he'd volunteered, I remembered how wrecked he'd been in that first fight with it. What if I lost Abbas *and* Sarrlevi was killed?

"Be careful," I blurted as he headed toward the street.

Talk about stupid and obvious advice.

Sarrlevi looked back over his shoulder at us. All he said was, "Thorvald, keep her alive."

"That *is* one of my goals for the night," Thorvald said and headed for the back door.

I paused, for the *brysarrusi* had come into view between the trees, with two hulking werewolves in human form walking at its side. Their eyes were glazed, the magic the creature exuded wrapped around them. Enslaving them?

Snarling, it strode toward the house, not looking at Sarrlevi's approach. Like everyone else, it wanted what lay underneath it.

Sarrlevi sprang to intercept the *brysarrusi*. As one, the two werewolves surged toward him. He slashed and kicked, too quick for them. One pitched to the ground, grabbing at blood spurting from its throat. The second would have followed, but the *brysar-rusi* roared and rushed Sarrlevi.

He leaped into the air, whirling to slash at its neck as he evaded swipes from powerful claws that should have torn him to pieces. But he twisted, dodging and attacking simultaneously as he seemed to defy gravity, landing numerous blows before he touched down.

"Amazing," I muttered, enraptured despite myself.

Thorvald jogged back and gripped my arm. "In case that thing wins and wants to team up with the orcs, we may want to go in while he's keeping it busy."

"Right." I ripped my gaze from the battle and ran toward the back door.

Do not die, Sarrlevi told me telepathically, even as he kept fighting.

Because you didn't learn anything useful from Artie, and I'm your only lead when it comes to finding my mother?

You are my only lead.

Yeah, I dig you too.

Metal clashed against claw, the screech worse than fingernails on a chalkboard. Sarrlevi didn't answer me. He was too busy trying to stay alive.

26

THE HOUSE SMELLED OF DIRT FRESHLY TRACKED IN—OR DUG UP from below—and more faintly of burning ozone. Weapons at the ready, Thorvald and I headed for the stairs, with Sindari checking the rooms we passed. I sensed the orcs and Tinja below, not in the basement but *under* the basement, but that didn't mean there weren't camouflaged enemies along the way. Or traps.

The post on one of the railings leading downstairs had been broken—kicked, it looked like—and I scowled. Even though I'd intended to replace the railing with something more modern, the destruction this house kept receiving irritated me no end.

"One more reason to kick that shaman's ass," I muttered, trying to marshal my anger to give me the courage to face him. With Sarrlevi busy, there wouldn't be anyone to protect me from another mental attack.

"Because one of his minions broke your staircase?" Thorvald asked softly.

"It's a legitimate reason to deliver an ass kicking."

"I suppose that's true." Before we headed down, she added,

"Sindari and I are camouflaged again. If we can surprise them, we will."

I nodded and didn't bother to rub Tinja's goblin charm. Its camouflaging magic had likely worn off when we'd been fighting, and I wanted the shaman to know I was coming anyway. If he thought I had run off, he might hurt Tinja. She might only be alive because he was using her as bait.

Nobody stopped us as we headed into the basement, nor did any traps spring. Probably because we were already walking into the one the shaman had set.

Yellow light glowed from the laundry room.

"Matti?" came Tinja's reedy voice from below the hole in the floor.

"I'm here," I said, relieved at the confirmation that she was alive and able to speak. "I need you to show me the updates to your blueprints, so you'd better be okay."

She didn't respond.

I could sense her aura, but it was dwarfed by that of the shaman. Even full-blooded goblins weren't powerful magical beings and had to be crafty to avoid being enslaved and used by others. I could also sense the two other orcs, though their auras weren't as significant. Minions. If I could distract the shaman, maybe Sindari and Thorvald could take those guys out, then help me with their leader.

I eyed the washer and dryer still hooked up a few feet from the hole in the floor. Since I hadn't removed any joists, they ought to be well supported, but I thought of arranging to drop them on the shaman's head. Sadly, when I peered over the edge, he wasn't standing near the hole. He had his back to the brick wall, a hand around Tinja's neck, while his two minions crouched in front of them, gripping heavy axes as they glowered up at me.

Come down here and tear away this enchantment, dwarf mongrel, the shaman spoke into my mind, *or your friend will die.*

Why did bad guys always want to wrap their big bully hands around innocent people's necks?

"Let her go so she can climb up here, and I'll see what I can do," I offered, though the rope Sarrlevi had lowered before was gone.

You will drop the wall, and then I will toss her out of this chamber. His hand tightened around Tinja's throat.

She squeaked, her fingers flying up to grip his arm, but she couldn't budge it. Fear made her eyes round, tears filming them.

"Fine." I lifted a hand. "I'm coming down to help." Meeting Tinja's eyes, I whispered, "I'm so sorry."

Thorvald was in my peripheral vision and pointed to indicate she would slip down after I did. Careful not to look at her, I lowered myself through the hole, dropping to the ground and rolling to soften the impact. I came up with my hammer gripped in both hands and wrestled with the temptation to try to spring past the minions to brain the shaman.

But a whisper of pain stabbed my mind. *Little fighter, do not bring a blunt weapon to a battle with one who commands the elements. You will die a death of agony and suffering.*

The shaman, his grip still tight around Tinja's neck, dragged her to the side and extended a hand toward the wall in invitation. As if I had any idea how to remove a gnomish enchantment. Or a dwarven enchantment for that matter.

"I'll take a stab at it. Or rather a blow." I hefted the hammer, hoping the enchantments on *it* could do the trick. I had no doubt that it was nearly indestructible; what I didn't know was if it could bash through magical protections.

The minions eyed the weapon warily as I hefted it, but all they did was back up, staying between me and their boss.

The Ruin Bringer and her kitty will step out of the shadows and assist you, the shaman said.

"The who?"

We sensed her when she fought and know she is with you.

Behind me, throats cleared in the shadows of the chamber. I didn't want to take my eyes from the shaman and his two minions, but I couldn't help but glance back.

Six male orc warriors in armor appeared, standing in front of a female orc wearing a fur robe and bone necklace, her gnarly hand resting on an orb atop a staff. She released it as she bared her teeth at me, and I felt the whisper of magic disappearing. Whatever camouflaging spell she'd used to keep me from detecting her and the warriors before.

Step out, Ruin Bringer, or this goblin dies. The male shaman squeezed Tinja's throat again.

I surged toward him with my hammer, but he attacked my mind. The pain came upon me so suddenly that I only made it halfway to him before my knees buckled. I had to jam my hammer down, using it as a crutch to keep from collapsing. Even that was barely enough as pain jackhammered in my head.

"All right, all right." Thorvald and her tiger came into view a few feet to my right, her back to an empty wall and her sword pointed at the male shaman. "Knock off all the evil-emperor crap. We don't even care about this artifact you're looking for."

The pain lessened but didn't disappear completely as the shaman watched me. *The dwarf mongrel cares.*

"No," I snarled, "I really don't."

That might have been a lie. I didn't want to care about some magical trinket, but ever since I'd seen my mother's face in those photos...

Then you will use your power to break down the brick wall so we can retrieve it.

"I'll do my best." I didn't want to help them, especially since I didn't trust him to let Tinja go once he got his prize, but with so many orcs down there with us now, I didn't have a choice.

When I stepped up to rest a hand on the wall, Thorvald came

up to my shoulder. The bricks were still warm to the touch and infused with magic, but I knew little more than that. My senses weren't refined enough to tell a dwarven enchantment from a gnomish one.

"Do you know how to break it?" Thorvald whispered. "Or what's behind it?"

"No." I moved my hand along the wall, as if it might speak to me in some way and tell me what to do. More likely, it would knock me on my ass, as Sarrlevi had warned.

"So, what's your plan?"

"Hit it with my hammer and hope for the best." I eyed her warily, expecting judgment.

But she smirked. "Sounds a lot like one of my plans."

Sindari let out something that sounded like a sigh. Did tigers sigh?

"Does your boss approve of such methods?"

"Willard? Nah, she thinks I'm a brute. Later, I'll tell you the story of how my sword glowed and pulsed like a lighthouse for a week after I bashed an artifact."

Enough scheming! The female orc shaman shook her staff at us.

A threatening tingle of magic ran over my skin. It reminded me of standing under high-voltage power lines, and I suspected the sensation would get a lot stronger if we dawdled.

"We're not scheming," Thorvald said, "we're bonding. It's something mongrels do."

None of the orcs smiled. Not that we'd know if they did. Those tusks made every facial expression look like a scowl.

The orcs do not appear amused by your humor, Sindari observed. His back was to the wall as he guarded Thorvald and we contemplated our options.

"I know," she said. "It's weird how few enemies appreciate my wit."

"I'm going to try to knock it down." I waved for Thorvald to stand back and looked at Tinja. "Are you all right? Can you breathe?"

The damn shaman still had his hand around her neck.

"I'm being tortured and am dying and won't be able to finish my homework, Matti," Tinja squeaked. "It's due in two days. This isn't right. Goblins aren't meant to be captured. We're not brave!"

Silence! both shamans roared in our minds.

Tinja whimpered and didn't speak again. I hefted my hammer, letting my frustration at not being able to help her fuel my muscles, and pounded it into the brick wall.

Usually, the magical hammer would pulverize such a mundane material. Not this time. It was as if I'd hit solid steel, and a jolt ran up my arms to my spine and jaw, making my every nerve hurt.

"That plan didn't work as well as I'd hoped," I whispered to Thorvald, shaking out my arms.

"It didn't look like it. Do you have a Plan B?"

"Hit the wall harder?" My aching joints objected to that plan.

"Do you know any power words for your hammer?"

"Power what?"

"Like *eravekt*." Thorvald waved her hand at the hammer and forcefully said, "*Eravekt!*"

Her sword glowed bright blue. The double head of my hammer also glowed, a soft silver-blue that illuminated the wall like a lantern.

"Uh, no." I might have admired the effect—the inner glow highlighted the beauty of the patterns and runes engraved in the metal—but the orcs were muttering among themselves and shifting impatiently from foot to foot. "Will that make it hit harder?"

"I don't think so, but it lights up a tunnel nicely if you don't have a torch. My sword—Storm or *Hyrek* in Dwarven—has a number of commands. About twenty."

Hyrek was one of the Dwarven words I knew. One of Mom's nursery rhymes had taught terms for weather and the seasons.

"I didn't know the power words until a nice dwarf enchanter helped me research the blade and taught me to use them," Thorvald admitted.

I wished *I* had a dwarf enchanter tutor. No, I admitted with a twinge of longing. I wished I had my mother.

"It's common for dwarves to enchant their powerful weapons with extra abilities, but if the previous owner didn't teach the words of power to you, you're out of luck beyond guessing the typical ones."

"I'm sure my mother would have taught me one day. If she'd lived." I grimaced again and drew my hammer back, thinking about trying to hit the wall higher up in the hope that it would be weaker up there.

"That's interesting." Thorvald pointed to the top of my hammer, a flat circle between the two heads. It had a tuft of werewolf fur stuck to it from my earlier skirmish.

A rune I'd never seen before—it wasn't engraved in the metal like the others—glowed silver inside the circle, as if it had been painted there with an invisible pen and only showed up under certain circumstances. Such as when one uttered that power word?

Unlike the other runes, which I believed were representative of Dwarven letters or words, it was pictographic. It looked like the mouth of a cave with a sun glowing in it.

"Do you know what it means?" Thorvald added.

"No idea."

Since the imagery had nothing to do with fighting, it seemed an odd choice for a weapon, though maybe it signified the dwarven afterlife, a place where warriors who died bravely in battle ended up.

If you are not able to knock down the brick wall, the shaman said, unimpressed by our glowing weapons. *I will tear up all the human domiciles to access what is on the other side from above. And I will use the head of this goblin as my shovel.*

"Hey, Tusks." Thorvald glared at him. "What's the hurry? You got a bus to catch?"

The werewolf shifters and their master infest this location like termites. The shaman looked in the direction of the street—was Sarrlevi still battling the *brysarrusi* up there? *The assassin's half-hearted wards will not keep them out indefinitely. But we will already have the artifact and have left by the time they arrive.* His eyes closed to slits as he looked back to us. *I will ensure it.*

"I don't think they'll have luck going around," Thorvald muttered, glancing toward the closest wall and the ceiling above. "All the support beams and posts have some magic about them. I think the dwarves only wanted one way into this place." She waved at my glowing hammer. "Try again anyway. Willard won't be happy if we let orcs raze the neighborhood in an attempt to find a way around the dwarven magic."

I almost pointed out that *we* weren't working for Willard—only she was—but I didn't want to see the neighborhood razed either. Beyond humanitarian concerns, such things made it hard to resell a house.

Resting my hands on the brick wall hadn't been illuminating, so I gripped my hammer and gazed down at it. Thorvald's suggestion that it had more powers than its enhanced durability hadn't surprised me, and I wondered if any of the Dwarven terms I knew might also be power words.

Too bad I couldn't remember my mother ever saying anything around the hammer. Not that I'd seen her go into battle often. Not until the night she died.

A memory I'd forgotten surfaced, Mom yelling a war cry and hitting one of the soldiers with the hammer. Lightning had shot out from the head, not only striking the man but arcing and hitting an outlet and light fixture. That had been how the building caught on fire.

Had it been a war cry? Or had she shouted a command? One of these power words?

I shook my head. I couldn't remember.

"What does the artifact that you want do?" Thorvald asked the shaman. "We're not helping you get something that will let you take over the world, are we?"

Nobody wants this prison hole of a planet, the shaman replied. *It will aid our people in great ways.*

"Because it does... what?" Thorvald asked.

The shaman only growled for an answer.

Maybe it would be worth trying *hyrek* as a power word. Lightning was related to storms, wasn't it?

"*Hyrek,*" I whispered to my hammer. In case it helped, I also imagined it adding power to my blows and allowing me to batter down the brick wall.

A tingle ran through the haft, buzzing against my palms. Not sure if that was a warning or a sign that magic was infusing it, I hefted it for another swing. Bracing myself for another jarring jolt of pain, I slammed it into the brick wall.

Light flashed, and silver and blue streaks of lightning sprang from the hammer as it struck. Branches crackled all along the wall, as if brick were a perfect conduit for electricity. Several voices around me cried out. A whoosh of hot buzzing air blasted past me as cracks appeared in the brick.

The magic did a lot more than *whoosh* for everyone around me. Thorvald flew backward. All the orcs except for the two shamans, who somehow braced themselves, did too. Tinja was blown out of the grip of the male shaman, tumbling away with the flailing warriors. Sindari roared and lowered himself, belly almost touching the ground, and managed to keep from flying away.

Snaps came from the wall, and mortar crumbled, dust flying

into the air as the lightning faded. The magic of the gnomish enchantment disappeared from my senses. I backed away as bricks fell from the wall. More dust clouded the air as they hit the ground, and I coughed, backing even farther.

With most of the orcs down or at least distracted, I was tempted to attack them, but not with the two shamans still standing and watching me intently. They barked orders to their minions, and the warriors scrambled to their feet. None of them had grabbed Tinja, so I hurried to her side and helped her up.

"Stick with me," I whispered, hoping I could keep the shamans from recapturing her.

She groaned. "I'm starting to wish I'd accepted Gondo's invitation to the Coffee Dragon tonight."

"I hear the goblins that frequent that place are rowdy. You wouldn't have been able to concentrate on finishing your homework."

"*Orcs* are rowdy too." Tinja glowered around at them.

I ignored them and looked at the pile of bricks, all that remained of the wall. Thorvald was back on her feet, Sindari at her side as we gazed at a now-revealed tunnel, more beams and posts supporting it as it stretched toward the house with the yapping dog. Toward and *beyond* that house, I guessed. There was no light other than what came from our glowing weapons, so we couldn't see where the tunnel led or how far it went, but the ceiling was high, the sides wide. A substantial passageway.

"I thought there would be a room or vault." Thorvald looked at me.

Shrugging, I rested a hand on Tinja's back to keep her at my side. So far, the shamans hadn't rushed over to grab her. They were contemplating the tunnel.

I couldn't detect the aura of a powerful artifact, but it could have been camouflaged or behind another wall that blocked our senses. I was, however, aware of... I wasn't sure what. Magic. It didn't feel like an artifact but something that was almost but not quite alive. It puzzled me, and I couldn't remember sensing anything like it before.

"Do you feel that?" I whispered to Thorvald.

"Yeah."

"Do you know what it is?" I assumed she'd encountered all manner of magical creatures in her years as an Army contractor.

"No."

"Ah."

"It does feel like dwarven magic though." Thorvald looked at my hammer, then me, then back down the tunnel.

"Normally, I would find that comforting, but the dwarves were determined to keep people out of this place. I'm not sure their magic will welcome me. Or any of us."

"Probably not." Thorvald took a couple of steps into the exposed tunnel and knelt to pick up something on the ground. She held her palm open to show me. More bullet casings like the one I'd found down here that first night. "It looks like those with the rifles got past the brick wall."

"I think," I said, remembering how recently the flooring had been installed and how bright and new the mortar between the bricks had been, "those are the people who put *up* the wall."

"To keep others from exploring down here after they were done?"

"Or to keep whatever they found trapped down here. They must have built the wall, then gotten a gnome enchanter to add magic to it. If my—if the dwarves had been responsible, it wouldn't have been infused with gnomish magic."

"No. If it weren't the middle of the night, I'd be tempted to call my friend Nin and ask if she ever makes house calls—or knows of a gnomish enchanter who does." Thorvald touched her pocket, maybe thinking of doing so, regardless of the time.

But the orcs crowded around the tunnel entrance behind us,

their weapons leveled at our backs. Tinja squeaked and squeezed between Thorvald and me.

There will be traps, the male shaman said. *Dwarves* always *build traps. You will lead.*

"So we trigger them and die first, huh?" Thorvald said.

The shamans bared their teeth in what might have been a smile.

27

The tunnel curved as Thorvald and I walked side by side, her tiger next to her and Tinja sticking close to me, glancing nervously at the armed orcs crowding our backs. Our glowing weapons provided the only light, illuminating the sturdy posts and beams of the passageway.

A couple more times, Thorvald crouched to pick up bullet casings. She dropped them in a pocket, the metal *tinking* softly in the quiet tunnel.

Once, she paused not to pick up something but to touch the ground. Long parallel marks gouged the packed earth. From claws?

After another bend in the tunnel, we came upon a man's body crumpled on the ground. A rifle was tucked under his arm, as if he'd died shooting. Shooting at something impervious to bullets? Other than the claw marks, there was no sign of whatever his target had been.

The dead man had short brown hair and wore a camouflage military uniform. The *remains* of such a uniform. It had been shredded in numerous places on his torso and legs, and his face was so clawed it was unrecognizable.

"One of your people?" I asked Thorvald.

Unfazed by the garish sight, she crouched beside the body. "There's no rank on his collar, no name tag sewn into the jacket. It could have been someone who liked shopping at the military-surplus store."

"As one does before sneaking into magical tunnels in the middle of a city."

Thorvald shrugged and stood back up. "Smell anything interesting, Sindari?"

A grunt from behind made me look back. Several of the orcs were scratching at their arms and heads, as if a swarm of mosquitoes had arrived to munch on them. But I didn't see any insects, nor any sign of worms or any other creatures that showed up to decompose bodies. The man looked to have died some weeks earlier, but nothing had started working on the remains. It was as if we had entered an ancient tomb, magically sealed to protect the contents from the world outside.

"I've been contemplating things," Tinja said, as the tiger sniffed, sampling the air, "and I believe I should wait back in the laundry room. Or even the kitchen. I didn't double-check my measurements for the addition of the island, and now would be a fabulous time to do that."

"If it were up to me, I'd let you go," I said.

The female shaman roared and thrust her staff upward. Light flashed, and raw magical power blasted from her. Several of her own people stumbled into the walls, and I wasn't immune this time. Her magic battered me, and I tumbled, landing on the body.

With a squawk of distress, I rolled away. Thorvald caught herself on Sindari and didn't fall.

I do not smell any animals or a suggestion that this is a den for a creature, Sindari said, ignoring the orcs.

"So, whatever is leaving claw marks on everything—*everyone* —isn't alive?" Thorvald asked.

Not in the flesh-and-blood sense, unless it's able to hide all evidence of its presence from me.

"I don't think it's trying to hide much." I waved at the body.

More grunts came from the orcs. One slapped at the sleeve of his chainmail shirt, then punched a buddy on the shoulder. That earned a snarl from his comrade and a return punch.

The shamans yelled something, and the group quieted. The female jerked her staff, indicating we should continue onward. Tinja, who'd meekly gone along with their demands thus far, jumped up and down and snapped at them in Goblin.

"Is some magic affecting the group?" I whispered as Thorvald and I continued past the body. I tugged at Tinja to make sure she followed.

"Something is." Thorvald shrugged.

"Why not the three of us?" I waved at her and the tiger.

Sindari snarled, then snapped at the air. His tail swished, and he whipped his head around to bite at his flank like a dog trying to get rid of a flea.

"The two of us," I amended.

"Maybe our weapons are protecting us," Thorvald whispered, the words for me alone. She probably didn't want the orcs to get the idea of taking our means of defending ourselves. A sentiment I agreed with.

She rested her hand on Sindari's back. Trying to extend the influence of her weapon's protection? In case it helped, I put my hand on Tinja's shoulder.

The tunnel curved again, and we came to another body, this one in a sitting position, slumped against a post with his rifle in his lap. The same weapon or claws had eviscerated the man, intestines visible where they'd spilled from his abdomen. He'd died trying to hold them in while pointing the rifle—no fewer than twenty bullet casings littered the ground around him.

"Looks like these guys were trying to guard the tunnel so the rest of their team could get away," Thorvald said.

"Yeah." Who would guard the tunnel so *we* could get away?

After confirming that the man didn't have a name tag, Thorvald continued on. She hadn't searched pockets for wallets, but something told me we wouldn't find anything that would identify them.

Behind us, the grunts grew more belligerent. I'd grabbed my hammer with both hands when the last body came into view and forgotten to touch Tinja's shoulder again. She snarled and paused to kick the side of the tunnel. One of the orcs threatened her. I gripped her arm and pulled her along with us.

A faint humming grew audible, seeming to emanate from the earthen walls all around us.

The artifact, the male shaman announced. *Yes. It must be making that noise. It has great power!*

Great power that was making everyone itch and punch each other. What a promising find.

"I don't think we're anywhere near your house anymore," Thorvald said.

It was hard to tell with the curves the tunnel had made, but we'd seemed to continue away from the lot in roughly the same direction.

"I think we're under the park," I said.

"One wonders if the landlord had any idea his renters were excavating a tunnel halfway across Bellevue, starting from his basement."

"Probably not. Makes those tenants who don't mention pets seem kind of innocuous."

After we passed two more bodies, men who'd fallen side by side, facing and firing in the direction we were going, a hint of light came from the tunnel ahead. The humming had grown louder. Behind us, the breathing of the orcs grew heavier, as if they were having to exert themselves a great deal to keep from losing control. Maybe they were. Two orcs started fighting with each other, and the shamans had to pull them apart.

My hand still on Tinja's shoulder, I met Thorvald's gaze. If the orcs completely lost it and attacked us en masse, we would have a challenging battle. Especially if we had to worry about the clawed whatever piling on.

Thorvald nodded grimly at me.

Ahead, the tunnel broadened, and a chamber came into view. Our destination?

As with the wide passageway, it had been hollowed out with clean precision, with support posts lining the sides and beams in the ceiling. Something that looked like a small table or maybe a pedestal rested in the middle, but it was hard to see details. The light source came not from within the chamber but from a six-inch-wide band of silver embedded in the floor, walls, and ceiling at the tunnel exit. Not only was it emitting the glow, but it seemed to be the source of the hum.

"A force field?" Thorvald wondered. "The magical version?"

I didn't think there was a *mundane* version of a force field, unless one counted Star Trek technology, but I heard clacks and didn't respond. Not only that, but I sensed the strange not-alive entity that I'd detected after the wall came down. It waited in the chamber ahead.

"Of course," I muttered.

"It's a furnace guardian," Tinja whispered.

"Which is what?" Thorvald asked.

Tinja started to answer but broke off with a squeak as she glanced back. One of the orcs threw something. I dodged to the side as it whizzed between Thorvald and me. It lodged in the earthen wall of the tunnel. A dagger.

I couldn't tell which orc had thrown it. They were more focused on arguing with and punching each other than us, and it might have been accidental. The female shaman strode between them, chanting and raising her staff again. Her power knocked the orcs away from each other. The male shaman clawed at his arm, but that didn't keep him from striding toward us.

Keep going. He pointed at the chamber. *Find the artifact, and figure out how to make this irritation stop.*

The pedestal is empty? The female shaman scowled past us and into the chamber. *Are we sensing only the trap?*

That creature guards something, the male said.

But the female's face had grown more skeptical.

Go inside and deal with it. The male scowled at us and pointed toward the chamber again.

"Tinja?" I squeezed her shoulder.

"I've never seen a furnace guardian before." Tinja stepped closer to me to avoid the encroaching shamans.

Thorvald and I pointed our weapons at the male, who lifted his hands, as if to shove us through the force field. Or cast another mental assault? He was glaring at me specifically, and I braced myself, but he snarled and clawed at his own head instead of attacking.

"But I've heard about them," Tinja added. "They're constructs that dwarves make to protect the cores of their great underground cities, where their massive forges make heat and power for their people. They keep strangers out."

"Are they mechanical constructs?" Thorvald asked.

"Yes, I think so."

"That would explain why there's not an animal scent."

The male shaman roared and flung his arms toward the ceiling. *Go, now. Destroy it, or I will destroy you.*

I crouched, tempted to spring at him and knock him on his ass, but the female shaman succeeded in getting the rest of the orcs pointed in the right direction again. Toward us. Irritation and fury burned in their eyes, and the whole pack raised their weapons as they focused on us. As if they believed *we* were the source of the magic disturbing them.

Two warriors sprang past the male shaman toward us. All I had time to do was push Tinja behind me before a spear thrust toward my face.

With my grip wide on the haft of my hammer, I turned it horizontal and thrust upward to parry. It knocked the spear high, leaving the orc's chest open as his arms flew up. I snapped my foot up and kicked him in the crotch, then shifted my weight to send a second kick higher, clipping him in the chin. He stumbled back into another orc trying to reach me.

Metal clanged beside me as Thorvald parried a blow. Sindari hurled himself into more orcs, his jaws snapping and claws slashing.

Though we fought side by side, using the walls of the tunnel to keep them from flanking us, the sheer number of enemies was daunting. And they were enraged enemies, taking out their irritation over the magic that was driving them crazy on us.

Thorvald took down one orc, but two more sprang to take his place. Even as we defended ourselves, we were pushed back.

"We're almost to the barrier," Tinja blurted, scrambling to keep from being stepped on.

"See if we can go through," I called, not daring to glance back to check how close we were.

A yelp came from behind us.

"No, and when you bump it, it *hurts*," Tinja cried.

An orc I'd knocked to his knees swung an axe at my legs. I jumped to avoid it, then cracked my hammer down on his shoulder. He roared, drew a knife, and lifted his arm to throw it.

"Look out," I barked, hesitating to dodge because I didn't want it to go past me and hit Tinja.

When the knife sped toward us, Thorvald's sword stabbed out. As I leaned away from it, she deflected the blade with a clang. It flew back the direction it had come, the tip lodging in an orc's thigh.

He roared in pain. While he was distracted by pulling it out, I slammed my hammer into his chest. The male shaman thrust him aside and pointed a finger at me, uttering two words in his language. Raw power lanced from that pointing finger and struck Thorvald and me in our chests.

I flew backward, the silver glow of the band in the wall flashing. Thorvald struck the invisible barrier and cried out, bouncing back toward the orcs. I... went through it.

Startled, I hit the ground hard, only my reflexes turning the fall into a roll so that I didn't crack my head. Tinja, Thorvald, and Sindari were stuck on the other side of the silver band, their backs inches from it. The tiger's tail brushed the invisible barrier, and he hissed and yowled, jerking it away and swiping angrily at the orcs.

Where is the artifact? the female shaman demanded, even as the battle raged. *Were we sensing only that barrier?*

Ominous clanks came from the chamber behind me, and I turned away from the battle.

Before, I'd only heard the creature, but now I could see it. A great mechanical construct that reminded me of a cross between a giant dog and a dragon without wings. It prowled toward me, metal scales covering its body—*armoring* its body. With its canine-like head, ears pointed and rotated in my direction, it must have been fifteen or twenty feet tall. Magic made its entire body glow silver, all save its eyes, which burned with a crimson light.

A realistic animalistic growl came from the construct's throat as those glowing red eyes focused on me. It continued forward, left behind to guard... what? I didn't even know. Aside from the empty pedestal, there was nothing in the chamber. Nothing save more spent rounds—my foot came down on one, and I almost slipped.

Why did I have a feeling the humans who'd invaded the place had already gotten what this thing had been left to guard? But if they had, how had they gotten in when Tinja, Sindari, and Thorvald hadn't been allowed through the barrier?

Unfortunately, the construct didn't realize that it didn't need to keep doing its job. Its jaws opened, showing rows of pointed metal teeth, and smoke wafted from its mechanical throat. A semblance of a roar bellowed from its barrel chest, and fire spewed forth, a great gout that burned the air for ten feet in front it.

I scrambled back, but with Thorvald and Sindari bunched up against the barrier and fighting the orcs, there was nowhere for me to go. They were stuck on that side of the barrier and busy with their own battle.

I would have to fight this thing myself.

28

Another gout of fire spewed from the creature's metal jaws as it strode toward me, its scaled tail erect behind it. Keeping my hammer up, I danced out of the path of the flames while considering where to strike it and what its capabilities might be. Since it had caught up to and killed those men in the tunnel, it had to be able to move quickly. Thus far, it was only doing as much as it needed to keep itself between me and the pedestal.

"Hello, good friend!" I called in execrable Dwarven—it wasn't like I'd had anyone to practice with over the years. "We can be friends. No fire!"

Unfortunately, I didn't know the words for *furnace guardian* or *don't incinerate me.*

"I think my mother might have helped make you," I said, switching to English. It probably wasn't intelligent enough to understand either language. "Look, this was her hammer." I raised it over my head. "Do you recognize it?"

The power I sensed within the creature grew stronger, as if it were building up to a detonation. An alarming thought.

It crouched, and I also crouched, ready to spring left or right if it charged.

That was exactly what it did. Like a locomotive that could go from zero to a hundred in a split second, it sprang straight at me. I flung myself to the side, diving in an ungainly roll, thinking it might crash into the wall behind me. But it landed precisely where I'd been, whirling as it stopped, and its jaws opened again.

Certain more fire was on the way, I rolled farther to the side. Flames bathed the ground behind me, heat scorching my exposed skin.

Though I wanted to run back into the tunnel, the dead men in there promised it wasn't safe. If anything, there would be less room to dodge.

I made myself spring to my feet and inch closer to the construct. If I could reach it, I could use my hammer on it.

The flames stopped, and the crimson eyes locked on me again. Maybe it was suicidal, but I sprinted toward it. One good strike with my hammer might make a difference.

Its maw opened, and fire shot out once more. This time, I forced my dive to take me under the flames and toward the construct. Using my momentum to close the distance, I jumped up under its jaws—and the fire shooting from them.

As it lowered its head to snap at me, I yelled, "*Hyrek!*" and struck the hammer to its shoulder, using as powerful a blow as I had on the brick wall.

The construct must have weighed a ton, for it didn't budge at all, and not a single metal scale came off. But, as it had before, lightning arced from the head of my weapon. A dozen branches spread and wrapped all around my metal foe, crackling and brightening the air.

Unlike with the wall, the creature's magic intensified instead of disappearing. It lifted a foreleg, claws longer than scissor blades flashing near my eyes.

An instant before it would have struck down and pinned me

with those claws, I dove and rolled to the side. Instincts warned me of another threat, and I made myself keep rolling, getting as far from my attacker as I could, as quickly as I could.

A good thing, for it spewed more flames at me. Though they didn't hit me full on, they singed my clothes, and I smelled burning hair. *My* hair.

I leaped up and ran toward the only thing in the chamber to hide behind—the pedestal. It wasn't much wider than I and only came up to my chest. A few runes were carved into it, but I didn't have time to study them.

"This is some lousy cover," I panted, crouching and glancing toward the tunnel.

The good news was that Thorvald and her tiger had taken down the male shaman and three of the orcs. The bad news was that they both bled from copious wounds, and the female shaman was still up, attacking with magic as she—or the insanity afflicting them—forced the rest of her warriors to keep fighting.

Tinja had retrieved one of the thrown daggers, and she crouched behind Thorvald. Hopefully, the magic wouldn't compel her to slash wildly at friend as well as foe. Even if they fought perfectly together, I didn't know if their combined forces would be enough. I needed to help them.

Clanks sounded as the construct ran toward me.

"Just need to solve my own problem first." I held up the hammer, wondering if a blow to a more vulnerable spot might do more to damage it. The eyes? I couldn't reach them. The snout? Smoke was curling from slits that resembled nostrils, but I couldn't reach those either.

"Try *keyk*," Thorvald yelled back without pausing in her own battle. "It means ice."

Ten feet away, the creature stopped, its mechanical maw opening again.

I barked Thorvald's word. The haft of my hammer grew cold in my hands, and crystals appeared on the double head.

The creature shot flames at me. I prepared to dive to the right to avoid them, but instead of a narrow gout of fire, it flung a broad band at me. All I could do was crouch behind the pedestal and pray it and my hammer would protect me.

The power of the weapon *did* seem to help, the haft growing even colder in my hands, but I still felt the heat. Fire crackled past the pedestal, roasting the air all around me so it seared my lungs and my eyes. I had to squint them shut under the intense light and heat.

"Stop, please!" I tried in a mix of Dwarven and English. "My mother was Roxy—Princess Rodarska. She wouldn't want you to kill her daughter. Aren't you supposed to protect dwarves?" Heat scoured my throat, and I coughed. "Princess Rodarska!" I cried again, as if it might be a password to ensure safety. It *should* have been, damn it.

But the fire continued. Even though the flames didn't hit me directly, they hit the pedestal and the air around it. I grew light-headed. Frustrated, I cried my mother's name one more time and smashed the hammer against the pedestal. Too bad it was made from metal instead of stone, else it might have shattered and flung pieces into the construct's face.

Surprisingly, a balloon of magic swelled from the pedestal, and the heat vanished.

Flames still danced in the air, but they weren't coming close to me anymore. No, they weren't coming close to the *pedestal.* It had created a dome-like protective barrier around it.

The construct must have been smart enough to realize it, for it stopped and cocked its head, like a dog hearing something strange. If it hadn't been trying to kill me seconds before, I would have laughed at the quizzical expression. Then it sat back on its haunches.

Sindari yowled—his enemies had backed him into the barrier.

A noisy *crunch* came from the tunnel as Thorvald slammed the point of her sword into the glowing metal band around the entrance. White sparks flew, and she flung an arm up to protect her face. She also yanked her sword free, and Sindari scooted away from the barrier. The glow of the band faded, as did the hum and aura of magic that had emanated from it.

"Should have done that to start with," Thorvald said, though she winced and shook her arm, suggesting she'd received some magical backlash.

Dreadful thing, Sindari said, facing the orcs again. But they'd paused in their attack.

That pedestal *is not what we seek*, the female shaman snarled. *Where is the* jyrelika?

The what?

With the trap destroyed, I sense nothing except that. The shaman flicked her staff toward the pedestal, her face disgusted behind her tusks.

"Anything else in there, Puletasi?" Thorvald asked, weariness in her voice though she remained in a defensive crouch, her sword back to pointing at the orcs.

"No, I think someone else already got what the dwarf renter was guarding. And I think you can call me Matti after all this."

Thorvald gave me a weary thumbs-up. In the aftermath of the battle, sweat mixed with blood from a gouge and dripped from her face.

The female shaman, muttering in disgust, waved toward the remaining warriors, and they backed away, not bothering to collect their fallen kin.

"Are you okay?" Tinja asked me, eyeing the construct sitting just beyond the barrier.

"For the moment. If the pedestal drops its defensive magic, the creature might go for me again." I rested a hand on top of the pedestal, giving it a friendly pat. "Keep that barrier up, will you?"

I had no idea if it had reacted to my mother's name or the hammer blow, but it pulsed under my hand. I almost sprang back, but it didn't hurt. The pulse almost seemed reassuring.

Thorvald glanced at the retreating orcs, then whispered, "You're sure that's not the artifact?"

"I'm not sure of anything." I'd assumed the pedestal had *held* the artifact, but it clearly had magic of its own.

A click sounded, and, that time, I did spring back. But only a step since I didn't want to risk leaving the protective barrier.

A door in the side of the pedestal opened, revealing a perfectly ordinary-looking storage cubby. A ring similar to the one I'd found in the iron chest rested next to…

"Is that a VHS tape?" I asked.

I withdrew both items. It was indeed a VHS tape. There was no label, not even a Post-It Note to hint at its contents. The ring wasn't only similar to the other but identical. Neither was magical. As far as I could tell, they were simply nice pieces of jewelry.

The door in the pedestal swung back shut.

Disappointment rolled over me. Even though I had no need for a powerful artifact, after all that, it seemed like we should have earned more than someone's home movie.

I glanced at the metal creature, not sure it would let me leave with the modest items. On a whim, I slipped the ring onto my finger.

The construct's legs folded, and it dropped to its belly, its tail curling around its body, and the crimson glow of its eyes disappeared. As if it had gone to sleep.

The pedestal pulsed once more, and the barrier disappeared. I crouched, ready to run for the tunnel, but the construct didn't rise again. Maybe the pedestal had somehow told it that I was a dwarf, or at least an acceptable person to enter the chamber and take stuff out.

"That's it?" Thorvald asked as I joined them in the tunnel,

giving Tinja a shoulder squeeze. Thorvald dragged a sleeve across her face, wiping away the blood and sweat.

"Maybe the tape will show us something."

"That looks like it's forty years old." Thorvald waved to the tape. "It might not even play anymore."

"It's dry and doesn't look damaged." I held it up and shrugged. "Do you know anyone with a VCR?"

I didn't have one. That technology had been wandering down the path toward obsolescence even when I'd been a kid.

Thorvald cleaned and sheathed her sword. "I'm sure Willard can find one."

I wasn't eager to hand over whatever secrets might be on the tape to the military, but Thorvald plucked it from my hand before I could seriously contemplate objecting. Since she'd helped me with magical words that awakened powers in my hammer, I decided not to club her and take it back.

She gave Sindari a pat, then dismissed him to his realm to heal. With a cloud of silver mist, and a few words about enjoying noble battle, he disappeared.

"Do you need to stop at the hospital along the way?" I asked. "You're dripping blood all over the tunnel floor."

"Nah. I heal fast. By the time we get to Willard's, I'll barely have any blood left oozing out to smear on her leather chair. She appreciates that."

"You seem like a weird employee."

"It took you all night to figure it out?"

"Well, not really. It was weird when you showed up on my friend's rooftop with a dragon."

"I hear that more often than you'd think."

"Odd."

"Yes."

29

DAWN BRIGHTENED THE WINDOWS AS THORVALD AND I WAITED IN Willard's office. After the battle, we'd found the *brysarrusi* dead in the street, dozens of sword wounds in its torso, neck, and skull. One driven into its heart appeared to have been the one that had finally killed it.

And Sarrlevi... Who knew where Sarrlevi had gone?

There'd been a lot of blood dampening the pavement. If some of it had belonged to him, he might have staggered off to set up his camp and meditate to heal his wounds.

Maybe I should have checked the pantry before leaving, but I'd been distracted by Abbas limping down the street to the house. Apparently, the *brysarrusi* had been keeping him hostage in the park until it had abruptly knocked him unconscious and left. By the time he'd woken, the fight had been over. I was glad he hadn't been hurt worse.

As Thorvald had ushered me to her Jeep, Abbas and Tinja had headed back to my house to treat each other's wounds. More than ready for something to eat and my bed, I wished I could have gone with them, but I was too curious about the VHS tape to let it out of my sight.

After listening to a terse report about the night's events from Thorvald, Willard had left to retrieve a VCR.

I nibbled on my fingernails and thought about Thorvald's concern that the tape might be too old to play. I had no idea how long that technology lasted but assumed underground storage wasn't ideal if one hoped for longevity. At least it had been protected inside the pedestal.

"All that effort from everyone, and we got nothing," Thorvald mused, looking out the window.

"*Someone* got something." I eyed her.

I doubted she had anything to do with the people who'd killed the renter, found the tunnel, and taken the artifact, but after seeing the uniforms on those bodies, it was hard not to believe the military was involved. And Thorvald worked for the military. As an independent contractor, it was possible she didn't know anything—I doubted Willard filled civilians in on everything the Army had going on in the area—but surely the colonel had a clue.

"Maybe." Thorvald shrugged. "Maybe whoever walled in the place didn't find an artifact either. It could have been long gone when they arrived, and they ended up having to deal with that mechanical monstrosity for no good reason."

I shook my head. "The renter wouldn't have been guarding the place for all those years if there hadn't been anything down there."

"I suppose that's true. If he was one of the ones who *put* whatever it was down there, he would have known if it disappeared. Let's hope anyway." She snorted. "Can you imagine spending your whole life guarding something that wasn't there?"

"Found a VCR," came Willard's voice from the outer office. "We're lucky we had a few. The other three have been eviscerated for parts by someone." Gondo wasn't in her outer office, but she glared in the direction of his desk as she walked past it. She carried a fistful of cables and a clunky machine that had been state-of-the-art in the eighties. "This isn't the first evidence we've found on a VHS tape. I've even got an old camcorder around here somewhere."

"Are there a lot of magical beings out there that celebrated their arrival to Earth with home movies?" Thorvald helped Willard plug the VCR into a flat-screen TV that had been hidden in a cabinet.

"More than you'd think. They have a history of finding our technology fascinating. Or amusing, maybe, since they can replicate almost everything with some kind of magic or another. We're lucky you didn't find a glowing orb instead."

"I imagine it's hard to figure out how to plug those into a TV," Thorvald said.

Not joining in the chitchat, I watched nervously as Willard turned on the TV and the VCR, pushed the tape in, and pressed play. A part of me longed to see my mother in the footage. Another part of me was so emotional from the dredging up of all my memories this past week that I worried I would break down if I did.

All of me, however, wanted to know what I'd fought so hard for. I hoped the werewolves and orcs that had survived would put the word out to the magical community that the thing they'd all been panting over wasn't there anymore.

At first, nothing but blackness played, and I sagged in disappointment. Willard hit the fast-forward button, and eventually the tunnel came into view with the camera operator walking down it and into the chamber. My breath caught when the camera panned to show the construct with its eyes glowing crimson. It looked newer than when we'd encountered it, the metal scales gleaming.

Someone trotted into view, running up to pat the construct on one of its stout legs. My mother.

She smiled and waved toward the cameraman as she gave the

construct another pat and strode toward the familiar pedestal. This time, it wasn't empty.

"Now we're talking," Willard murmured, leaning close to the screen for a better look.

A glowing orange cylinder rested horizontally on top of the pedestal, a panel on the front showing dwarven runes, each also glowing orange. Were they buttons? Or instructions for operation?

"Can you read that, Puletasi?" Thorvald asked. "Matti."

"No. I only know a few words of Dwarven." Even as I admitted that, I recognized one of the symbols, and a forgotten memory surfaced of my mother with chalk and a chalkboard, starting to teach me to read. English *and* Dwarven. I pointed. "That's the equivalent of ON/OFF."

"We've got plenty of language books that have been translated," Willard said as she pulled out a pen and pad to copy the runes down. "I'll grab them and look these words up later."

The camera was still focused on my mother. She now stood behind the cylinder, her hands resting on top of it. My hammer —*her* hammer—leaned against the pedestal at her feet. Her eyes were closed, and she was chanting, the words barely audible since the cameraman wasn't close.

Two male dwarves trotted into view, carrying something large between them. It reminded me of a lawn mower, with a huge conical attachment on the front. A giant drill bit? It was hard to imagine that cutting grass.

"That's the engineer friend," I said, recognizing one of the dwarves, though he wasn't wearing his armor. "And that's... Oh, that's the renter."

"I think I know what that device is," Willard said, a hint of reverence entering her tone. "I've seen drawings in dwarven engineering books. If it's as powerful as the tales say..."

"The lawn-mower thing?" I asked when she didn't go on. "Or the glowing cylinder?"

Willard held up a finger and pointed at the screen. Wanting confirmation before she shared her hunch?

I struggled to remain calm. People had been killed over what the renter had been guarding. *I'd* almost been killed over it. I wanted to know what it was.

Thorvald leaned her hip against the desk and watched, only looking moderately interested. Because *her* mother hadn't been tied up in whatever the artifact was, and it hadn't been found under *her* house.

After the male dwarves set down the hulking tool, my mother nodded and stepped back. The glow from the cylindrical device intensified, and a narrow beam streaked toward the tool. I winced, expecting it to explode, but after a couple of seconds, the tool roared to life, the conical attachment whirring.

The dwarves cheered, and the engineer flicked a finger toward one of the earthen walls. The tool rumbled up to it, set the attachment—the bit—against it, and dug in.

"Not a lawn mower," I said as dirt and rock flew. "A tunnel borer."

"I guess my visions of dwarves chiseling out their great underground cities with pickaxes aren't quite right," Thorvald said. "Though you can't blame me. Tolkien never mentioned tunnel-boring machines."

The dwarves only excavated a few feet before turning off the tool.

For the first time, the person holding the camera, another dwarf presumably, spoke. Since he was close to the mic, his voice was louder and clearer, but his words were in Dwarven. Thorvald and Willard shrugged and looked at me.

More all-but forgotten memories came to mind of my mother singing to me and teaching me rhymes in her native language. Most of the dwarf's speech was too rapid for me to decipher, and whatever they were discussing, it wasn't rhymes, but a few of the words were familiar.

"Can you play that again?" I asked.

Willard handed me the pen and paper and rewound the tape. As she played the section a few times, I wrote down the words in Dwarven the best I could and then translated the ones I recognized.

New home... build... power.

"We've got linguists who can translate it fully," Willard said, tapping that last word, "but I think I've got the gist."

I wasn't sure *I* had the gist, but I said, "My mother must have found out that Sarrlevi was after her and fled here with some of her friends, maybe dwarves sworn to protect her because she was a princess—"

"Not only a princess," Willard said, "but the heir to the dwarven throne, King Korvik Ironhelm's oldest of two daughters. I asked around after you left the office yesterday. It's common knowledge among the dwarves that Princess Rodarksa's younger sister Barothla had ambitions, but none of the informants I spoke to had heard about an assassin being hired to take out Rodarska."

"But Sarrlevi admitted he was," I said. "I wonder why she chose Earth to hide out on. How did she know Sarrlevi wouldn't think to look here?"

"Because we're not one of the worlds in the Cosmic Realms and under the rule of dragons, not many people from other places keep track of it," Thorvald said. "According to Zav, there's not a lot of inherent magic on Earth, not like on the more preferred worlds. It's one of the reasons dragons and other magical beings haven't attempted to take it over." She grimaced. "Lucky for us."

"Is that actually true?" Willard asked her.

"Yeah. I've experienced it. My magic—those roots Freysha taught me to grow to entangle enemies—worked *much* better in the fae realm." Thorvald pointed at the screen—it was paused on my mother again. "If she was a sorceress or enchanter or something, Sarrlevi might have assumed she would go to one of the worlds where her power would work as well as on the dwarven home world. Maybe that's why he never found her. He didn't think she would come *here*."

"This being such a backward dirt ball," Willard said dryly.

"To the magical races, it is," Thorvald said.

"So, she and some of her friends fled here," I said again, more interested in working out what had happened than discussing Earth's magical potential, "to avoid Sarrlevi, and it sounds like they might have planned to stay long term. Maybe she thought her sister would try again to have her killed if she returned. Or that Sarrlevi would always be waiting. So she was going to start over and build a home here? Like a dwarven colony?"

Willard nodded. "Could be. Even though Earth is populated, it's not like many humans live underground. They might have believed they could find a mountain without many people around, dig in, and build an outpost. Or even a city. If that does what I think it does, such would have been possible. Such and more."

"Don't hold us in suspense, Willard," Thorvald said. "Can't you see Matti is dying to know what her mom's doohickey is?"

"A power source," Willard said.

"Like a big battery? That's it?" Thorvald raised her eyebrows as she looked at me and shrugged.

"No, not like a *big battery*. Try the equivalent of a nuclear reactor. Actually, if the descriptions I've read are accurate, it might be more like the equivalent of a *fusion* reactor. In that compact little device. I'm not sure what kind of waste it creates or what it does with the heat it must output—for all I know, it's capable of magically inserting it all into some other dimension—but trust me, Val. It's a big deal. *Huge*."

"We don't have fusion technology yet, do we?" Thorvald asked.

"People are working on it, but no. It's a technology they keep saying is ten years off, but they've been saying that for more than fifty years. Unfortunately. It would be a game changer, like the solution to all our energy problems on Earth." Willard pointed at the paused screen. "I'm not saying that *is* a fusion reactor, just that the descriptions of what one of them can power suggest it's the equivalent, presumably by using magic. The dwarves have them in their population centers, and they power all of their energy needs. And with all the excavation and mining and manufacturing they do, they have a lot of needs."

"Bet you didn't know you were buying a house with a reactor underneath it," Thorvald told me as I digested the information.

"Tinja didn't mention that, no," I murmured. "It wasn't in the description on the MLS."

"How incomplete. You should talk to the listing agent."

"How to make the devices is reputedly a closely guarded secret," Willard said. "The dwarves don't sell them, and they don't let outsiders in to see them. The dragons may know how they work, but the other magical races don't, and a lot of them would like such power sources for their own energy needs. They're supposed to last for thousands of years."

"*We* could use some of those," Thorvald said.

"Oh, yes." Willard gave her a sidelong look. "I suspect you aren't the first one to have felt that way."

"You think those were our soldiers on a mission to get it? They were in uniforms but didn't have rank or name tags."

"I'd like to think *we* wouldn't leave our people behind."

"Even in the face of dwarven traps and a deadly guard construct chewing up your team?"

"Even in." Willard's expression grew thoughtful as she looked at me. "Do you know *why* someone killed your mother?"

I shook my head. "I was just a little kid when it happened, and I haven't been able to see my father since. He might know. I remember him once telling me that others treated her differently because she was an outsider, and people are always afraid of outsiders."

"If she was the one responsible for crafting the reactor," Willard said, "I'd expect people would want to *capture* her, not kill her."

I rocked back. Had my mother been a powerful enchanter or... I didn't even know what dwarven career field built reactors. "I would have assumed the engineer created it, but, if it was magical, maybe not. Or maybe they combined their knowledge and abilities to make one together."

Willard nodded. "I would be surprised if something like that could be created by a single person. I wonder what happened to him."

"The only dwarf from the Polaroids that I was able to find was Artie," I said, "and Sarrlevi scared her off before I could speak with her."

"He's a pain in the ass," Willard said.

Thorvald snorted and glanced at me. Our discussion on erogenous zones coming to mind?

"He did get the *brysarrusi* off our backs," was all she said. "He has his uses."

"When his goals align with yours?" Willard asked.

"That's about the gist."

"I don't think he ever cared about the reactor." I waved toward the screen. "He's looking for my mother. Or her remains." I grimaced.

"So he says." Thorvald raised her eyebrows toward me. "Are you sure he's not still trying to kill her?"

"Not entirely." I shrugged. "But he told me he wasn't, and you said he's honorable."

"To a point. In battle."

I closed my eyes, thinking of all the times Sarrlevi had helped me. If he'd been hunting down my mother because he believed she was alive and wanted to kill her, wouldn't he have wrapped a hand around my throat and questioned me the way he had Artie?

"Do you have a way to ask the dwarven king to corroborate his story?" I asked them. "I don't *think* Sarrlevi is trying to kill my mother anymore, but the king would be the one to know. Sarrlevi said he was the one who hired him to find her."

Willard looked to Thorvald.

"I haven't been back to the dwarven world since the dragon lich was killed," she said, "but when Zav gets back, I'll ask him about it."

"Good. Do so. I'll get someone to do a full translation of the words we can make out on the tape." Willard waved to the paused screen. "I have a feeling this isn't over. I'll have to make a copy of this and send it along with a report. If it *wasn't* the US military that collected the reactor, and I doubt it was, my superiors may want us to find it."

"To give back to the dwarves?" Thorvald asked. "Or to keep it to study and use ourselves? Like all the stuff in your special vault downstairs?"

"You're not supposed to tell the world about that room." Willard tilted her head toward me.

"Even the dark elves know of its existence."

"Probably because you blabbed about it," Willard said. "Regardless, I'm a fan of returning what rightfully belongs to other races to them. When that dragon egg was stolen, we narrowly avoided having its angry dragon clan demolish Seattle, if not our entire world. Maybe if we returned the reactor to the dwarves, they would be so pleased they would give us the schematics."

"Schematics that would be perfectly useless without magic," Thorvald said.

I listened to them without commenting. Whatever Willard claimed, I highly doubted that reactor, even if her people found it, would ever make it back to the dwarven home world.

"Isn't your roommate an enchanter?" Willard asked Thorvald.

"Dimitri is a quarter-dwarf and uses his skills to make magical yard art and door knockers. A super-powered reactor is above his pay grade."

"Too bad. How'd Puletasi do out there, Thorvald?"

I pulled my gaze from the image of my mother frozen on the screen. They were both looking at me.

"She was a beast," Thorvald said. "I think even Sarrlevi was impressed by her ferocity."

"He didn't see the fight with the construct," I said.

"He saw you whale on two werewolves twice your height. I think one's head is embedded in a tree."

"It had better not be. I don't have a large budget for landscaping."

"Do you believe she's trustworthy?" Willard asked, pointing to me.

"You think I can make an accurate assessment after one night?" Thorvald asked.

"You did battle together. Multiple times. Isn't that all it took for you to fall head-over-heels in love with your dragon?"

"Love and trust aren't exactly the same thing, but I think she's honest and will tell you how she feels."

"Oh, wonderful," Willard said. "I *love* it when my troops tell me how they feel."

"You know what I mean. She'll do what she says and tell you to beat it if she's not interested. I don't think she'll leave you hanging."

As I listened to them debating my trustworthiness, I realized the reason for the conversation and slumped. Was the colonel going to try to *hire* me again?

Though I had more questions about my mother and her past than I ever had, that didn't mean I wanted to jump into the Army's arms. And I had a job already, an entire business of my own. I didn't need a side hustle, especially not one that pitted me against orc shamans, werewolves, and human-munching monsters from other realms. Battling bent nails and stripped screws was work enough for me.

"Such glowing praise," Willard murmured. "And yet, I'll extend my offer again, Puletasi. Will you consider working for my office? Especially on jobs related to mysterious dwarves who built powerful magical artifacts in Seattle in the past?"

"Are you going to threaten to throw me in jail again if I say no?"

"No. I think you've done your penance. But once you see the huge combat bonus I give Thorvald, you'll be eager to sign on."

"I'm not motivated by money." I glanced at Thorvald. "But out of curiosity, *how* huge? Like enough to buy a new truck capable of carrying more than ten two-by-fours at a time?"

"Uh. If you want to make that kind of money, you're better off working for gnomes." Thorvald shrugged apologetically at Willard.

"Your bonuses are enough to make the *payments* on a truck," Willard told her.

"Unless an angry dragon hurls your vehicle into a tree, utterly wrecking it, and your insurance won't accept it as an Act of God and pay out on the claim."

"Puletasi isn't going to have run-ins with dragons. Just dwarves. And maybe elven assassins."

"You don't think Sarrlevi can use his magic to hurl trucks around?" Thorvald asked.

Willard propped a fist on her hip. "What do you say, Puletasi?"

"I'll think about it."

"You said that last time, then fled through a portal to another world."

"Which Willard took personally." Thorvald smirked.

"I'm a fair and accommodating employer. My people *enjoy* working for me."

I promised to think about it again and backed out of the office. All I wanted was for my life to get back to normal, but the mystery of my mom's death, who had the reactor, and what had happened to all the dwarves in the photos would be hard to forget about.

Still, I could do research on my own, couldn't I? I didn't have to work for Willard. For the *Army.*

Willard might not believe US Army soldiers had been under the house, but I wasn't so sure. They were the ones who'd killed my mom all those years ago and put my dad in a military prison. It was a big organization; one colonel couldn't know everything that went on. I would be better off figuring things out on my own.

And I would. Just like I'd always done.

EPILOGUE

Time blurred past, meditative and calming, as chisel and mallet worked, turning the second of two stout posts at the top of the staircase into carvings of trees. Once I finished the squirrel perched on the branch, I would consider the work done.

The house was on its way to being done too, with me nobly resisting the urge to build custom cabinets instead of helping Abbas install perfectly functional models from the home-improvement store. Tinja was also nobly resisting the urge—Abbas and I had dragged her out of the kitchen—to haul in bedsprings, corrugated metal, and coat hangers to build the goblin version of Lazy Susans. We needed to finish the house and get it on the market, not customize every inch.

"Said by the person carving nature imagery out of the tree that burned in the yard," I muttered, then shut my mouth as I grew aware of a presence behind me, someone with a magical aura.

"That's good craftsmanship," Sarrlevi said, then added, "for a plumber."

I didn't have to turn around to see his smirk. It was in his voice. Bastard.

"It's good craftsmanship for *anyone*." I kept my back to him and continued my work, hoping my meditative state wouldn't evaporate with him there. "You're still an ass."

"Yes."

I sensed rather than heard him walking closer. Elves, especially elven assassins, never seemed to make a sound as they moved. I preferred the *thump, thump, thump* of a dwarf in boots.

"You found resolution for your problem under the house?" He stopped closer behind me than I would have liked, within touching distance, and I grew conscious that I was on my knees in front of him, like some servant.

I refused to feel intimidated by having him back there. Nor would I move. I was almost done with the squirrel, and I wouldn't let his presence rattle me.

"Not really, but I replaced the brick wall and the floor, and nobody else has been skulking around. I think the word got out that what everyone had been panting over has been gone for some time. Or at least since the renter was killed."

I assumed that was when the military had gotten it and that they'd thought walling in and tiling over the entrance to the tunnel would be sufficient to keep that construct from getting out. Funny that they hadn't called in Thorvald and her dragon to destroy it. But then, Willard hadn't known anything about all this, and she would have been the one to unleash Thorvald. A case of one hand not knowing what the other was doing, I supposed, and couldn't help but sneer down at my phone.

Earlier, Willard had left me a voicemail. No doubt she wanted to know my decision. I hadn't listened to it yet, and I didn't know what I would tell her. Working with Thorvald hadn't been as bad as I'd expected, and I appreciated that Willard hadn't shipped me off to a military prison or had me shot—I owed Sarrlevi for vouching for me, as much as I hated to admit it, and ought to thank him. Even so, the idea of getting into bed with the Army made my stomach turn.

"When you finish your work on this dwelling, you will search for your mother?" Sarrlevi asked.

"No. There's nothing to search for. She's dead. Letting myself believe she's not and starting some endless quest hunting all over the world for someone who isn't there..." I swallowed, emotions surging at the mere thought. "I could waste my whole life on that. And in the end, it would just make things harder than they already are. Do elves have a term like wild goose chase?"

For the first time, I looked up at him.

His hands were clasped behind his back as he watched me work, his face hard to read. "It implies something fruitless?"

"Yeah."

"What if this is *not* fruitless?"

"It is. If she were alive, she would have come looking for me a long time ago. I'm positive."

"Unless she was unable to."

"For thirty years?"

"Has your father not been incarcerated for thirty years?"

"Yes, but I know where *he* is. And I didn't see a building burn down around him." I rubbed my forehead, annoyed with Sarrlevi for bringing all this up, for stirring up feelings that I'd thought I'd long ago come to peace with.

Sarrlevi rested his fingers on the top of my head. I froze, not sure what he would do or what the gesture meant. It was hard to imagine someone like him offering comfort.

"I told the king—your grandfather—that I would do my best to find her," he said. "I need your help. Even if I could locate her here on this world with which I'm largely unfamiliar, she knows that I was once hired to kill her. She would hide from me. But you..."

He brushed his fingers through my hair, his nails teasing my scalp. Pleasure raced along my nerves, delightful warmth spreading through my whole body.

It was pleasure I didn't want to feel, not from the touch of someone who'd once been hired to kill my mother, who'd *accepted* that job. I told myself to pull away—or *spring* away—but my body refused to obey. I even caught myself leaning toward him, craving his touch.

No. I froze, not letting myself crave anything of his. He was probably smirking down at me, amused that he could so easily stir my libido.

"She would come to you," Sarrlevi said quietly, his fingers shifting from a brush to a rub, a massage.

"So, you want me at your side to trick her?"

"So she will accept my help if she needs it. And know it's safe for her to return to her home. I am no longer after her."

"What if someone else is? Is her sister still gunning for her?"

"Her father knows of his younger daughter's duplicity now. He will protect Rodarska."

"Look, she's dead, all right? And I have work to do. I'm not going anywhere."

The phone buzzed, another call from Willard. She was determined to get an answer, wasn't she?

"Your services are requested by many," Sarrlevi said dryly, as if he also knew what Willard wanted. Maybe he did. He had chats with Thorvald, after all.

"Yeah, but I'm not working for her either," I said. I hadn't truly decided that yet, but I wanted everyone to leave me alone so I could go back to doing the work I loved and that I was good at, only pausing to thump bad guys on the side when I saw people in need of help.

"No? Is she not in your military?"

"Yes."

"The military that has imprisoned your father?"

"Yeah."

"Perhaps if you worked for her, she could arrange for you to see him. You must be curious about what happened that night, from an adult's point of view." Sarrlevi kept massaging my scalp as he spoke, fingers occasionally brushing my ear or neck.

It was the most erotic experience I'd had in months, and I was both indignant, because he was trying to manipulate me, and... I didn't want it to stop. Carnal thoughts of us sharing his little cot on his moss rug came to me, but I did my best to quash them, reminded that he could read minds.

"And if my father gave me a lead on if she's alive and where she is, I could tell you," I said.

"Of course." Sarrlevi crouched down and touched the carving with his free hand. "You are correct. This is good work for anyone. Even by dwarven standards."

I swallowed and muttered a grudging, "Thanks," though having his face that close to mine was unsettling, even if he was looking at my work instead of me. "And thanks for telling Thorvald I wasn't responsible for the deaths of the police officers."

He nodded and met my eyes. Instead of saying *you're welcome*, he said, "Assist me. Your grandfather would wish it."

"I doubt he knows I exist."

"Would you like an introduction?"

I hesitated. Would I?

Even when the picture of the king—of my grandfather—had shown up in the air over the blood-identifying device, I hadn't considered that it might be possible to meet him. But if Sarrlevi could create portals to other worlds, he could take me to the dwarven realm. *If* I was a good little girl and did what he wished.

Sighing, I slumped against the post, leaning my forehead against the cool wood.

Sarrlevi rubbed the back of my neck, making my whole body tingle with desire as he waited patiently—and probably *certainly*

—for his answer. He knew I was attracted to him, whether I wanted to be or not, and he was using that to his advantage. His fingers pushed up into my hair, nails scraping along my scalp, and my heart pounded in my chest, excited by the sensations and exhilarated at the thought that we might—

No. No, we would not. I wasn't going to let him use me.

I lifted my head and scowled at him. "You're trying to do to me what you resent other people doing to you, manipulate me with sex."

Admittedly, he hadn't promised *sex*. He'd made it clear he wasn't into me. He probably thought a little scalp massage would be painless enough—he barely had to touch me—and get him what he wanted.

And he'd very nearly been right.

"By rubbing your head?" he asked dryly.

"You know what you're doing."

"Yes. Is it working?"

"You're an ass."

"Yes." Sarrlevi smiled faintly. "If this doesn't work, I also brought cheese."

"The blue one?" I barely refrained from salivating. That was almost as tempting as the promise of sex with a very agile, athletic, and *hot* elf. And I'd probably be able to look myself in the mirror the morning after eating cheese.

His smile widened. "Yes."

"Hell." I stared through the railing, afraid I would regret this, but… "All right. I'll help you look for her. Just quit rubbing my head."

"Very well." His fingers strayed, and he caressed my ear before releasing me, sending such an intense wave of pleasure through me that I was sure to have erotic dreams for weeks. "You still want the cheese, right?"

"Damn straight, I want the cheese. A brick of the blue every month that I'm helping you." I narrowed my eyes at him. "*And* a wheel of the pink."

"Agreed." His smile shifted to a knowing smirk. He'd known I would cave to him before he'd walked in. What a smug bastard.

As he walked to where he'd set down his backpack to retrieve my prize—my bribe—I picked up my phone to return the call.

"This is Colonel Willard," came the Southern drawl.

"Hi, ma'am. It's Matti. Uhm, I accept the offer of a job."

"That's good news, Puletasi." Apparently, it was a rule in the military that one could only use surnames. "I'll let you know when I have work for you. In the meantime, I'll wish you luck on your quest."

My quest. Positive she didn't refer to rehabbing the house, I squinted suspiciously over at Sarrlevi.

He lifted the block of cheese in a semblance of a salute.

THE END

AFTERWORD

Thank you for checking out my new series! If you enjoyed *Hammered*, I would appreciate it if you would leave a review.

If you want to continue on with the adventure, you can order Book 2, *Betrayed*, now.

Also, if you haven't read *Death Before Dragons*, the series that kicked off everything in this dragon-filled world, you can check out the first book, *Sinister Magic*, and find out how Val and Zav first met.

Made in the USA
Monee, IL
21 November 2023

47083268R00184